MysteryTribune Books

FREEDOM
DROP

by Brian Silverman

Mystery Tribune
mysterytribune.com

First Edition: May 2021

ISBN 978-163821930-9

Cover Illustration by Fabio Consoli.
Cover Design by Mystery Tribune.

Printed in the United States of America

To Heather, my brilliant partner in life whose sage advice to write a mystery I stubbornly ignored for years. This one, finally, is for you.

THEN

She hugged the child tightly to her chest as she ran. The light from the eastern sky was just beginning to brighten her way through the trees. Besides the sound of her heavy breathing, she could hear their faint calls in the distance and the sound of the dogs. They were getting closer.

"Reviens!"

"Arret!"

"Retourner l'enfant!"

She knew the language. They said they would not harm her or the child. They wanted her to return. To bring the child back to them. But she could never do that. She had planned this ever since her daughter was born and she saw her fair skin and her green eyes. She knew what would happen. She would never let them take her baby.

The others told her what she had to do to escape. She could not stop. She could not look back. She had long limbs and ran fast. She was almost there, at the place where so many others had run to. She burst through the heavy brush and the sky opened up in front of her. The sun was rising just above the blue sea beyond. She was told to run into the sky. To jump into it. That was the way. That was how they could both finally be free.

Her feet were bloodied, but she didn't have far to go. She could hear the dogs' feverish panting behind her.

She kept running. She ran into the sky, her baby against her chest, her legs still moving.

Her legs continued to churn and then she and her baby dropped. Where they all dropped.

NOW

She was panting as she ran through the thick brush. She could hear him behind her. She could hear his labored breathing. He was calling for her. Why? She did not want this. She pushed too far this time. She knew she took too many risks. And she knew one day those risks would burn her. She reached for her phone again. She needed to text for help. She fumbled with it and then it fell from her hands.

She could sense that he was right behind her now. She stopped and looked for the phone. There was no time. He would be on her if she searched. She left the phone where it fell and kept running.

She could hear him calling. He was telling her not to run. To come back. That he would not hurt her.

The other man was standing at the cliff's edge. He was waiting. She saw his crooked smile. He held open his arms for her. She could run to him.

The other man behind her was pleading with her, telling her not to run. To come back to him. He was weeping. He cried that he was sorry. So sorry. This made her pause. She didn't know what to do. She almost stopped. But she didn't. She kept running.

PART ONE

1

"**B**e a man'" Tubby Levett said.

Those were the first words Tubby had uttered since I picked him up at his house. We were in my Jeep and he was to my left, in the passenger seat. Here on the Caribbean island of St. Pierre, a former British colony, we drove on the left side of the road. And like most roads on this small island, it was a particularly narrow one. There is very little flat land on St. Pierre so not only, for me as an ex-New Yorker, was I not driving on the *right* side of the road, but I had to contend with oncoming vehicles, while swaying down the slopes of the island's many hills and mountains.

"Are you asking me or are you telling me?" I asked Tubby, my eyes on the road. We were heading to St. Pierre's airport, which wasn't much more than an airstrip. I could see the small control tower ahead of us and the blue Atlantic a few hundred yards beyond the airport's one runway,

"What?" Tubby was surprised by my own question.

"To be a man."

"I'm not asking. And I'm not telling," he replied.

"Then why did you say it?"

He pointed to the Jeep's speaker. "You play that Jamaican music, reggae music, all the time, but you don't know who sing them songs and such? I hear you play this song many times. The song called 'Be a Man.' A title like that should not be forgotten."

I was smiling because he was right. I didn't know the name of the song, but I should have. I had listened to it countless times and liked it, but never bothered to find out the song's title or who recorded it. I was bad with names, titles, stuff like that. I was better with faces, sounds, sensory things.

"You make this reggae playlist I hear you play so many times?" Tubby asked.

I hugged the curb, careful not to spill the Jeep into the recessed drain gutter. That would not be good for my shocks or alignment. We were almost at the airport.

"No, someone I once knew made it for me a long time ago," I said.

"Who?" I could feel his eyes on me.

I thought about his question for a moment.

"No one you know. It doesn't matter," I said.

"It doesn't matter?"

"Nope," I said with what I hoped was finality, but I knew he was staring at me. Then I heard him hiss through his teeth, the sound he made whenever I avoided his questions. Whenever I was keeping something from him. When I first met Tubby, he was working part-time at the St. Pierre Yacht Club bar. I had just arrived on the island. Tubby impressed me with his charming, easy-going manner and after I tasted his, now-legendary, version of that famous Caribbean cocktail, the rum punch, I immediately offered him a full-time job working with me at my bar. Tubby's help getting my venture up and running was invaluable. Our different skill sets complemented each other. And that he once saved me from having my brains splattered on the bar's expensive burnished wood, from a gun pressed to the back of my head by a Guyanese drug trafficker, sealed the deal. Tubby wasn't only my business partner; he was the best friend I had on St. Pierre. So I was used to those hisses. They were no big thing.

Before he could continue his questioning, I pulled into the airport's small carport, and then both of us got out of the Jeep and headed inside.

The airport waiting area was mostly deserted. Tubby and I were manspreading on an otherwise unoccupied row of plastic chairs facing the landing strip. We were quiet, just sitting there with our legs stretched out, staring at the little runway, when Tubby, out of nowhere, said: "I hear they have traffic lights on Barbados."

I nodded. "I think I remember some traffic lights there," I said, having visited Barbados a few times. "Some paved roads too. But they still drive on the wrong side of them, paved or not."

Tubby snorted. "Wrong side for you, maybe. Why then you come to an island with bad roads and no traffic lights when you can pick any island? Why not live on an island that got those good things we don't have here?"

I turned to look at him.

"Who says those are good things?"

He thought about what I said and nodded in agreement. "You know I been to Trini for Carnival when I a young man. I save my money from working at the quarry for one whole year after I finish my schooling for that trip. On Trini—Port of Spain—I see a few traffic lights too."

"What did you think?" I asked.

"Didn't help the traffic much," Tubby said.

"Traffic lights just make more traffic, I think," I said. "They never helped move traffic in New York, Tubby."

"That might be, but traffic bad around the harbor here, especially at the roundabout, and we have no traffic light. Maybe we need one there," he said.

"Could be," I said, but to be honest, I wasn't really thinking about traffic lights. I was barely listening to what Tubby was saying. I was a little anxious and I think he understood that, so he cut me some slack.

I looked at the time on my phone and then back out the window in front of us. I could see the sharp glint of sun off the silver metal of a plane in the bright blue sky. The plane was heading toward the runway.

I nudged Tubby with my elbow and pointed to the sky.

"She come?" he asked.

"Yeah."

The plane, a Liat ATR-42 turboprop, swerved away from the strip and out over the Caribbean Sea, and then circled back toward the runway. I watched as it broke through a few small puffy clouds and then saw as the wheels were lowered.

I stood up and went close to the window. I clenched my fists as I watched the plane descend. My palms were sweaty. When the plane touched ground, bounced and then leveled as it eased down the runway, I released my fists and exhaled.

Tubby got up now and stood next to me. The plane taxied toward us and then stopped, the propellers slowing and finally coming to a halt. I watched Kingsley Durant, who worked as one of the grounds crew on duty that day at the landing strip, push the ladder with one hand and wheel a baggage cart with the other. Soon the door opened and one of the flight crew appeared. A tall, slender, light brown-skinned woman emerged first, carrying her luggage in one hand and a big purse around her shoulder. She had sunglasses on, and her hair was long and straight and was blowing over her face in the wind. She wore a form-fitting pencil skirt.

"You see what I see?" Tubby said.

"How can I not?" I said, but really I was looking beyond the woman at the other passengers as they exited and descended the steps attached to the plane's front door.

Two white men wearing dark blue suits and carrying brief-cases followed the woman off the plane.

"Men in suits," Tubby said.

"Thanks for pointing them out to me, Tubby," I said.

An older couple, who moved slowly down the ladder and across the strip, was followed by a young woman carrying a baby in her arms. I could feel my heart beating in my chest. There couldn't be many more on that small plane. Then, finally, I saw her. Her golden hair was in a ponytail, and she was wearing dark leggings with a bulky burgundy sweatshirt. I watched as she struggled to get her roll-on bag down the steps. I wanted to go there to help her, but that wasn't allowed. When she got it down, she rolled her luggage easily across the runway toward the small terminal where we were perched. I took off my sunglasses and wiped at my eyes.

Tubby turned to look at me and then back at what I was looking at. He looked back at my damp eyes and grinned.

"You got allergies or something, Mr. Len?"

"Let's go," I said, ignoring his crack.

We headed back outside on the other side of customs and immigration. We waited in the midday sun, our sunglasses back on, as the woman with the pencil skirt pushed through the door. I peered beyond her, trying to locate the girl with the blonde ponytail, but the door closed quickly.

I turned my attention back to the woman in the pencil skirt as she moved toward us. As she got closer, I noticed the scent of vanilla, along with something else I couldn't identify but knew was expensive. The combination was what they would describe in a perfume ad as "intoxicating." I wasn't sure how obvious I was being, but Tubby made no effort to hide his appreciation with a broad, toothy smile. Sensing our mutual admiration and not caring one bit, she smiled at me, or maybe it was both of us, but I didn't think so.

"What she see in you?" Tubby grumbled, confirming what I thought was true.

"Maybe she likes a man with a few miles on him," I said.

"Yeah?" He grinned. "That is until she find out he need a serious tune-up."

We turned to follow her movements as she was met at the curb by St. Pierre's superintendent of police, Keith McWilliams, and one of his deputies, James Baines. Baines held the back door of the police cruiser open and the woman slid into the back seat, smoothing that pencil skirt under her as she did.

"Looks like she get a police escort," Tubby said.

"It does, doesn't it?" I turned back to the darkened glass door of the airport. The two men in suits were next to emerge. They headed to the curb where a limousine, which on St. Pierre was a well-preserved Toyota Camry, waited. Opening the rear door for them was Royston Barksdale, normally a taxi driver but playing chauffeur today. The two men slid in, but, I noticed, neither made any effort to smooth their slacks under them as they did.

The elderly couple came out, and the woman, ignoring me, asked Tubby if he could take them to the Lime House. There were not many hotels on St. Pierre, but of the few, the Lime House was one of the popular ones.

"He's with me," I said to her, indicating Tubby.

"Oh?" She looked to her husband, whose face was pink and what little hair he had was white, sparse and bushy around his ears.

"Can you take us?" the man asked me.

We were leaning against a railing as we waited. "They think we taxi drivers," Tubby said.

"Yeah I got that," I said to Tubby.

The man and woman looked at both of us—waiting.

"No, we can't take you, but he can," I said as I pointed to a white minivan parked near the curb where Kenneth Ambrose was licking at his fingers and then wiping them with a paper towel. I imagine he had just finished eating a very juicy mango. The couple headed toward Ambrose without even a thank you, not that I really cared.

I turned back to the darkened door just as it opened and the girl with the blonde ponytail came out. She looked around, her eyes scanning the sparse crowd, then finally caught my eye and smiled. Her pace quickened as she headed toward us.

I think then I smiled too. I know that I had my arms open

and wide for her. And she ran right into them.

"Daddy," she said.

2

It had been two very long years since I last hugged my daughter, Kasie. That I could go two years without seeing her—and her brother—burned at me. What kind of father does that? Did I really have a good excuse? Work? Opening and expanding a bar? And now this other stuff. This side work I had been doing. When I visited New York two years ago the memories came back hard. And they hurt. Still, that was no excuse not to see my children. And my brother, Pat. What did they all think of me now? What kind of man had I become?

I held her in my arms longer than I had anyone else in a very long time. And now I really didn't want to let go. She lived with my ex-wife Kathleen, her brother Luke and a man named Richard that Kathleen married a few years after I left my family to come to St. Pierre. Finally I let her out of my grasp and just looked at her. Though we communicated regularly on Skype, now, with her here, right in front of me, I didn't know what to say. I was known as a man of few words, but now I was at a total loss.

"How was the flight, Kasie?" I finally said, because I couldn't think of anything else.

Tubby shook his head at me. "How was the flight? That bad. That pathetic, Mr. Len. You can do better than that."

Kasie smiled and looked up at both of us.

"If you didn't know, honey, this so-called friend is Tubby Levett. I've told you about him."

She looked him over. "Hi Tubby, who isn't tubby," she said with a small smile.

Tubby shook his head at me.

"Why didn't you tell me Tubby wasn't tubby at all," she said to me.

"Blame it on my Ma," Tubby said before I could answer my daughter. "She call me that when I a baby 'cause my cheeks and she say everything else were tubby. The name stick even when all the fat gone," he explained.

"Yeah, and Tubby sounds a lot better than the name his Ma christened him with," I said. When I had a local attorney draw up papers granting Tubby a percentage of ownership of the bar, the Sporting Place, which I opened with Tubby's help, I found that his legal first name was Monroe.

Tubby glowered at me. "Don't you go there, Mr. Len," he said and then turned to my daughter. "It's a pleasure to meet you, Kasie. This man tell me a lot about you. But he don't tell me where you get your good looks, 'cause I know it not from he."

"Her mother," I said without hesitation.

"Maybe so," Tubby said. "But you sure there no funny business going on back den? At church the preacher say God works in mysterious ways. That for sure seeing you, pretty girl, and knowing this hideous, stubborn old man your flesh and blood."

Tubby was laying it on thick, but I didn't care. I wasn't really even listening. I couldn't keep my eyes off my daughter. She had her mother's blonde hair and blue eyes. She had shot up in the two years since I had last seen her in person. Now she was just a few inches shorter than me. She had the slender body of a runner. I knew she ran track in high school and even earned several honors for it. She was a beauty. I never doubted she would be. To hear her voice and look into her eyes. To have her close to me. It was as good as it got for me.

"This is some serious drama," Kasie said, grinning widely. "Are you two married?"

"Oh-ohhh," Tubby raised his eyebrows. "Okay, now I know you this man's daughter. He like to poke at people just like that. Is that a thing you born with?"

"Yeah, Tubby," I said. "She's Bronx like me. Lots of attitude."

"Not anymore, Daddy," she said. "Long Island now."

"Yeah, yeah, don't remind me. But I'm glad to see that despite living in that fancy suburb you still got the Bronx in you."

Before my wife and I split, and for most of my life, we lived in the same working-class Italian-American neighborhood in the Throgs Neck section of the Bronx where I grew up. Once Kathleen remarried, her husband moved them to a big house on the North Shore of Long Island.

"Of course, Daddy, you can take the girl out of the Bronx, but you can't take the Bronx out of the girl," she said with a grin.

We started walking to my Jeep. I rolled Kasie's bag. Tubby tried to take her backpack, but she waved him away. "I got it, Tubby, it's okay," she said.

From what I could see she could handle herself. Now that I had her for a week, I hoped to find out more about her life. I wanted to be a bigger part of it, if I could. I wanted to be her father again.

We got into my Jeep, Tubby holding the door open for Kasie.

"I can sit in the back," Kasie said.

"I insist. You are a guest on our beautiful island. Sit up front with your Pa."

I pulled out of the airport and drove toward Garrison, the island's capital and main port. There was a cruise boat docked at the port. Tourists were wandering the old streets that circled the harbor, clicking pictures from their phones at every opportunity.

Kasie was staring out the window at it all. We came to the roundabout, took the first exit to West Road and, as I did, swerved almost onto the curb, narrowly avoiding an oncoming truck.

"It's weird being on the other side of the road. And the steering wheel on the right side. Do you ever get confused, Dad?"

"Not anymore," I said. "It's like second nature for me now."

"It would be hard for me to figure it out," she said.

I looked at her.

"Don't tell me you have your license?"

"Not yet, but I have my permit so I can drive with an adult in the car who has a license."

"Nobody told me," I said, glancing at her and then at the road.

"That's 'cause you probably never asked," Tubby offered from the back seat.

I looked back at him for a moment.

"Yeah, I hear it all back here," Tubby said, grinning at me. "And keep your eyes on the road."

"Tubby thought it would be a good idea to accompany me

to the airport to pick you up. I should have left him at the bar for all the grief he gives me."

Tubby let out another hiss from the back seat. This one was loud and long. I glanced over to see Kasie smiling.

The traffic suddenly slowed. There was a jam in front of us. I could see colored flashing lights from a police car on the side of the road up ahead. We crawled up the hill and came to where the car idled. There was another police car parked ahead of the other. The cars were in front of a small white single-level home.

It was rare to see two police cars with their lights flashing on St. Pierre. While there was plenty of petty crime on the island, low-level drugs, domestic disputes, drunken brawls and the sometimes violent settling of scores, either financial or romantic, serious crime was unusual..

"What going on up here?" Tubby wondered.

I came to a stop next to the police cars. Two officers in blue pants with red piping, light blue shirts and dark blue hats rimmed with red and green stripes, St. Pierre's colors, escorted a very big man in handcuffs out of the house.

"That Big Tree they shackle," Tubby said leaning forward to get a closer look.

I watched as they gently bent the tall man's head under the metal arch of the car's back door and into the back seat of the police car. I started to move the Jeep slowly up the road, passing the other police car. I stopped for just a moment and looked into the car. James Baines was behind the wheel with Keith McWilliams in the seat next to him. We had just seen them both at the airport. There was someone in the back seat of the car. I looked in and saw that it was a woman. She turned to stare back at me with a grim expression. I recognized her from the airport, the tall woman in the pencil skirt who McWilliams and Baines accompanied into the police car. She turned away and kept her eyes straight ahead. McWilliams looked up and gestured for me to keep moving. I drove past them now and started to accelerate up the hill.

"You know that man?" Kasie asked Tubby.

"Tubby knows everyone on this island, Kasie," I said.

"What Big Tree do to get him shackled up like that? He a good boy always," Tubby said.

"Big Tree?" Kasie said.

"His God-given name is Rawle Johns, but the man big as a mango tree so since he a boy, we all call him Big Tree. Why they arrest he? I never know Big Tree to disrespect the law."

I wondered that myself. Big Tree was a tour guide for the island's office of tourism. Because of his almost encyclopedic knowledge of St. Pierre's history and his pleasant demeanor, he was chosen to give island tours to visiting dignitaries, the press, travel agents and others who came to St. Pierre and were deemed VIP. I was no VIP but had heard he was the best, so I arranged a tour with him soon after I arrived here. A person could drive around the twenty-two-square-mile island in less than three hours. With Big Tree, the tour, with all the stops along the way, was a full-day affair. I remembered him pointing out significant sights on the island, explaining them slowly in what was an almost comically high voice, coming as it was from such a big body. What could he possibly have done? And why was the woman from the airport there to witness his arrest?

Kasie was looking at me, studying my expression.

"Almost there," I said, forcing a smile.

3

We drove up to the top of the hill and I turned into the three-car parking lot in front of the Sporting Place. Back in New York, I had owned and run a number of bars in Brooklyn. My partners and I opened them just on the cusp of the hipster explosion in Williamsburg and Bushwick. Our timing had been good, but we also knew how to make a bar work. After things began to go to shit in New York and I made the move here, I sold off my share of the bars for a considerable sum. I took a portion of those profits to invest here.

With the exception of the bars in the island's few hotels, the only option for those who wanted a drink was what was called a rum shop, a small roadside shack where you could have a beer, a shot of rum and maybe play some dominoes. I thought an alternative to the rum shop, a cosmopolitan, somewhat urbane sports bar, would work on the island.

With four televisions, the Sporting Place attracted tourists and locals for worldwide events, mostly those of the athletic kind. Depending on the season, I had European and South American football, the NFL, NBA, NHL, MLB, college basketball and football, Grand Slam tennis, championship fights, both boxing and UFC, the World Cup and other big athletic events, and, mostly for the locals, days-long cricket matches. I also tuned into CNN and/or the BBC for assassinations and elections, terrorist attacks, papal visits, royal weddings, civil wars, hurricane news and other newsworthy catastrophes.

The Sporting Place originally seated just thirty, but after two years and establishing the bar as a popular destination on the island along with hosting a few big private parties, I decided to expand. I had land in the back, and with Tubby's help we extended the bar out, so it now seated seventy-five. We also built a spacious deck where people could take in the view of the Caribbean sea, Garrison Harbor and the colorful roofs of the surrounding eighteenth and nineteenth-century structures, Fort Phillipe and the majestic Holy Ground Catholic Church. I could have expanded even more, but I didn't want the place to be cavernous and cold. Most nights it was empty or with just a few regulars at the bar, but on weekends and during peak winter season, between December and April, it could get so busy we had to hire additional help to serve drinks and clean up after. Still, I think I was being overly ambitious, not to mention a tad pretentious when I strived for cosmopolitan and urbane.

"This is the place," I said with pride.

Kasie gazed at it as she let herself out of the Jeep. "I like the sign," she said, peering at the red neon with the flickering Sporting Place name in script. I had it made at a place I knew back in Brooklyn. To have it shipped down here was expensive, but worth every cent to me.

We went inside and our eyes had to adjust after the bright sun outside. It was spring break and the place was unusually crowded for midday. Mike, Tubby's cousin, was behind the bar. Kendall Cummings and Samuel Mitchell, two regulars, were seated at the bar, bottles of the local beer, Carib, in front of them. The television above the bar was broadcasting an early-season baseball game. No one was watching. The tables in the back were occupied, and I could hear chatter from the deck. Through the open back windows, I could see a party sitting at the table out on the deck.

"Who's this pretty girl?" Mike said, smiling broadly at Kasie. Mike wasn't as tall as Tubby, but he had the build of an NFL nose tackle. His arms and shoulders bulged from his black T-shirt.

"My daughter, Kasie," I said.

"I know that, Mr. Len. But how come she look nothing like you?"

"Ask Tubby," I said to Mike. "He'll tell you a story about that."

Tubby snorted. "It hard to believe but it all true. This beautiful creature come from this ugly man."

"I cannot comprehend such a thing," Mike said.

"Is this gonna go on for the next week?" I asked them.

"I believe it will, Mr. Len," Mike said.

"You want something to drink, honey? Mike makes a memorable lime squash," I said.

"Does it have alcohol?" she asked.

"It can," Mike offered.

"But this one won't," I said, glaring at Mike. "She's sixteen, Mike."

"Sixteen? She look older. Watch out for de island boys here,

Kasie," Mike said as he cut a lime in half and squeezed the juice from one half into a cocktail shaker. "They see that golden hair and they follow you everywhere. Don't waste your time with dem. I have a nephew also sixteen named Percy. Now he a boy you can trust not to disrespect you. He a good boy. Your Pa know him."

"Mike, don't start trying to fix up your nephew or anyone else with my daughter. She's here for only a week. Why would you want to break their hearts?"

Mike thought about that as he poured a shot of simple syrup and added ice into the cocktail shaker. He shook the concoction and then strained it all into an ice-filled highball glass. "Maybe you right, Mr. Len," he said. "That boy already have his heart broken, my sis tell me. I don' think he can take another." He added a small lime wedge to the drink, put a straw in it and handed it to Kasie. "One lime squash for the pretty girl," he said.

"Thanks," she said as she settled onto a barstool.

I went behind the bar and grabbed a bottle of Carib from the ice tray below and came around to sit next to my daughter. I clinked my bottle against her glass. "Cheers, honey," I said. "I'm happy you are finally here with me."

She smiled at me and those tiny dimples, just like her mother's, formed on her cheeks. Tubby was right; it was a good thing she inherited her mother's looks. She was spared my Calabrese nose which her younger brother, who was dark-haired with brown eyes like me, most likely would not. But with his good looks, he might get away with it.

"You hear about Big Tree, Mr. Len?" said Kendall Cummings, who was sitting a few stools down from us.

"We just saw, Kendall. What's going on?" I asked.

"Mike just tell me he hear it bad," Tubby said.

"Henroy Charles tell me they suspect him of foul play," Mike said with a nod.

"Foul play? You're gonna go all Sherlock Holmes on me now, Mike? What did Big Tree do?

Tubby looked at me from behind the bar. And then he looked at Kasie, who was listening to our conversation.

"They think he have something to do with that girl's death," Mike said. "The one who fell from the Freedom Drop last year."

"The writer from that press trip?" I asked.

Tubby nodded.

"What's Freedom Drop?" Kasie asked, taking in everything we were saying.

"It's a famous site here on St. Pierre. I'll take you over there later this week," I said to her. I turned to Mike and Tubby. "I thought that was a closed case. Didn't they say she was drunk and just fell? That it was an accident?"

"That what they say then," Mike said while rinsing a few dirty glasses behind the bar. "But something change."

"What could Big Tree have to do with all that?"

Mike, Tubby and even Kendall said nothing, but the way they were looking at me said something else.

"You okay, Dad?"

I didn't like what I was hearing, and my face rarely hid what I was feeling.

"Just thinking on this news," I said.

"We all just speculating now, Mr. Len," Tubby said. "Soon we know what's what."

"Yeah, we will," I said.

But something wasn't right. At least that's the way my mind

was working. I don't know if it was the quiet here, the calming sounds of nature that are so much different from what I experienced most of my life in New York, but since I came to St. Pierre, if I heard something, or someone told me something, I would start to think a little more deeply on it. To wonder about what was said. Wonder about what was right and what was wrong. And it had become more than just wondering. I had begun acting on my suspicions. It started when I confronted that drug trafficker from Guyana; my sense of justice made me take him on. I wasn't even thinking about the drugs he was bringing to the island. I needed to right a wrong. But why would I do that? I never cared about things like that in New York. Let the cops handle it. Let the corrupt politicians. It wasn't my job. But here...it was almost as if it was an obligation. Or so I felt.

Soon after the incident with the drug dealer, there was an injustice done to a local girl who was a friend of a friend. I was asked to settle it. In a roundabout way I did with the help of an island celebrity who I originally thought was the man responsible. Though the real criminal, a powerful island businessman, was never jailed or even charges brought, he suffered. And the island knew what he did and how he paid for his crime, and that was enough for them.

I've learned in my time on this small island that word travels quickly here. For some reason I became a man people could talk to when they couldn't talk to the police. Or when the police would not listen to them. Island folks were beginning to see me as more than just an owner of "that bar up on Windy Hill." Because I took care of a few troubles a couple of times, it was assumed I could do it again. I've never claimed to be someone like that. I had no background in police work. I was no detective. I didn't read crime fiction and probably watched no more than two episodes of *Law and Order*. I didn't know the first thing about conducting an investigation. I ran bars. That was my business in New York. And that was my business here. Except now there was this other thing that people expected of me, whether I wanted it or not.

I felt Kasie nudge me in the ribs. "Dad?"

"Huh?" I looked at her and shifted a little on my barstool.

"This man's talking to you. Where did you go?"

I turned away from Kasie to look at who was talking to me. He had reddish-brown hair that was slicked back from his head. His eyes were blue, his nose was narrow, and his lips were thin. He looked to be in his early to mid-thirties. He was wearing an aqua polo shirt tucked into his beige hiking shorts, along with leather sandals. His frame was slight under the shirt.

"I asked if you were the owner of this place?" the man said, holding a beer bottle in his hand.

"Sorry, yeah, it's mine," I mumbled. "And my friend over there." I pointed to Tubby. "Ours."

"Great place." The man smiled. I could see that his teeth were almost too white and perfect. His smile too seemed well rehearsed. "That view out there is outstanding."

I nodded and started to turn back to my daughter. I often got compliments on the view from the deck. I knew I was being a little rude, but I wanted to talk to my daughter, not some man off a cruise boat. And that phony smile made me wish he would just go away.

Yet my lack of attention didn't deter him. He kept that smile on me. "Eric Dunn," he said, extending his hand.

I looked at his hand and gripped it half-heartedly. I knew that by the time I released his hand, his name would be forgotten. I was bad that way. I might just remember his face though. And that off-putting smile. I was better in the visual department.

"Len Buonfiglio," I said. "Welcome to the Sporting Place."

I smiled at the man. I had no choice but to do my best to not be rude. My daughter was watching. I didn't want to set a bad example. I started to turn my attention back to her when he moved a little closer to me. The guy wouldn't let go.

"My group here has been sailing through the islands." He gestured to some people he was drinking with out on the deck who I could not see from my perch at the bar.

"So it's your first time on St. Pierre?" I asked, then immediately regretted it, knowing that would lead to more conversation I did not want.

"Yes, it is, and who knew that this was truly paradise? Nice beaches. Friendly people. A rain forest. Beautiful waterfalls. A volcanic lake. No wonder you decided to settle here," he said.

I wondered what he meant by that. Did he know something about me? Probably not, but for some reason he now had my hackles up.

"It's worked for me," I said.

"I can see it has," he said.

He stood there, quiet for a moment, and then said, "Something tells me you're a New Yorker. Am I right?"

"Yes." And something told me he already knew that bit of information about me.

"My father's from New York originally. He still has a little bit of that New Yawk accent. And that toughness, too." he said.

"Don't believe everything you hear. Not all New Yorkers

are tough."

"No, I guess they're not," he said. "Whereabouts in New York?"

"The Bronx. What about your father?"

He grabbed one of the beers and sipped. He grinned. "Not the Bronx," he said.

"I see," I said. "And where are you from?"

"Vegas," he said.

"That's a place I've never been."

"No? Say it ain't so, Len."

"It's so..." He kept using my name and all I could do was dance around the fact that I already forgot his. It was getting embarrassing. Maybe I did need to take some of those memory boosters like the turmeric tea Tubby kept pushing on me.

"Everyone needs to visit Vegas at least once in their life," he said. "So then I take it you're not a gambler?"

I shook my head and sipped more from my beer. I glanced at Kasie. I knew she was ready to go, and so was I.

"Nope." I was hoping that would help cut this short.

"Well, Vegas is not just about gambling. Or Elvis impersonators."

"Now I wouldn't mind seeing an Elvis impersonator," I said.

He laughed. "Come to Vegas and I'll make sure you see the best. But seriously, the city is changing. It's becoming more sophisticated, I think. Not so much Sin City anymore. It's more like New York...of course nothing is really like New York, though some of the best chefs from the Big Apple—and the world—have opened restaurants in our city. If you like to eat, you can't do much better than Vegas."

"Should I put it on my bucket list then?"

"Vegas should be on everyone's bucket list, Len."

A dark-skinned man with long braids, wearing jeans and a colorful T-shirt emblazoned with a rasta-haired lion in gold sunglasses, moved between me and the man I was chatting with to grab the four beers Mike had opened for him. The man was thin with taut, muscular arms cluttered with dark blue tattoos that melded into his skin. He grabbed the four bottles of Heineken, two in each large hand, and then exchanged a look with the chatty man. The man from Vegas nodded and the man with the braids took the beers and headed toward the deck in the back.

"It was nice to meet you, Len. Now that I've discovered St. Pierre and especially this place, I'm sure we will meet again."

"It would be a pleasure," I said with as straight a face as I could manage.

I watched as he went back to the deck. I could see the man with the braids and another man next to him. The man from Vegas had his back to me and was sitting next to a woman with a short dyed-blond afro and dark skin, as dark as the man with the braids.

I turned to Tubby and Mike, who had witnessed the interaction between us.

"Am I supposed to know who he is?" I asked them both.

"I guess you are," Tubby said.

"Do you?"

"No," Tubby said.

"He a celebrity or something?" I asked.

"No celebrity I know," Tubby said.

"How many celebrities do you know, Tubby?"

"I mix a rum punch for Johnny Depp one time at the Yacht

Club," Tubby said. "When he filming one of those *Pirates of the Caribbean* movies on Tobago. He take a break from Tobago for a few days and visit St. Pierre. We chat but I couldn't understand a word from the man's mouth."

"Maybe it was because you make your rum punch so strong, it even makes Johnny Depp slur his words."

"I think Johnny Depp a natural slurrer, Mr. Len."

"If you say so, Tubby," I said.

"All I know is this man here leave a generous tip each time he buy a round, that I can say," Mike said. "That make him a celebrity to me."

I turned to my daughter to see if she was listening to. She looked like she was about to fall asleep on the bar. "You ready to go?" I asked her.

"Dad, I've been ready."

"Sorry about that, Kasie. People just want to meet the owner sometimes. They can't resist me."

She rolled her eyes at me.

"Okay, let's get out of this dump," I said as we got off our stools and headed back to my Jeep.

4

The twenty-minute drive back down to Garrison was a quiet one. We headed for the Atlantic side of the island, where I had built my home. I knew Kasie was tired from her trip; the five-hour flight to Barbados had left early from JFK. She had to have been up well before dawn. And then the hour changeover in Barbados for the forty-minute flight to St. Pierre. It was still early in the evening, but it had been a long day for her.

I didn't volunteer much either. I had plenty of questions for her, but I just couldn't get them out and I sensed, now without Tubby as a buffer, some awkwardness between us. There was no reason to force an interrogation. She was going to be with me for a week. There would be plenty of time, I hoped, to get reacquainted.

She was asleep with her head against the window by the time I pulled into my driveway. I built my house on a bluff overlooking the ocean. The windward side of the island was craggy; the beaches were volcanic black sand and the surf rough. The best beaches for swimming and sunning were on the Caribbean side, but still, I could spend a whole afternoon just staring out at the Atlantic. And I often did.

She opened her eyes when I turned off the Jeep.

"We're here?" She looked around. "I fell asleep, I guess."

"No worries, Kasie. I know it's a long day."

She stared at my house. I built it intentionally to be small and simple. I didn't expect to be doing much entertaining. The house was a single-level with a half porch in front. I had a good amount of land, most of which was brush and a few fruit trees, including a big tamarind tree off to the side and two small orange trees in the back. Inside, my pride was the picture window off the living room facing the bluffs and the Atlantic. I had two bedrooms and a bathroom and a half, along with a small room in the back I thought I might use as an office. But whenever I had paperwork to do, I usually did it at the kitchen table, where I could distract myself now and then by staring out the window at the ocean.

"This looks nice, Dad," Kasie said as she opened the door to the Jeep.

"It works for me," I said.

We got out of the Jeep and I went to the back to get her bag. My dogs came bounding over. I had three adopted dogs of undetermined ages. They were strays, mongrels that found their way to my house soon after I moved in and never left. They sniffed around Kasie. She looked at them tentatively as they sniffed.

"Don't worry, honey, they won't tear you to bits unless I tell them to," I said.

"Seriously?"

I laughed and shook my head. The dogs were all around the same size — thirty to forty pounds. The only female of the three had a brown coat. Another had a spotted coat of white with a few patches of dark gray, and the third had a gray coat. I named them by their coats: the Brown One, the Spotted One and the Gray One.

We started into the house, the dogs following. The Brown One, maybe happy there was finally another female in the house, stuck close to Kasie, bounding along near her legs. I held the front door open for her and we were almost inside when I heard a voice coming from not far behind me.

"Sir?"

I turned to see a young boy, maybe twelve or thirteen years old, in his school uniform of navy blue chinos and a light yellow button-down shirt and navy blue necktie. He held a small silver Dutch pot in his hands.

"I was scared of the dogs," he said as he approached me slowly.

"It's okay, they won't bother you," I said to him. "What can I do for you?"

"My Grandma make this for you," he said, offering me the Dutch pot.

Kasie was at the screen door, peering at me and the boy.

"Who's your Grandma?"

"Miss Johns," he said.

"Miss Johns?" The name wasn't registering.

"Yes, sir. She tell me to bring this pelau to you. She say to tell you she would bring the pelau to you herself, but the hill too steep for her." He held the Dutch pot out to me.

I took it from him, opened the lid; the rich aroma of meats mixed with rice, pigeon peas and savory spices immediately made me realize I hadn't eaten since breakfast.

"Why did your Grandma have you bring this to me?" I asked.

"What's going on, Dad?" Kasie asked from inside the house.

"I'll be right in," I said to her.

I turned back to the boy.

"She just say bring this pelau to you and you will know," he said.

I thought for a moment. Not too long ago another woman brought me food in a Dutch pot. She fed me and then I helped her with a crime she felt had been committed. I never expected to be paid for what I did. I never asked for money. And I never asked for food. But it came anyway. I wasn't complaining.

"Miss Johns?"

The boy nodded.

"Family of Rawle Johns?"

He nodded again.

"Big Tree?"

"Yes, that's what they call my Pa," he muttered, his eyes down now.

"And what's your name?"

"Ezran," he said.

"Thank your Grandma for me, Ezran. I'll stop by to return the Dutch, okay?"

"Yes, sir," he said as he turned and started down the hill. I watched as he walked quickly, turning for a moment to look back at me and then heading down the hill.

I brought the still-warm Dutch pot inside.

"What was that all about, Dad? Who was that boy?"

"The son of a friend," I said.

"Why did he bring you that?" She pointed to the Dutch pot.

"I'm not sure, but I do know now what we are having for dinner tonight,"

But I *was* sure. The food brought to me was a signal. It was a request for my help. I couldn't refuse the food. I couldn't give the Dutch pot back to the boy. I would find out soon enough what would be requested of me whether I wanted to or not.

While Kasie showered, I put the pot on the stove to keep it warm. I had some flat roti bread in the refrigerator that I heated in the oven. I made a salad out of shredded cabbage and carrots and dressed it with vinegar. I set the table for the two of us and then called to her that dinner was ready.

"I'm in here," she said.

I went into my bedroom to see her staring at a painting, a colorful acrylic of a beach scene, that hung over my dresser. There was a man, a primitive, childlike figure really, sitting on a rock close to the blue water. On the beach near where the man was sitting there were several upright sticks with fish impaled on them. The title, scrawled in black paint at the bottom, read: "*Saltin' the Fish*." The artist's name, Benoit Yarms, was at the bottom-right of the painting.

"I like it," Kasie said with a smile. "Don't you have something just like that at the bar? I thought I saw it today."

I was impressed that she made the connection between the two. "I do. The one with the kids playing soccer on the beach. You've got a good eye, kid."

"I get As in art," she said. "Mom wants me to take more advanced classes and maybe think about art school. I like to draw, but mostly I like to look at art."

I smiled at her. I was thinking of something to say. I should have asked her about artists she liked. What styles interested her. And maybe, if she had any of her own creations, she could show them to me. But I didn't and I don't know why. Instead, I said, "You know I went to Pratt Institute in Brooklyn for a few months."

"Mom told me," she said.

"She did?"

"Yeah, but how come you never told me that?" Kasie asked.

I thought about that. I really didn't have an answer. There were many things I hadn't told my daughter. "I don't know," was all I could say.

She clearly wasn't happy with my non-answer, and there was another one of those awkward moments between us. To get out of it, I steered the conversation back to the painting she was admiring.

"Did you know that the artist, Benoit Yarms, painted those two paintings for me in one day?" I told her.

"For real, Dad?"

"Yes, for real. He painted thousands of paintings with scenes depicting life here. He was what they call prolific."

"I know what prolific means," she said, shaking her head at me with some impatience.

"Ah...okay...well anyway he was in his nineties when I com-missioned him to paint them for me."

"You hired him to paint those particular paintings?"

"Yeah, I drove up to Sandy Valley, which is the dry, southwest part of the island, where Yarms had a shack about a half-mile from the road. I had to get out of my Jeep, walk past goats and chickens, and knock on his shack, where he painted. He showed me some samples of his work that he could duplicate, I picked out the one you see here and the one we have at the bar, and he said he would have them done for me by the end of the day. And he did. He charged me just a hundred dollars for the two."

"That's all?"

"That's all," I said. "The man's paintings can be found all over, even in a gallery in London. He was a legend on St. Pierre," I said.

"Was?"

"He died a couple of years ago," I said.

Kasie pondered what I just told her. "That's sad," she said in a quiet voice.

It wasn't my intention to bring up death or anyone's mortality so I tried to put a cheerful spin on it. "He lived some life, though." I said. "He was ninety-six when he died and had eleven children, twenty-four grandchildren and I don't know how many great-grandchildren. And those were just the off-spring from his legal marriages. There were others, I know, that weren't legally his children, but all knew he was their father. So, yeah, prolific is the right word for him." I smiled at what I said hoping she got the reference.

She laughed. "Okay, Dad, I know what you mean." She looked at the painting again. "Is that beach on St. Pierre?" she asked.

"It is," I said. "Coral Beach. Great snorkeling and diving there too."

"Really? Can we go?"

"If you like," I said. Besides taking time off from the bar to be with her, I hadn't really made any plans for us. In our many Skype conversations, I told her how laid back the island was. There wasn't much really to do besides relax, enjoy the weather and the beauty of the mountains and beaches. In New York, the bar business was stressful at times. The only thing that saved me from burnout was my Type B, or maybe even C, personality. Still, coming from New York, the quiet pace of the island took some time to get used to. I never thought of making up a schedule of things for us to do, but maybe I should have

"Let's go tomorrow," she said. "I've never really snorkeled anywhere where I can see fish."

"You'll see plenty off Coral Beach," I said.

She looked back at the painting and then at me. "How come you left Pratt?"

"That's one big regret," I said. "Back then they were giving out money to join the armed forces. I got three thousand dollars to join the Marines, along with a decent monthly check. And they'd set me up with a career once I completed my service. With that option, going to art school seemed a foolish thing even though I enjoyed it. I thought making money was the responsible thing to do. Maybe learning a trade that I could carry on when I returned to civilian life. I made the wrong choice, looking back."

"But I thought Marines were like — I don't know — the best or something."

I chuckled. "For some maybe. But not for me." I shook my head. "I was never one of the few...or the proud. None of that bullshit."

"Dad!"

I had to stop. I was with my daughter. With the exception of Tubby, no one ever was around to call me on my often cranky outbursts. And the dogs never complained as long as I filled their bowls.

I shrugged. "I never saw combat. There were no conflicts when I served, so I guess I was lucky about that. And they did teach me how to drive a truck. Beyond that, I would have much rather have studied art with all those pretty girls than bunked with a group of jarheads. And I think I would have learned just as much about the world."

"Dad, you're such a Grinch. Mom warned me about that,"

"Oh, she did?

"Yeah, and by the way, thank you for your service," she said with a wicked grin.

I growled but realized she was just teasing me. She was sizing me up. I was telling her things I never told her before. She was learning more about her father. And, despite my gruff talk, that playful smile remained, so I guess she liked what she was hearing.

I dished out some of the pelau onto our plates, along with the salad and the roti bread. Kasie picked through the rice, examining its contents.

"What is all this?" she asked.

"They call it pelau," I said. "It's a comfort food here on St. Pierre. An easy one-pot dish with rice, pigeon peas, pieces of chicken, pig tail..."

"Pig tail?" Kasie put her fork down.

"Yeah, honey." I looked at what I served her. "If you find one in there, you can give it to me. I'm sure what's mostly in there is chicken thighs. But don't hate on the pig tail. It's good stuff."

"Luke ate frog once when Dick took us all out to a Chinese restaurant in Queens."

"Did he like it?"

"Luke likes everything, Dad. Especially anything with meat."

The thought of my son voluntarily eating frog made me smile. I only wish I was there to see it. To experience it with him. I had no one to blame about that. This was all my doing.

"But that's Luke," she said. "You know I'm not eating a pig's tail."

"Your loss," I said. "But try the rice, they make it with home-made coconut milk," I shook out a few dashes of the local pepper sauce onto my portion and then offered her the bottle.

"Is it very spicy?"

"You have no idea," I said.

Taking it as a challenge, she sprinkled red splotches of the pepper sauce onto her rice.

There was no pig tail in her portion; I found two in mine and devoured them happily. Mrs. Johns' pelau was first-rate, but I knew it came with a price. I would have to find out what that price would be when I returned her Dutch pot.

♦

After dinner, we walked outside in the dark toward the hill-top overlooking the Atlantic. There was a half-moon that cut a sliver of light over the dark water below, the only light on the sea. Sometimes when I'd look out in the distance, I could see the lights of a cruise boat or a freighter. On this night, though, there was nothing.

"I can't believe how quiet it is here," Kasie said.

"You get used to it after awhile," I said. "In the morning it's not so quiet when you start hearing those roosters and goats scurrying about."

"Goats? Really?"

"You'll see," I said.

"But don't you get lonely out here all by yourself?"

She looked at me. It was one of those feel sorry for you looks. I didn't want any of that.

"You know, I really don't. I'm busy most nights at the bar. And when I'm not working, the quiet is kind of a nice break. After all those years working in New York, this is welcome. And the dogs keep me company."

She frowned. "I don't like thinking of you down here by yourself with only these dogs to keep you company."

I smiled at her. Or tried to. What she said cut right to my gut. I didn't know what to say.

We walked back into the house and sat in the living room. The Brown One jumped onto the couch and curled next to Kasie before quickly falling asleep. I sat opposite in my big black reading chair that swiveled so I could easily turn to stare out at the ocean.

"We miss you," Kasie said as she stroked the Brown One's coat.

"I miss you too, honey," I said. "Not a day goes by when I don't think of you and your brother. But this is my home now. I'm happy here, really. The only thing missing is having you guys close by. Is everything good at home?"

"It's all cool. They're happy. Dick doesn't bother us." She curled her lean jeans-clad legs under her.

The Dick Kasie was referring to was Richard, my ex-wife's husband. I met him a couple of times when I visited New York. He was a quiet, unassuming man from what I could observe. There was nothing I found objectionable about him, and he deferred most of the parenting to Kathleen, which I thought was a good thing.

"I'm glad to hear that," I said. "And Luke is good? Nothing I need to know about there?"

"You mean is he hanging out with the wrong dudes? Vaping? Smoking THC-laced weed? Skipping school? Or just being a pain-in-the-ass little brother?"

"I expect he is a pain-in-the-ass little brother. It's the other stuff I worry about."

"He's okay," she said. "We just miss you. It would be nice to spend more time with you is all."

What she said hurt. I had to live with my fuck-up. I could have stayed. I could have figured another way out. But instead I ran from there. I ran from it all.

"Soon you'll be old enough to be able to spend more time here," I said after letting that sink in. "At least I hope you want to. You guys are my life. But now this is too."

"It's okay, Dad. Just so long as you aren't going all reclusive on us."

"Reclusive? Now you tell me, is getting a Dutch pot of pelau delivered to your door the sign of a recluse?"

"Maybe not," she said. "But it is a little weird."

"Not weird, just the way it can be here on this island." With that I got up from the chair. "I'm going to bed. You can stay up, watch TV, do whatever, your room's all set for you."

"Okay, Dad, but don't wake me."

"You gonna sleep all day?" I looked at her.

"No, we're going snorkeling. Wake me for that."

I kissed her on the forehead and as she started playing on her phone, doing whatever she was doing on it, the Brown One snuggled next to her on the couch.

5

I was up early the next morning. I knew Kasie would sleep in. She had been up late on her phone texting and whatever else a sixteen-year-old girl does on her phone, most of which I didn't want to know about. I had gone shopping in anticipation of Kasie's visit and stocked up on cereal, eggs and bread for toast. I made coffee and kept it warm in the coffee maker. There was juice in the fridge. Whatever she might want for breakfast was available for her to help herself to if she woke before I got back. I wrote a quick note telling her to call me if she needed me and left it on the small dining room table off to the side of the kitchen.

I scrubbed the Dutch pot and took it out to my Jeep. I headed down East Road toward Garrison, St. Pierre's capital and main port. Rush hour on the island meant the narrow two-way streets were jammed. Another cruise boat, this one the size of one of the Bronx housing projects I was so familiar with, had docked overnight at the pier. The cruisers, as I called those aficionados of the cruise-boat scene, wandered around the harbor taking selfies, while Harold Boothe and his army of taxi drivers lined up to give them island tours, take them to beaches or up to Fort Phillipe or Mt. Hadali, the island's dormant yet still-smoking volcano and its steaming volcanic lake. Tourists had no idea what was coming next, when seemingly appearing out of nowhere, higglers descended on the unsuspecting hordes, shoving homemade wood carvings, jewelry made from local shells, bottled local spices, condiments and anything else in front of them, hoping for a quick sale. To a St. Pierre higgler, a no meant let me try again...and again, until their victims would give up and buy something just to get rid of them.

There was a jam about a quarter of a mile long as I approached the roundabout. Ever since I arrived on St. Pierre, there'd been talk, sometimes heated, about installing a traffic light at the roundabout to help ease traffic. Though many were against it, the prime minister, Leeland Garvey, made it a campaign pledge. But without the money it would take to run electricity to a light and put in the computer circuitry needed to make it function properly, nothing had been done. I was skeptical that a light would change anything. And for whatever strange reason, it gave me some satisfaction to tell friends back in New York that I lived in a place where there were no traffic lights.

As the traffic cleared, I made my way up West Road toward Windy Hill and thought about what Miss Johns would ask of me. I knew her son, Rawle, was in trouble. It had to do with a dead girl. At least that's what I was told by the intrepid Greek chorus that drank at my bar. But that chorus sometimes got their information wrong. They weren't always reliable in delivering the facts. Ezran Johns brought me the pelau from his grandmother as an offering for my help. I knew that much. I would find out more after talking to the boy's grandmother. But would I get the facts?

I had briefly met the girl whose demise was now in question, just a day before she died. Her death, a fall from a historical site on the northern tip of the island called Freedom Drop, was a shock to all of us. It was said that the girl had to have been drunk and that an empty pint bottle of Stallion overproof rum was found nearby. Or maybe she was on drugs. Some speculated that she committed suicide. That she was so moved by the legend of Freedom Drop, a place where indigenous peoples and African slaves would leap to their deaths rather than submit to their white conquerors, that she thought it would be a fitting way to end her life. There were all sorts of rumors. I don't put much stock in rumors — I'd heard a few about me over the years — so I never listened to any regarding the poor girl's death. After a few days the story faded away.

The girl and I were alone together for no more than fifteen minutes, but she left an impression on me — an unsettling one, to be honest, and I didn't think that it was anything more than a tragic accident. Now, though, I recalled that meeting. Though I was introduced to her that day, I instantly forgot her name. I remembered seeing her picture in the paper after her death, smiling and happy. But it was really a picture of a smiling dead girl, and it made my stomach wrench to see it. It made me think of another girl. She was smiling too in her picture in the papers. She looked happy. But she was also dead. I didn't like seeing pictures of smiling dead girls.

Recalling the girl's face jarred my memory, and by the time I pulled in front of the single-level, wood-framed white house on the incline of the hill where Big Tree was escorted into the police car the day before, her name came to me: Deanna Gould.

As I got out of the Jeep with the Dutch pot in my hand, Ezran came out through the screen door. He was in the same school uniform he had worn yesterday, though he was carrying a backpack this time. "Are you gonna help my Pa?" he asked as he approached me.

"What?"

A short, stout woman with glasses, her hair in a net, pushed the screen door open.

"You late to school again. Leave dat man and go," the woman shrieked.

Ezran stared at me for a moment then, obeying the command given to him, he promptly headed down the hill to school.

The woman squinted at me as I made my way slowly to the door.

"I wanted to return this and thank you for the pelau," I said.

She held the door open for me to enter, and I went inside. The living room was dark, the shades were mostly drawn. I stood awkwardly in the room as she took the pot from me without a word and put it on top of her stove in the adjacent small kitchen. I could smell cinnamon and nutmeg. Something comforting had just been baked. She walked back to me on gimpy legs.

"I not sure if you enjoy the pelau with pig tail," she said. "Some don't like pig tail."

Pig tail was not something I grew up with in the Bronx, but I learned to keep an open mind when it came to food.

"Nothing wrong with pig tail," I said.

"Please sit, mister," she said.

I was going to ask her to address me as Len, but why would she be any different than so many on the island? Though my first name is Len, the name on St. Pierre I'm most commonly referred to is "Mr. Len." No matter how many times I have asked to call me "Len," it always came out, "Mr. Len." I wasn't sure if it was a sign of respect, the inability to properly pronounce my last name, *Buonfiglio*, or maybe the people of St. Pierre were just not comfortable calling me by my last or first name without a proper title attached. It had a colonial-plantation feel to it whenever anyone addressed me as such, and it bothered me. But I have long since given up asking. So I was actually relieved when Mrs. Johns simply referred to me as "mister."

I sat at the round kitchen table in one of the four wooden seats with plastic-covered seat cushions. She maneuvered around the table and sat opposite me.

"They think Rawle do a bad ting," she mumbled, her dark hands clasping together as she said it. "They think he have something to do wit de girl who fall from de Freedom Drop dat time. He never hurt a soul. The Lord make it hard on Rawle. He take he wife from he when she so young and Ezran just a baby. And now this? Why would dey think dat, Mister? Why dey think my son harm a creature, any of dem dat are God's creatures?"

It was a question I sensed I would be asked, but of course I had no answer. I could never imagine Big Tree hurting anyone. I knew he had lost his wife and was a single father to Ezran. He mentioned that to me on that first tour when I asked him about his family. He didn't seem bitter about it. He didn't dwell on it. With the help of his mother, he was raising his son. I bowed my head a little as I sat there and remained silent.

She wiped at her eyes, at the tears streaking down her dark, furrowed cheek. "Miss Shirma Bates come and pray wit me yesterday. She tell me to talk to you. She say you can help my son. She say you can find the truth and prove to the people that Rawle did not do this."

Shirma Bates. I took a breath. She brought me food just like Mrs. Johns did. She came to me with a local dish called oil down — a stew of meats, including cow feet and chicken legs, root vegetables, yams, green banana, pumpkin and dasheen greens, slow-cooked in coconut milk and spices. With her offering, she wanted me to help her clear the name of a man who was found hanging from a manchineel tree. The man, Fincey Pierce, was the island vagrant, a homeless man who ate from garbage cans and shrieked at tourists. On the island, he was better known as Filthy Man. But Ms. Bates knew him before he became Filthy Man. And she knew other things about his past as well. She knew enough to be convinced that Filthy Man did not hang himself. That someone else hung him and made it look like a suicide. Maybe it was the oil down. Maybe it was the way Shirma Bates expressed herself and the sincerity in her belief that the man she knew, and was in love with many years before he became damaged, would not kill himself. Whatever it was, I agreed to help her and indeed did prove that Fincey Pierce did not take his own life.

But despite what I learned in my investigation, nothing else had changed. Fincey Pierce was dead. The person responsible did not go to prison. Yet Shirma Bates was satisfied. She knew that without broadcasting my findings on social media or in the press, the island would now know the truth. They got their real news from one another. At church. In the rum shops. At the open market off the harbor. At social gatherings. Fincey Pierce's name was cleared. Nothing else mattered.

But this, I had a feeling, would be much more difficult.

"Why do they think he hurt that woman?" I asked. "Did they tell you?"

She shook her head. "They say dey find evidence now. Evidence? What evidence? What they mean?"

It meant that there was something that had come up to open the case again. There was something discovered that connected Big Tree to the girl's death. I knew St. Pierre didn't have the resources to do extensive forensic testing. But someone did somewhere. And whatever was found implicated the woman's son.

I listened to what Mrs. Johns said, and I was troubled. I wanted to help her son, but what did I know about forensics? What did I know about a serious murder investigation? I was just a man who owned a bar. She was studying my face, and I was sure she could read all the doubt there. Still, she looked at me with hope.

"Does he have a lawyer," I asked her.

She nodded. "He was appointed a solicitor, yes," she said. "But when I talk wit dat man, he talk to me in funny ways. Ways I do not understand. He ask questions as if he too think Rawle do dis. Why would de solicitor do dat? He job to prove a man innocent. You know my son. You know he a man who would never do someting like dis."

Big Tree was most likely given a court-appointed defense attorney. He needed much more than that for something like this but obviously didn't have the funds. I didn't know any criminal lawyers here. I had no power or pull on the island. I was not involved in local government, nor could I be. I wasn't a citizen of St. Pierre. I was an outsider, really, an American who made money in the States and, like others, chose to invest that here. I didn't have any power or pull that a born and bred islander would.

She sensed my apprehension and got up from her seat. I watched as she went back into the kitchen and slowly put a cake in a box. She closed it and taped the sides of the box and brought it to the table. "Spice cake," she said, pushing the box to me.

That was the aroma I inhaled when I entered the house.

"That's very kind, Mrs. Johns, but you don't have to cook for me."

"Ezran tell me your daughter come to visit," she said. "If she never have spice cake before, now she try it fresh."

"Yeah, okay. Thank you."

I smiled and stood up. She remained seated.

"Help Rawle," she said from her seat. "He become quiet and sad these years since his wife pass. And now this. Help him. Please."

I said nothing. I made no promises. I gave no indication that I would help. I just took the cake and left.

6

Where are you? was the text from Kasie that I saw on my phone as I walked back to the Jeep holding the box of spice cake. I texted back that I was on my way home.

The cake sat on the front passenger seat next to me. Did taking the cake mean I couldn't back off from Mrs. Johns' request? That I had to help her son? Beyond what she told me, I had no other details about his arrest. I hadn't seen the paper yet, and most likely the story would not appear for another day. The *St. Pierre Press* was usually a day or two behind the news.

What evidence was found? And why did it take so long for that evidence to materialize? I needed to get in to talk to Keith McWilliams, St. Pierre's police superintendent. He and I had a checkered relationship. McWilliams was respectful yet wary of me. He knew of my burgeoning reputation and, at times, thought of it as an infringement on his responsibilities. Still, he had the resources. I had none. And he had information. There were ways I could find out things without his help, but for this one, I had to start with him. As I pulled into my driveway, I remembered my daughter was waiting for me. We had just one week together. How could I help Mrs. Johns and also spend time with my daughter?

She was sprawled on her belly on the couch staring at her phone when I walked in holding the cake box.

"What's that?" she asked.

"A cake," I said. "Did you eat anything?"

She pulled herself up from the couch. "No, and I'm really hungry."

"Did you see my note?"

"What note?"

I picked up the note I left on the kitchen table and waved it in the air. "The one here that says to help yourself to cereal, toast, eggs, whatever."

"Oh? No, I didn't see it. Where were you anyway?"

"I had to go see someone," I said.

"Who?" Kasie asked.

"Someone who wanted to talk to me about some things,"

"What things?"

"Nothing important," I said.

"And she baked you a cake?"

"Yeah, a spice cake," I said.

"So you went to see a woman who baked you a cake."

"What?"

My daughter was displaying her cunning. She had set a trap for me.

"You said 'she,' Dad." She grinned.

"A woman, yeah, but nothing like that," I said, knowing what my daughter was implying. I thought of Mrs. Johns. "Nothing like that at all."

I put the box on the kitchen counter and opened it. Kasie was hovering behind me. The scent of cinnamon and nutmeg wafted from the open box.

She got up, peered into the box and sniffed. "Wow, it smells amazing," she said.

"I know you've never had a St. Pierre spice cake. She...Mrs. Johns...wanted you to try a piece."

I cut two slices of the cake and put them on plates.

"Who's Mrs. Johns?" Kasie sat at the kitchen table as I slid a plate and fork to her.

"That was her grandson that was here yesterday," I said.

"With that pelau pig-tail thing?"

"Yeah." I sat down opposite her.

"What's with that, Dad?"

"What's with what?"

"Why is she cooking stuff for you?"

"She must think I like to eat," I said. "And she might be right."

My daughter glanced at me. "You have put on a little weight," she said.

I looked back at her. Now she was going to judge me on my creeping waistline?

"I know...I know. I plan on addressing that...sometime soon," I stuttered.

"Yeah, okay, but now we are just avoiding the real subject. What's going on with you here? You're being kind of secretive with me."

"I am?"

"You are. I can tell. You're holding out on me."

I shrugged. She didn't need to know any of the other stuff of what had been happening in my life. What I was doing would be hard to explain coherently and since I had no background in investigations, or solving crimes, she might just think I've gotten a little crazy down here by myself. And I considered what I was doing temporary. I had no plans to make this side thing permanent. But now I had to say something. I just didn't know what.

"She wanted to ask me a favor," I said.

Kasie swallowed a piece of the cake. "This is good," she cut off another piece with her fork. "What kind of favor?"

I should have learned to bullshit better during my Marine training; it just never came natural to me. But what I did learn was to detect bullshit when I heard it. I had a feeling my daughter inherited some of my bullshit-detector tendencies. If I tried to make something up, Kasie would see it for what it was. I had to tell her the truth.

"You remember we saw a man being arrested yesterday when we were driving up to the bar?"

"Yeah, the Mango Tree?"

"Big Tree is what everyone calls him. His real name is Rawle Johns."

Kasie was picking at crumbs on her plate now. "Is Mrs. Johns his wife?"

"His mother," I said.

"Why did they arrest him?"

"They think he might have been involved in the death of a woman here. Something that happened last year."

"So he's in jail now?"

I nodded.

"What did she want from you, Dad? What kind of favor?"

"She wants me to help him."

Her eyes were probing mine. "How can you help him?"

"I really don't know," I said.

"Then why did she ask for your help?"

I shrugged but said nothing. I could see her heating up. Her eyes were narrowing. I'd seen that look many times from her mother.

"You're pissing me off, Dad. I didn't come all the way to this place to see you if you're not gonna talk to me. I mean, why are you that way? I'm your daughter. You can trust me. You live down here and run a bar, but there's got to be more to your life. Enough with the secrets."

Her outburst jarred me. I didn't expect it. But she was smart, my daughter. She knew how to get to me.

"Well?"

She was waiting impatiently for my answer, but I was tongue-tied. I was silent a little too long for her.

"There's not much to say, I…"

She pushed her plate away from her. "Okay, forget it, let's just go snorkeling, okay?" She cut me off before I could tell her anything more.

Why was it so hard for me? Why did I resist opening up to her? From what I observed after one day with her, she was wise beyond her years. Still I wasn't sure if I should let her in on what I had been doing. I didn't want her worrying about me. I didn't want her talking to her mother about my business.

"Honey, I…"

"Forget it. I want to go now."

Before I could explain, she got up from the table and walked briskly to her bedroom. I was familiar with that walk. I'd seen her mother do it a few times. So all I could do was sit there and think about how I was further damaging whatever relationship I had with one of the few people in the world I loved most.

7

Kasie was in the front seat of the Jeep. The top was down. Kasie wore a Mets baseball cap and sunglasses, and very short frayed jean shorts. She had on a long T-shirt over her swimsuit, which happened to be a string bikini. I didn't know what to think about what she was wearing. I mean, I did know but I didn't know what to do about it. I wanted to tell her to put something else on, but I stopped myself. By the time we got the snorkeling gear together, changed into bathing suits, and packed drinks and snacks, she seemed to have forgotten that she was angry at me. I knew, though, that we were still on shaky ground, and telling a sixteen-year-old girl what she had to wear at the beach would not improve our relationship. It was just a shock to me. When I had last seen her two years ago, none of what was on display in that bikini was evident. In some ways, I was relieved that I didn't have these worries on a daily basis. And knowing my ex-wife, I was sure she had all that well under control.

"What's with the Mets cap?" I said. Coming from the Bronx, I had always rooted for the Yankees, and I guess I expected my children to do the same.

"I like the Mets," she said.

"Have you discussed this with your Uncle Pat?" I said, referring to my older brother, who was a regular bleacher creature at Yankee Stadium.

She laughed. "Uncle Pat was not happy," she said. "But the Mets have some cute players."

"Cute?" I glared at her. "So that's what it comes down to? Your allegiance to a team depends on how cute they are?"

She smiled coyly. "Yeah, what else would I care about?"

I shook my head. "Nothing, of course," I said.

I parked at St. Pierre police headquarters, at the base of Fort Philippe, built by the French in 1688 and later used by the British. I wanted to have that chat with McWilliams. I knew it was close to his lunch break now, and most likely he would be eating it at his desk.

"Why are we stopping here?" Kasie asked.

"I need to talk to someone for just a few minutes, honey," I said. "You can stay in the Jeep if you want or wander the fort. There's a great view of the island, the harbor and out to the Caribbean from the top of the fort."

"Do you really need to do this now? I'm getting hot. I want to go to the beach."

"We'll get there, I promise. And it's probably better we don't get to the beach until the sun weakens a little," I said. "You've got fair skin. I don't want you to burn."

She knew I was full of shit and scowled at me. "Mom made

sure I brought sun block. Don't worry, I won't burn."

"I'll make it quick, I promise."

I could tell by the deep breath she took that she wasn't pleased. We were not off to a good start. I had to try to remember that this time with her had to be special. I couldn't mess it up like I had messed up so many other things in my life.

Before we could get out of the Jeep, I saw that Samuel Cummings was opening the passenger door for Kasie. Tall and thin, with a thick gray moustache, Cummings was dressed in his brown short-sleeved park-ranger shirt and matching brown khaki shorts.

He looked at my daughter curiously. "Mr. Len, you've come to visit Fort Philippe?"

I climbed out of the Jeep. "This is my daughter, Kasie," I said. "Kasie, Samuel Cummings, esteemed tour guide and park ranger of Fort Philippe."

"Your daughter?" He looked back at me. "I see only golden skin and hair, while you, Mr. Len..."

"Yeah, yeah, I know, she has her mother's good looks," I said.

Cummings grinned. "I was just going to say you are much darker complected." His eyes were on Kasie. "Have you seen our Fort Philippe?" he asked her.

"No, I just got in yesterday," she said.

"Well, welcome to our lovely little island," Cummings said. "And here on this historic fort is a good place to start your visit."

Kasie lowered her sunglasses to glare at me.

"I have to stop in to see McWilliams," I said to Cummings. "It shouldn't be longer than a half-hour."

"Perfect. I will be glad to take your daughter on a tour of the Fort. When you are done with your business, I will have her back here safely at your Jeep."

I knew she wasn't happy, but it would be better than waiting for me in the police-station waiting room.

"The view really is something," I said.

"One of a kind," Cummings said with a smile. "But it had to be, because from the top of the fort, the French could see for miles if any invading forces, the Spanish or the British, were on the horizon."

As he chattered, Cummings led Kasie up the stone steps that traversed the park. She looked back at me one last time. I knew I would hear it from her later. I would make it up to her, I told myself as I headed inside. I had to.

Though the fort was built in the late seventeenth century, the police-station interior looked like something out a 1970s *Kojak* television episode. There were gray metal desks and filing cabinets, and walls painted a sterile off-green. The adjoining offices and waiting area were lit by weak fluorescent lights. I knew there was a jail at the rear of the station that was even darker, and a courtyard where, I had heard, floggings still took place.

The station receptionist, Emmalin Sealy, a hefty woman normally with a fixed stern smile on her face, didn't even give me one of those as I approached her desk. She made a show of shuffling some papers on her desk.

"Mr. Len, what can we do for you today? I hear your daughter is in town," she said.

Why should I have been surprised that Emmalin Sealy knew my daughter was on the island? On St. Pierre just about everyone knew everything. Yet I often felt like I was kept in the dark.

"Cecile Marks from the duty-free store in the airport tell me last night at bible study she see her arrive. How lovely for you," she said looking up at me.

"I'm happy to have her with me for the week," I said.

That finally got me one of those stern smiles.

"Samuel take her on a tour?" she asked, though it was obvious it was a question that did not need an answer.

"What do you think?"

"Well, she in good hands then. What can I do for you, Mr. Len?"

"I wanted a quick word with the man," I said. "If he's available."

Emmalin shook her head with displeasure. "The man, Mr Len?"

"Superintendent McWilliams," I said, realizing that there were moments I needed to remember I was not in New York, that respect and decorum were needed when addressing figures of authority.

"Do you really want to upset his lunch?" She peered at me. "His wife just dropped off a plate of curry goat. Mr. McWilliams like to eat his curry goat alone."

"Alone? No, we can't allow that. He must know that a man should never dine alone. He who eats alone..." I leaned forward a bit on her desk.

Emmalin looked me over and raised up her eyebrows. "Dies alone? This coming from a man with only dogs as companions? I am sure you are good company, Mr. Len. Come to church on Sunday, and I can guarantee you will find a nice Caribbean woman to eat your meals with over there on East Road."

"But that would mean going to church," I said.

She glared. "Don't make light of God's work. You a man who could use some church."

"I apologize, Emmalin," I said. "Save me a seat. I promise I'll get there soon."

She made a sucking sound between her teeth and shook her head as I moved past her to the offices in the back of the station. It was lunch time, and most of the officers, of which there were only a handful, were out on patrol, meaning they were most likely idling in their cars eating their own lunches.

I could smell the curry before I even entered the open door of McWilliams' small private office. The police superintendent was picking meat from small bones when I entered. He adjusted his glasses as he looked up to see me. His droopy eyes reminded me of a hound dog. His skin was very dark. He was bald but had bushy sideburns that connected with his trimmed salt-and-pepper beard. Under his glasses, his eyes were usually bloodshot. The bad lighting in the office, I'm sure, didn't help any.

"Mr. Buonfiglio, it's lunchtime," he said in his deep baritone.

"I can see that," I said, looking at the plastic takeout container still filled with pieces of goat meat, rice and peas and a yellow, turmeric-based curry sauce.

"What can I do for you?" McWilliams asked calmly. That unruffled demeanor was one of his many attributes. He was a patient man. He did his work deliberately and knew just how far to go before he pulled back. He would only push on a case so much. He knew his resources were limited and understood what was acceptable to the people of St. Pierre and what would not be tolerated. He steered clear of controversy, handled situations politically, yet he was also thorough. He knew who he could press and who he had to work around. As a result, he had kept his position for as long as I had lived on the island. But because he would only go so far and refused to cross certain lines, justice was not always served as it should have been, at least not for me. He was aware of what my role was becoming here and usually didn't interfere. Unless he had to. Unless what I was doing would push back on him.

"Rawle Johns," I said. "Big Tree. We all know he wouldn't do something like that."

"Like what?" McWilliams asked as he shoveled some rice into his mouth, his eyes on me.

"The girl who fell from Freedom Drop. Rawle's mother tells me you think he might be involved. Is that why he's in custody?"

It was how he operated. By asking me that question even though he knew what I was talking about, McWilliams got me to reveal that Big Tree's mother was asking for my help and that I now would be involved in the case. In his indirect way, he could be very sly.

"He is a suspect, yes. I gave a statement to the media last night. Did you not see it in the paper? You could have saved yourself a trip down here, and your poor daughter would not have to endure a tour of Fort Philippe led by Samuel Cummings." He sat back with a satisfied grin.

Of course he too knew my daughter was with me and was now touring the fort with Samuel Cummings. By now it was public knowledge for pretty much everyone on the island.

"This is better than anything I could read in the papers. Here, I get to talk to you in your radiant office while you enjoy your curry goat. And you can tell me from your lips why Big Tree is a suspect in the death of Deanna Gould. What changed from the original conclusion that she died from an accidental fall?"

He finished his lunch and pushed the container away from him, wiping his lips with a paper towel. "This is a tragic business, Mr. Len," he said, dropping the formalities he used on my entrance. "I know Rawle since he was a little boy. I prayed with him when he lost his wife. He has been a model citizen of St. Pierre. A promoter of the island to so many with his magnificent island tours. But I can't let my emotions affect my decisions here."

I was afraid to ask but I did. "What decisions?"

"There was forensics work done on the body by doctors and technicians in the States." he said. "The results have implicated Mr. Johns as a suspect."

I knew that from what Mrs. Johns had told me, but I wasn't sure of the extent of that work.

"How were forensics arranged? If the death occurred here, why did they allow the body to be examined elsewhere?"

"The girl's mother," he said. "Apparently she has some influence in Boston, where she is from, and was able to make the arrangements."

"What did they find?" I asked.

He studied me. "And if I tell you, Mr. Len? What will you do? Will you tell Mrs. Johns what they discovered?"

I didn't like the sound of that. I looked back at him but didn't answer.

He thought for a moment as if he was debating what to do. He looked at me again.

"There was bruising in areas not consistent with the fall and the impact from it," he said.

"She was killed before the fall? Someone threw her dead body off the cliff?"

"I did not say that," he said. "The fall killed the poor girl, but they found other things in their examination that had nothing to do with the fall."

"What things?"

He sighed as if he knew he was telling me too much. "They did a DNA test," he said. "There was a match."

"A match? What does that mean?"

"It mean they find Rawle Johns' DNA on the girl," he said.

I could tell it was painful for him to say it, but he got it out.

"He led them on that tour. They could have touched or hugged or something like that. That doesn't mean he killed her."

He pushed his dirty take-out container even further from him on his desk as if he didn't want to look at it. "They find Johns' DNA samples all over the girl," he said looking directly at me.

"All over?" I said.

He nodded, his eyes intent. I understood the implication.

I pictured Big Tree. Heard that melodious voice, saw him smile on that tour he gave me years ago. I knew what McWilliams was implying. He didn't have to. But it just didn't seem possible. There had to be a mistake.

"You're telling me that he raped the girl and then threw her off the cliff?"

He frowned. "I'm telling you no such thing, Mr. Buonfiglio. I'm just telling you that because they find the DNA like that, he had to be questioned."

"And?"

"Mr. Johns made a statement. He confirmed what the forensics found," McWilliams said.

"He confessed to killing her?"

"No he did not," he said. "But his statement and the forensics report make him now a suspect in her death."

"What was in the statement?"

"Mr. Buonfiglio, I already tell you too much. And I trust you will not repeat this to anyone. I tell you only because I am also a friend of the man's family. Maybe it will help you to talk to the mother. To get her to understand what has happened. Since they engage your help in this matter, though I do not understand why, maybe she will listen to you."

"Can I talk to him?" I asked.

"He has counsel," he said. "You have no authority to speak with the prisoner. Only his counsel and his family."

"He's a prisoner? But he hasn't had a trial. Has he even been charged?"

"He is a suspect in a potential murder investigation. Under our laws, he is to be kept in custody until either a trial acquits him or a magistrate deems the evidence does not warrant him being held."

"That sounds like bullshit to me," I said. "What kind of law is that?"

McWilliams did not answer.

"I need to talk to him," I said.

"Mr. Buonfiglio, as I said, this is now a very serious matter. I know you've handled a few small incidents here in your own way, but this is something you should let the authorities take care of. Talk to the man's mother. If I need you for anything else, you can be sure I will let you know. As I said, only his counsel or family can speak with him now."

"And what if the family gave me permission as a proxy for them?"

He sighed and then smiled.

"I was hoping you would not ask that, but I should have known better. Yes, they can do that, but there are forms to be filled out for something like that to be approved. And a magistrate needs to sign off on it."

"Give me the forms," I said.

He took a breath and picked up his phone. I heard him mutter in his deep voice into the phone.

"Mrs. Sealy will have the papers up front." He looked at me sternly. "Take my advice, Mr. Buonfiglio. Your daughter is vacationing with you. Spend your time with her. Don't involve yourself with this. We will make sure that justice is properly served."

I got up from the chair. "Justice?" It wasn't a statement, it was a question, but McWilliams didn't answer it.

When I got to the front desk, Emmalin held the papers out for me. "They need to be filled out and signed by the family. Make sure everything is signed and initialed in the appropriate areas." She looked at me for added emphasis. "Or the proxy will not be valid." Her eyes probed mine. Her mouth opened as if she was about to speak again, then she stopped herself. She just nodded at me and I took the papers from her.

As I walked out of the police station, I checked my phone. There was a text from Kasie: *Help me,* it read along with grimacing not-so-smiley face.

8

As I exited the police station, I could see Samuel Cummings gabbing at Kasie near the Jeep. She saw me and quickly opened the door to get in. That did not deter Cummings, who leaned over and continued talking to her through the window.

"She's a smart one, Mr. Len," Cummings said to me when I approached them. "I am sure any university would be honored to have her as a student."

I went around the car to Cummings and handed him twenty dollars. "Thanks for showing her the fort, Samuel," I said.

He smiled and took the money. "It was my great pleasure."

I looked at Kasie. She knew I was nudging her to thank Cummings too. She smiled weakly.

"Thanks Mr. Cummings. You were right; the view up there was amazing."

He peered into the passenger seat. "Enjoy your stay here on this paradise of ours," he said to Kasie.

"Now to the beach?" I said as I got into the driver's seat.

"Dad, could you have tortured me more? God, so boring. Don't do that to me again."

"Come on, Kasie. When's the last time you got to walk a seventeenth century fort?"

She rolled her eyes and I said no more.

From the fort, I headed north on West Road, hugging the shoreline. After about twenty minutes driving, I pulled over and parked on the side of the road. We took our bag with our snorkeling gear through the thick green brush and then down a narrow slope to Coral Beach. The wide swath of a beach was on the sparsely populated northwest side of the island. Because land jutted out on either side of the beach, the waters were calm and protected from the elements. The shadow of Mt. Hadali loomed over the beach; millions of years ago it had spewed lava that resulted in what was now black volcanic sand. There was a row of almost uniform palm trees on the perimeter of the beach offering natural umbrellas from the sun. We were the only ones there except for a young couple with a toddler.

Kasie looked around at the clear aqua-blue water and the green of the palm trees. "This is awesome."

"Yeah, this beach is special," I said. "Because we had to walk down that hill to get here and the sand being dark instead of white, some people stay away. You'll never see a tourist here, and we like it like that. But if they knew what was out there," I pointed to the water, "they might come in droves."

"Really? What's out there? Buried treasure? Pirate skeletons? Mermaids?" She grinned at me, poking at my enthusiasm for this beach. And I didn't mind at all.

"You'll see, smart-ass," I replied with my own grin. I spread out a big beach towel under one of the palms and took out the masks, snorkel and fins I packed in our beach bag.

"Let's go," Kasie said, her T-shirt off, rushing into the warm water.

After putting our fins on in the water, then our masks, making sure they fit properly, I told her to follow behind me. I swam out about thirty yards until we hit the coral reef the beach was famous for. We hovered there. I could hear Kasie through her mask and snorkel as she saw a huge ray glide under us. There were trunk fish and spotted drum fish hovering around abstract, multi-colored coral formations. Kasie yelped and turned to see a school of tiny fish nipping lightly at her ankles. After almost half an hour in the water, I signaled that we should take a break.

She took her mask off and was giggling like a little girl on Christmas morning. After our earlier spat, the sight made me beam.

"What were those fish? They were tickling me."

"Damselfish," I said. "They must have sensed something sweet coming from your skin. Notice they didn't come any-where near me."

"They were cute," she said.

"See, it was worth the wait and the hardship of climbing Fort Philippe and having to endure Samuel Cummings' history lesson," I said.

She nodded, the mask over her forehead.

"Can we go back in for another swim?"

"We can," I said. "But let's get out for a bit and drink some-thing. Even though you may not know it being in the water, your body can dehydrate. And then, Kasie, you can go back in the water and start searching for those pirate skeletons." I smiled at her and she splashed me as we made our way out of the water.

We headed back to the beach towel and the shade. I opened two bottles of water as we sat on the towel together. "Scuba diving must be even better," Kasie said.

"Yeah, there are some really good dives off the island."

"Where did you learn to dive, Dad?"

"In the Marines," I said. "Back then for about a minute I thought I would try for special ops but after a few months I decided it was a no go for me. I stayed in the program long enough to get scuba certified, and once you're certified you're good to go. I guess I need to give a little more credit to the Marines for teaching me; that and how to drive eight-wheel military trucks, which is what I mostly did in those four years."

"I'd like to get certified," she said. "Is it really hard?"

"Not really. You can learn easy enough. You're in great shape, and your mom says you're an excellent swimmer. That's the first step. I don't remember how long it takes, but there's book work and classes involved before you can get into a pool, and then you need to complete a few dives before you are certified. So it's a process. I'm sure there are dive courses on Long Island. Get it done, and next time you visit we'll go diving together. Or when you come see me again, I can set you up with a real good instructor who will have you diving before you leave."

"That would be very cool," she said.

The toddler who was splashing in the water with his parents wandered over to say hello on chubby, shaky legs. His mother, who had been feeding him, came to fetch him.

"I sorry," the young mother said. She pulled the little boy up into her arms and smiled at us. From what I could tell she wasn't much older than Kasie.

"He's beautiful," Kasie said to her.

The young mother smiled again and without saying anything held out an open plastic bowl to us. I could see slices of ripe, bright-orange papaya in the bowl.

Kasie looked at me warily.

"It's papaya," I said. "Try it."

She tentatively took a piece dripping with juice, and so did I.

"Oh, wow, that's delicious," Kasie said. "I don't think I've ever had papaya before."

The young woman smiled again and carried her son back to where they were situated on the beach.

"People are friendly here," Kasie said.

"Yeah, they are," I said, very happy to be where I was at that moment.

"Is that why you came here. To St. Pierre?" she asked.

I shrugged. "Partly. It's a small island and I wanted that. I didn't want to go to an island overrun with big resorts and tourists everywhere. And look around. See how green? That papaya you just ate was probably picked in someone's backyard this morning. The beaches here aren't the best in the Caribbean, but I don't mind that. I don't care if the sand isn't perfectly white like many do. For me, Kasie, this island has all I need and want."

She was running her fingers through the sand as she listened to me and then she just nodded at my words. "Let's go back in, Dad."

"Okay," I said.

Kasie ran back into the water with her gear.

As I rose up from the beach towel, I noticed two white men emerge from the brush. They wore nearly matching beige khaki shorts and white, long-sleeved button-down shirts.

"Come on, Dad," Kasie yelled from the water.

I joined her and turned to face the beach as I put on my fins. I watched the men. One was holding a small electronic tablet and was using a finger to work it. The other was taking off his shoes. The two of them started to walk slowly around the perimeter of the beach.

"What's wrong?" Kasie asked.

"Nothing, let's go," I said. I put on my mask, but I was thinking about something other than snorkeling. I was thinking about men in suits.

We swam for another hour and then relaxed on the towel in the shade until we both were dry. The family with the toddler had gone, and so had the two men. We were now alone on the beach. It was quiet and I was tempted to take a nap right there, but Kasie said she was hungry, so we packed up our stuff.

As we walked back to the path up the hill, I saw two slats of plywood sticking up in the sand about four feet from one another. Kasie was about to walk between them. I shouted for her to stop and grabbed her before she could go any further.

"What? Dad?" she said, startled as I pulled her away from where she had been walking.

"I'm sorry, honey. I didn't mean to scare you. Just step around those markers," I said

She now noticed them. "Why?"

"It's a nesting area," I said. "Sea turtles."

"Really?"

I nodded and pointed to the markings on the wood where there was a primitive drawing of a turtle done with what looked like a black Sharpie.

"They usually come at night to lay their eggs. There are nesting areas all around the island, but I think Tubby told me this was one of the turtles' favorites. He knows about stuff like this."

"Can you watch them lay their eggs?"

"You can, but you have to know when the best time to see them. I think Tubby said a full moon is best...or maybe it was a new moon, I don't remember. We'll ask him. I've never seen them, but I hear it's pretty special. Maybe they will nest while you're here and we can see it."

"I want to see that, Dad. Ask Tubby. Please."

I smiled to myself. Happy that she and I could share something like that together.

"Sure, Kasie," I said as we made our way up the hill and back to the Jeep.

We stopped at a small restaurant on the beach on the way home to eat, and by the time we finished it was starting to get dark. When we got back into the Jeep I heard a ping from my phone.

"Here, let me look," Kasie said grabbing for my phone that sat in the cup holder. "It's from Tubby."

"What's he want?"

"He says to come to the bar."

"Ask him what's up."

I glanced over to see Kasie type the message, then put the phone down.

"You're not going over there now, are you, Dad?"

I shrugged. "You tired?"

"Yeah."

I nodded. "I'll take you home. I need a shower anyway."

I pulled into my driveway and Kasie staggered out. After my shower I checked the phone again. *Just come,* was all Tubby had texted.

"Do you want to come along?"

"Can I hang out here?"

"Sure. I'll be back as soon as I can. If you need me, I'll have my phone."

She nodded but didn't look up from what she was doing on her phone.

9

The bar was busy when I arrived. There was a group of German tourists at one of the tables in the back watching a soccer match on the big screen above them. Beer bottles were scattered around their adjoining tables. There was another group, maybe from the cruise boat that had docked that morning, on the deck in the back. Tubby was playing a mix he'd made of old-school R&B and soca. Alma Modeste and Franklyn Worthington, who worked at Windward Savings, were dancing to Eddie Floyd's "I've Never Found a Girl (to Love Me Like You Do)" between two of the tables. All the stools at the bar were occupied. Tubby was at one end of the bar and Mike was working the other. Normally I would be back there with Tubby, but I had Mike take my shifts while Kasie was visiting.

Tubby saw me come in and waved me over. As he did, a man swiveled on his barstool and looked at me. There was a woman sitting on the stool next to him; I noticed she had moved her stool very close to his and that she had her hand on his thigh.

She was dark-skinned and was wearing a very short, clingy black dress that revealed long legs. She had short natural hair that was buzzed even shorter on the sides. Her Afro was longer on top and dyed gold. As soon as she saw me looking at her and the man next to her, she squeezed his thigh, got up and slinked away, rubbing her body against my back as she passed me, as if to make sure I was aware of what was under that thin dress. I turned to look back at her. She gave me a knowing smirk before she disappeared into the crowd.

The man she'd been talking to was grinning at me. His head was shaved, but what he lacked on his head, he more than made up for on his chin. His red beard was thick and long enough to touch the middle of his chest. He was wearing a black T-shirt and baggy cargo shorts and had a bottle of Carib in his hand. His sizable belly hung over his shorts. I could see the colorful ink splashed over his arms from twenty feet away. He smiled when he saw me and turned back to Tubby. "This the man?" he asked.

Tubby didn't answer. Red beard turned back to me and got off his stool, the smile still on his face. Tubby was shrugging now as he looked at me.

"Bro! The June first hero himself."

I stood my ground as he headed my way. I didn't like what I heard.

"Did I blow your cover?" He looked around sheepishly. "Hey, man, it's okay. Everyone should know what you did. No reason to keep that shit a secret."

I looked at Tubby. Mike slid over and looked at me too. Tubby raised his eyebrows and just nodded.

The beefy man held his hand out. "Craig Frost," he said.

I took his hand and shook it. His eyes were blue and a bit

bloodshot at the moment. He had a ring in his nose. "Len Buon-figlio," I said.

"I know who you are," Frost said. "And damn proud to meet ya."

"This man been wanting to talk to you, Mr. Len," Tubby said.

"Tubby's right, Len. Soon as I got here, this was the first place I wanted to come to. It's awesome. People are cool. Drinks are cooler. And that view? You hit it with this place, dude. Tubby here, the host with the most, telling me stories about St. Pierre. So I thought I'd tell him a story about New York and his buddy, Len Buonfiglio."

"Yeah? What kind of story?"

"A good one, you know that. You all modest hiding out on an island. I mean Tubby told me he knew already what you done, but Mike had no idea. And even Tubby wasn't clear on how many you saved that day."

What about the one I didn't save, I thought to myself.

"Is that why you came up here, Frost? To tell them my story?"

"Not just that. I heard good things about this Sporting Place. And I went to some of the Brooklyn bars you were involved in, back in the day. They were cool too."

I nodded and headed behind the bar. Frost swung around on his stool again. I had tried to keep my past out of my present and had done a pretty good job of it. I should have known it wouldn't last, that someday someone would come and broadcast what I did that day in New York. I couldn't prevent people from finding out. It was easy enough to dig up. But there was one truth they would never know. And I lived with that one every day.

"Busy here," I said to Tubby.

"Yeah, but it's good, Mr. Len. We got this thing under control."

"I know you do, Tubby."

Frost was trying to listen in to what we were saying, but Tubby and I could communicate and understand each other no matter how loud it got in the bar. And between the raucous Germans who were bellowing at the soccer and the music playing, the decibel meter was pointing to high.

"How much has he been drinking?" I asked Tubby.

"Just a few beers," Tubby said. "He act drunk, but I don't think he drunk. I think that just the way the man be. Maybe he nervous. People get chatty like that when they nervous."

"Did he say what he wanted?"

"Just to talk to you, Mr. Len."

I looked at Frost. "You say you got in today?"

"Yeah, bro, it was a long trip. I flew to Miami, then into Trinidad, took another plane to St. Vincent and then the ferry over."

I knew that the route he took, Miami to Trinidad and then to St. Vincent, and then the hour-and-a-half ferry, was the cheapest but also the longest option to get to St. Pierre.

"I hope you got the budget fare," I said.

"Absolutely. And worth the hassle. This island, from what I've seen of it so far, is a gem. Who knew? I mean, I've been to Puerto Rico, Jamaica and the DR on vacations. They were fun, but a different vibe, you know? And all those all-inclusives and casinos. Who needs them, right?"

I thought about what he said, calling the island a gem. Someone else said the same thing just recently but I couldn't recall who.

"We certainly don't," I said.

"No, that touristy shit would destroy this place," he said.

"So what is it you wanted to talk to me about?"

He glanced around the bar.

"Can we go somewhere and talk?"

I nodded. "Follow me," I said to Frost. I looked at Tubby as I left. He was watching me. I gave him a nod and then guided Frost out the front door.

The Sporting Place was situated on top of a hill. The closest home was about a hundred yards away. I walked with Frost up the road toward where I had parked my Jeep. We could still hear the music coming from the bar, but it was now just background noise. As we walked, I tried to get an idea who Craig Frost was and why he wanted to talk to me. Did it have something to do with my past? I thought all that was ancient history. I had my fifteen minutes of fame and had no interest in one minute more. I wondered if I had met the man before. I pegged him to be in his thirties, more or less. I was stumped.

"So what's on your mind?" I said to him as we approached my Jeep.

He stopped walking and leaned against the front fender. He shoved his hands in the pockets of his cargo shorts and picked his head up to look me in the eyes. "Deanna Gould," he said.

He caught me off guard. I was expecting something else. A coincidence? Or part of a puzzle? I hoped it was the former, because I was never any good at puzzles.

"The girl who died in that accident last year?" I did my best not to let on that Deanna Gould was on my mind as well. I wasn't sure if I was succeeding. Poker was another thing I wasn't any good at. At least the poker-face part of it.

"You met her," Frost said.

And how did he know that? I wondered.

"Briefly, yes. She and a group of travel writers stopped at the bar while they were touring the island. I was very sad to hear what happened."

"I don't know, bro. You say briefly, but you made an impression on her."

"Did I?"

"Enough for her to text me your name the day before she died."

I shuffled my feet as we stood in the dark. I recognized "Bad in Bum Bum," the Carnival Soca hit from St. Lucia playing in the bar. Tubby probably put it on so he and Mike could see Alma Modeste do her infamous back bend that highlighted her own bad bum. I thought about what Frost said about Deanna Gould. That I had made an impression on her. And here I thought it was she who made the impression on me.

I pictured her again as she was on the day I met her. She was pretty in an unconventional way, with long dark curly hair with blue highlights. Her skin was the color of light coffee, and I particularly remembered the smattering of dark freckles around her cheekbones that just enhanced her distinctive beauty. She had full lips and a wide enough nose to make it obvious to me that she was biracial. But what stuck the most was the intense, playful, overtly flirtatious way she looked at me. I don't know if it was me or how she looked at everyone, but it definitely had me off-balance. I remember her holding her rum punch in one hand, aiming that teasing smile at me. There was a sexual tension that seemed to flow from her. And I wasn't sure if it was something she had control over or even knew was there. I had a feeling that she did, though, and used it often to her advantage.

"Why would she do that?" I asked Frost.

"She gave me your name as someone to see if I ever came down here."

"What do you mean?"

His head was down. The garrulous voice softened. He was choking up.

"If I needed to talk to someone on St. Pierre."

"If?"

"Yeah, if something happened to her." There were tears in his eyes now.

I nodded again. It was obvious there was a past between the two. Frost was in love with her.

"So you two were together?"

He wiped at his eyes and tried to compose himself.

"Sorry, bro, I didn't mean to lose my cool. It's just that she was a special one," he said. "But no. We weren't, you know, boyfriend-girlfriend. Not that I would have minded that. Deanna liked to have too much fun. We were colleagues."

"You're a travel writer, too?"

He laughed. "Wouldn't that be nice," he said. "Deanna wasn't a travel writer. That was all bullshit."

I stared at him, waiting for more.

"She and I worked for a website. ThirdRail," he said. "You know it right?"

All I knew was Google, Facebook, Yahoo, Twitter and Skype. Beyond that I was internet ignorant.

He saw that there was no recognition and laughed.

"Down here you probably don't care about some of the shit that goes down. You can filter it all out of your life, which is a good thing. Anyway, we do some breaking news. Investigative stuff that makes headlines. That upsets people. People usually in power. Deanna used the travel-writer thing as a cover. She got press credentials and thought she could uncover something she was working on here."

I took in what he was telling me. I remembered her asking, no, *grilling*, me about my past. Why I chose St. Pierre. I made up something about seeking a more peaceful lifestyle, which she saw right through. I wasn't going to tell her more than that, though I almost did and had to catch myself. There was something about the way she asked. Or maybe it was the way she wouldn't take her eyes off mine while we talked. The way she moved her body, an almost hypnotic sway to it while just standing there talking. I could see how she could get a man to open up to her. I had a feeling she could probably interrogate with the best of them, in her own way. It took some effort to resist, but I was able to. She wasn't about to hear my confession no matter how good she was. But I was actually relieved when the group had to move on from my bar to their next destination, before she could try a little harder to get me to spill my guts. She was unlike any travel writer I met before, that I recall clearly.

"What are you saying?" I asked Frost.

"I'm saying that Deanna was murdered for what she knew and was about to expose. There's a big name involved in some shit here. A powerful dude that wanted to hush her. She didn't die in any accident. She liked to party, but I never saw her staggering around drunk or high. Never. She was into her life. Her career. She wouldn't fall off any cliff."

"You know they arrested a suspect a couple of days ago. Someone they believe might have murdered her. And they have some pretty substantial evidence."

"You talking about the Big Tree? Come on, Buonfiglio. You don't believe that do you? It's bullshit. The evidence was probably made up."

I was about to tell him that the Big Tree confessed to certain things that might change his opinion, even though I had no idea what those certain things were.

"She never mentioned his name to me once, and we were in contact all the time almost up until..." He choked up again. "No, someone else did it. Someone who knew what she was looking into."

"You gonna tell me who this someone might be?" I was dubious. What was going on here on St. Pierre that could be so nefarious that there would be an investigative reporter snooping around?

He looked up at me. His red beard looked damp, almost glistening in the very dim light of night. "Yeah, I'm gonna." He looked around as if he thought someone might be listening or watching us, and then there was a ping from his phone. He fished it out of his pocket and stared at the screen. He looked down the street. "Can we talk tomorrow? My ride is here."

I looked at what he was looking at and saw a dark-green Suzuki idling by the side of the road. He started to walk down toward it. I walked with him.

"Where you staying?" I asked.

"A guest house," he said.

"Which one?"

"Lulu's or something like that."

"LuJean's?"

"Yeah, that's it."

"I'll swing by tomorrow," I said.

"Okay, bro," he said as we came to the Suzuki. I peered inside to see if I recognized the driver. In the dark of the car, I could only see that his skin was light and had a yellow tinge to it, making him look Asian. He looked hard back at me, like he too was sizing me up. He was no one I knew or recognized.

Frost opened the back door, and as he did, I was surprised to see a pair of long ebony legs back there. Abetted by the light from my neon sign, I noticed the bright golden color of her hair and a prominent tattoo on her thigh, some sort of skeletal image. It was the same woman he had been talking to at the bar when I arrived. The same woman who had rubbed up against me. Frost saw what I was looking at and shrugged sheepishly at me as he slid in next to the woman. Whatever Frost had arranged was his business.

As soon as Frost got in, the Suzuki quickly pulled away.

"What that man want?" Tubby asked as soon as I returned to the bar.

"He wanted a recommendation for a good tour guide to take him on a hike up Mt. Hadali," I said, referring to the dormant volcano and the island's highest mountain peak.

"Don't start with that now." He was shaking his head at me. "You think I not find out what you up to? When you learn that you need me? You way too old to take on de dirty stuff without some help. And you know it, but 'cause you so old, you stubborn and refuse to make it easier on you."

"I have no idea what you're talking about, Tubby." I smiled. "And I take offense at all your references to my advanced age. That hurts me deeply."

He waved a kitchen towel at me, opened a cold Carib and

handed it to me.

The bar was quieter now. Mike had gone home. The Germans had left, as had the group from the cruise boat. Alma Modeste and Franklyn Worthington were huddled close together at a table in the back. I knew the bank they worked for would be open tomorrow morning. And both would be dressed discreetly, Franklyn in a jacket and tie and Alma in a conservative suit that almost, but not quite totally, concealed that bad bum. They would go about business throughout the day without even a nod or glance at each other.

"How much did he tell you and Mike?" I asked as I leaned back and sipped the beer. It was cold and tasted very good.

"I already know all that about you, Mr. Len," Tubby said. "I know all that when we first met. I check you out before I take you on as a partner."

"Oh, *you* took *me* on, Tubby?"

"That's right, I don't go in wit no man who shady or such," he said.

"So you did some research on me?"

He nodded. "What I never understand is why you never like to talk about it. I don't know why you do not, but I respect that. Mike never hear 'bout it before. Don't worry about Mike. I tell him to be cool and not gossip it all around the island."

"Thanks, Tubby."

"Why you don't like to talk about it, I do not understand. But that your business and I don't go there until you want me to. Just know, I'm your friend and you can trust me."

"I'm lucky to have you as one, Tubby," I said. "I know I can trust you. It's not about that."

He was right. It wasn't his business, it was mine. He was also right that he was a friend. A friend I should confide in. I didn't have any others. He looked at me, waiting for me to open up. He realized that wasn't going to happen.

"Someday you tell me. I not gonna pressure you. No worries, Mr. Len."

I nodded. "You know that woman?" I asked.

"What woman?" Tubby said.

"What woman? You didn't notice those legs? That gold hair?"

"Lots of girls color their hair gold here," he said. "And I notice those legs. When do you know me when I don't notice legs?"

"That's what I'm saying, Tubby. Who is she?"

He shook his head "She not from here that I know," Tubby said. "But I see those legs and everything else once before."

"When?"

"She here yesterday with some people," he said.

"What people?"

"My memory only for those legs," he said

I thought about what he was telling me. I didn't remember seeing her at the bar when I was there with Kasie. But I wasn't looking for legs or anything else.

"You never tell me how that snorkeling go with your daughter. You show her Coral Beach?"

I cursed into my beer. I had left my daughter at home alone. I told her I would be right back. "Got to go, Tubby," I said as I hustled out of the bar.

I cursed myself on the ride back. I was so caught up in what Frost told me and what was going on in the bar, the fact that she was alone all night didn't even cross my mind. It was as if she didn't exist for those few hours I was away from her. What kind of father would do that? Maybe it really was better I was away from my kids.

There was a light on in the kitchen when I got home, but Kasie was asleep on the couch, her phone near her face, the Brown One spooned next to her. I lifted her into my arms and carried her into her room. With one hand I pushed the covers back on the bed and then lowered her onto it, pulling the covers up over her. The Brown One came into the room and stared at me. And then she leaped on the bed and curled next to my daughter.

10

I was up before Kasie and got busy in the kitchen making pancakes. It was the least I could do after deserting my daughter the night before. She staggered out just when I was flipping a stack on the griddle.

"I must have slept twelve hours," Kasie said as she slumped in a chair.

"All that swimming we did and the sun here can truly knock you out without you even knowing it," I said.

The Brown One came right up to Kasie and rested her snout on her lap. She stroked her forehead. "This one really likes me," she said.

"Yeah, I noticed that. She's not usually that friendly with people," I said.

Kasie smiled at the dog and continued to caress her forehead.

"I'm sorry I was out so late. I didn't plan on it," I said.

"It's okay, Dad."

I brought a plate of pancakes to the table along with syrup.

Kasie began eating immediately.

"Any ideas on what you want to do today?" I asked, watching her devour the pancakes and feeling good about it.

"The beach, of course," she said. "Can we go snorkeling again?"

"We can," I said. "But do you want to see another beach? You think Coral Beach was nice? The one I want to take you to is the best on the island, in my opinion, Not much to see snorkeling, though."

"No? Then what makes it the best?"

"You'll see when we get there."

I was getting up to clear her plate when there was a loud knock on the open screen door.

"Mr. Len," a deep voice said from the other side of the door.

In the shadows near the doorway I saw two uniformed figures. I put the plate down and went to the door. Kasie looked up.

James Baines and Claude Evans, two of McWilliams' officers, stood at my doorway. "What's going on?" I asked the two of them through the screen door.

"Superintendent McWilliams needs you to come talk to him, Mr. Len," Baines said.

"Why?"

"He'll tell you when you get there," Baines said, peering through the screen at my daughter.

"Get where? Can't I just call him?"

"No, sir, he wants to talk to you at the station. We are to escort you there."

I turned back to look at Kasie. She had gotten up and started moving to the door to stand next to me.

"Escort? What is this bullshit? I can drive."

"Dad!" My sixteen-year-old daughter was trying to get me to calm down. How bad did that look? But what was McWilliams pulling here? Making this show. And in front of my daughter.

I took a breath. "Fellas, I'm here with my daughter, who's on vacation. Let me call McWilliams and make an appointment for later."

Baines opened the door and took hold of my elbow. I didn't like that and pulled away abruptly. He knew enough about me to stand back and not try that again.

Evans moved in between us. "It's what Superintendent McWilliams has requested," Evans said. "Now please, Mr. Len." I could have made more of a scene but thought better of it. I had to retain my composure.

"How long's this gonna take? I was going to go to the beach with my daughter," I said. "McWilliams could have let me know."

"You can settle this with Superintendent McWilliams at the station," Baines said, still halfway in my doorway. "Pleased to meet you, miss. Your father is a good man."

I turned to Kasie.

"Listen, honey, I'll try to get back as soon as I can. I don't know what this is about, but I'm sure it's nothing. I'm gonna call Tubby and have him bring you to the beach, and I'll meet you there. Are you okay with that?"

"Yeah, I guess."

"I'll be there as soon as I can," I said. "Take your phone, and text or call if you need me for anything. I'm sorry, honey. I have no idea what's going on here."

"Um...okay, Dad," she said looking at me and then at the officers as they led me out of my own house.

I sat in the back of the car like a criminal as Baines drove, texting Tubby to check in on Kasie and bring her to the beach. And then I looked out the window. I tried to think what could be so urgent to drag me down to the police station. I really had no idea but knew it couldn't be good.

The two officers escorted me past Emmalin Sealy's front desk, down the corridor and into McWilliams' office, where he was waiting for me.

"Really, McWilliams? This was necessary?" I glared at him.

"Sit down, Mr. Buonfiglio," he said gesturing to the chair opposite his desk.

"What is this about?"

"Sit."

I sat but the glare remained. He shuffled some papers and pulled out a photo and pushed it in front of me.

"Do you know this man?" I looked at the photo. It was a color shot of the man I met the night before. I tried to remember his name. In the picture, which looked like a Polaroid, his eyes were closed as if he were asleep, but I had a feeling he wasn't sleeping.

"Yeah, I met him last night," I said. "Why?"

"What's his name?"

I tried hard to remember. I was going to meet him at LuJeans. "Something Frost...?"

McWilliams nodded. "Craig Frost," he said. "He was at the Sporting Place last night?"

"Yeah, that's where we met," I said.

"Was he drinking there?" McWilliams looked at me.

"As far as I know. He had a beer when I was there. Tubby Levett, who was there earlier, said he had a few beers."

"No rum?"

"Not that I know of. What's going on, McWilliams?"

He took the photo back and looked at me.

"The man was found dead this morning," he said. "They find him in his room at LuJean's."

My head was spinning and so was my stomach. The result was a sick feeling of dread. I was quickly reminded of the chat I had with the man. The conspiracies he was weaving around Deanna Gould's death. He wanted to talk to me today. He wanted to tell me more. Now he couldn't.

"Dead?" I muttered. "How?"

"We suspect alcohol poisoning. Maybe he drank some bad bush rum. People come here and they try the bush rum. We warn them it not safe to consume, but they like the risk. They believe it when they are told that the rum make a man strong and...virile. Why they believe that rubbish, I don't know." McWilliams shook his head.

"We don't serve bush rum, McWilliams," I said. "Is that why you brought me here? You think he drank something at my place?"

"When a man die on our island, a man not from this island, we need to know facts. We need to be thorough in our investigation. We want to be seen as being competent here, Mr. Buonfiglio. Not a third-world colony. He was seen at your bar. He was seen chatting with you. Asking about you. What did you two talk about?" He pushed his glasses up his nose as he looked at me.

I thought for a moment. I knew I had to be careful here. "He knew of me from New York. From some bars I owned there years ago. He just wanted to meet me."

I heard my phone buzz and glanced at it. It was from Kasie.

I didn't read the message; she was probably asking when I was going to get home so we could go to the beach. I looked back at McWilliams.

"Was he with anyone else at the bar?"

I thought for a moment and then remembered those long legs, the brush of gold in her hair, and the way she rubbed her body against mine. I felt a chill go through me knowing she was also in the car with Frost.

"He was chatting with a woman at the bar when I arrived," I said.

"What woman?"

I shook my head. "I didn't recognize her, McWilliams."

He tapped a pencil on a notepad.

"Did you see him leave?"

"Yeah, a car picked him up," I said.

"What kind of car?"

"It was a green Suzuki. Dark green."

I watched as McWilliams made notes on a yellow pad.

"Did you see the driver?"

"Couldn't really see him very well in the dark," I said. "I didn't recognize him."

"Anything else I should know?"

"There was a woman in the back seat of the car that picked him up," I said.

He tapped his pencil again.

"Was it the same woman?"

"It was dark. I couldn't be sure."

"Can you describe her?"

"Long legs," I said.

"What else?"

"She had a tattoo on her thigh," I said.

He chuckled. "They all have the tattoos now. To me, a person put a tattoo on their thigh, they do not understand it look like a blemish there. Nothing more. Why ruin a very nice thigh with a tattoo? And what happen when you do not like the tattoo? I hear it not so easy to have it removed."

I waited until he finished his lecture on the perils of body art. "She had gold hair," I added.

He just shook his head. "I do not understand these woman," he said. "Long or short hair?"

"If it was the same woman who was in the bar, it was short... natural," I said, meaning she wasn't wearing a wig as many women on the island did, in many different colors, these days.

"Anything else you notice, Mr. Buonfiglio?

"Before the car came, he got a text, I believe. At least I heard it and saw him looking at his phone. The phone probably has what you need to find whoever it was that picked him up."

"Yes, indeed. If there was a phone," he said.

"What do you mean?"

"When they find him, they can't find any phone anywhere."

That bit of information made me pause. McWilliams wasn't saying it, but we both knew that Frost had been murdered. Someone gave him something that killed him. I needed to get out of there. I needed to think this through, and I couldn't do it facing McWilliams.

"That's all I got, McWilliams. See, I did good. Now can I go?"

He studied me. "A man come to your place and talk to you, and he dead the next morning," McWilliams said.

"A tragedy," I said, not really trying to be a smart ass but wanting to get out of there.

"What did he talk to you about?"

"He wanted to know a good tour guide to take him hiking up Hadali," I said, repeating the lie I gave Tubby the night before. McWilliams saw through it as quickly as Tubby did, not that I cared. I wasn't about to tell him what Frost had told me, which wasn't much.

"Are you going to cooperate with me, Mr. Buonfiglio?"

"I am cooperating, McWilliams. I'm here to help," I said.

"If I need your help, I will certainly ask for it."

"Don't hesitate," I said. "You know my daughter is here. You had your men drag me down here in front of her. Not cool at all. Do you need more from me? Or can I go?" I had enough of his questioning.

He called to Baines. The officer came into McWilliams' office. "Take him back to his home."

As I walked out with Baines, I read the text Kasie had sent. *Dad, some men were here looking for you. The dog went crazy barking*, it read.

Some men? My heart was pounding. With my daughter at my home alone?

I got into the back seat of the police car and quickly texted back, asking if she was okay. She responded immediately that she was. I knew talking to her would be best, but I didn't want Baines listening to my conversation. I texted Tubby next to find out where he was. He responded that he just pulled up to my place. I breathed a little easier knowing Tubby was now there.

11

Tubby was pacing the room when I got back. Kasie was on the couch studying her phone.

"She say two men come looking for you, Mr. Len," Tubby said. "What that mean?"

Kasie looked up from her phone. "Yeah and this one started barking at one of them. Growling too. They didn't like that, I could see," she said indicating the Brown One, who was still by her side.

"What do you mean?"

She shrugged. "I don't know. Just the way one of them looked at her."

I looked at Tubby and then back at Kasie.

"Did they say what they wanted?" I asked.

"No. They asked for you. I couldn't really understand them. Their English wasn't very good. They had accents." She glanced at her phone to see if she missed anything important since the last time she looked at it, which was no more than thirty seconds ago. "They said they would be back to see you."

I sat on the couch next to Kasie and stroked the matted coat of the Brown One. "What did they look like?"

"One was about my height, thin, but kind of muscular. He had tattoos and braids. The other was stocky. He had short hair and light skin. It looked almost yellow."

Almost yellow, she said. I swallowed, remembering the man driving the Suzuki. The man who picked up Frost.

"Anything else you notice about them?"

"No, not really. When I told them you weren't here, they just left. Can we go to the beach now, Dad?"

I looked over at Tubby, who was sitting in the chair facing the couch. He shook his head at me. Both of us were thinking the same thing — and it wasn't good.

"Yeah, we can go. Just let me get changed."

I got up and headed to my bedroom. Tubby followed me.

"I see them men once. A man with tattoos and braids? Another with yellow skin. Somewhere I see them but I can't remember where."

I nodded. I held back telling him that the driver of the car that picked up Frost had yellowish skin. I held that back from McWilliams too. Why?

"There trouble now," he said. "Two men come here looking for you. McWilliams bring you to see him. Big Tree in jail. That man you have a chat with last night dead this morning. This no good, Mr. Len. No more nonsense, you need to tell me more so I can help you."

I looked out my bedroom and down to the living room to see if Kasie had gotten up from the couch. To see if she might be listening to us. I know they say that kids spend too much time on their phones, but at this moment I was glad my daughter was no exception and was totally consumed with whatever she was doing on it. I shut the door.

"You heard about Frost?" I asked.

"My wife friends with the wife of Joseph Tilly, the paramedic who take the body to the hospital. I hear he die for some such reason I don't know. Why McWilliams want to bring you to see him? He think you know something about why the man die?"

"They wanted to know what he had been drinking. They think he died from alcohol poisoning. He wanted to know if we served him bush rum."

"McWilliam know we do no such thing. We never serve the bush rum. He have another reason then to see you. What that man say to you last night? Don't tell me he looking for a tour guide to take him up Hadali."

I didn't want to bring Tubby into this. Mrs. Johns asked for my help. And now these two men, whoever they were, had me worried. I didn't like it. I didn't want my best friend, who had a wife with three young children and expecting a fourth, to get involved. I wanted to protect him.

But Tubby would be persistent. He would take it wrong, thinking I didn't trust him. He would think I didn't have confidence in him to have my back, when that couldn't be further from the truth.

And then I thought about my daughter. I couldn't do this. I had to step away. I needed to at least wait until she was gone, safe back home on Long Island with her mother, brother and step-father. It wasn't fair to spend my time on this with her here. I didn't want her answering my door to strangers while one of my dogs wanted to rip those strangers apart.

But what was I supposed to do? This was a small island. This was a place where people looked after one another, who took care of their own. St. Pierre was now my home. Tubby, Big Tree, Mrs. Johns, all of them were now my people. I had an obligation. I just had to hope that whatever was happening here would conclude quickly or be put on hold until Kasie was back in New York. Somehow, though, I knew that wasn't going to happen.

"He knew that girl," I said to Tubby in a quiet voice. "The one who died at Freedom Drop. They worked together, and I think he also had a thing with her."

"A thing?" Tubby stood over me.

"Yeah, he was in love with her," I said. "They were working on some story here. Investigating something. He said they worked for a website."

"What they investigating?"

"I don't know. He kind of hinted that someone big on the island was involved. He was going to tell me more today. How did that work out for him?" I said.

"This not good, Mr. Len. He girlfriend die in a mysterious way and now he dead. I don't like this," Tubby said.

"Neither do I," I said. I opened the door and looked down the hall again to check on Kasie. She still hadn't moved from the couch.

"Don't you worry about her," Tubby said, sensing my real concern. "No harm ever come to her, I see to that."

I nodded. I knew that to be the truth. I knew Tubby would protect her as if she were his own.

"You think you can locate those men?" I asked.

He laughed. "I find them by the end of the day," he said. "Count on it."

12

There's a place I often go to for lunch called Uncle Harvey's Delightful Roti Shop. Uncle Harvey died a few years back, and the shop is now run by his daughter, Justine. They bake their roti, an Indian-spiced flat bread, in a stone oven and then stuff them with an assortment of fillings. Kasie and I stopped there to pick up lunch for the beach; a spicy chicken roti for me and a vegetable roti for her. I took West Road north. Neither of us did much talking on the ride. Kasie stared at the scenery while my mind was occupied with all that had happened and the bad feeling I had in my gut. She sensed my apprehension. She knew I was holding back on her. Like Tubby, she didn't like that. I wanted her to have fun here. I wanted this to be special for us. But things were getting complicated and a little out of my control. I had to find a way to insulate her from all this other stuff.

I pulled the car into the driveway of the Bougainvillea Beach House, St. Pierre's most upscale lodging. The house and its small restaurant were located on Heaven's Beach on the island's Caribbean coast. There were six guest rooms of varying sizes, all of which had en-suite bathrooms and king-sized four-poster beds. There was a four-star restaurant helmed by Tito Cuevas, an acclaimed chef from Peru who, along with his partner, Clayton Teel, owned the Bougainvillea. I was friends with Clayton and Tito, and they always let me park in their driveway if I wanted to use the adjacent beach, the best on the island.

I grabbed our bag holding our beach towels, sun block and water, while Kasie took our lunch. She followed me through the property's lush gardens to a stone path that led to the beach.

Kasie's eyes went wide as she walked onto the beach. She scanned the idyllic spot — the sand, so white it seemed like it could be bleached, leading to calm, clear blue water. The small crescent-shaped beach was surrounded by lush green vegetation that hung over it. It was like something out of a postcard.

Clayton and Tito bought the 150-year-old house in dilapidated condition, restored it to its original grandeur and stocked it with antiques and art they had picked up on their travels around the world. Heaven's Beach was open to the public — there were no private beaches on the island — but the access the house had to this beach made it well-known among the more sophisticated, discriminating travelers.

The only other person at the beach was a woman lying on a large towel under the shade of one of the many grand palms that surrounded us. We set up our towels, also under one of those palms, the fronds once again serving as natural umbrellas.

"This is incredible," Kasie said. She had her phone out and started taking pictures.

I lay back on the beach towel glad that her mood had changed and that she could so quickly forget the trouble left behind at my house. I wish it were that easy for me. Despite the beauty around me and the joy I felt in being with my daughter, there was that feeling of unease—of things being not quite right—that hung over my mood.

"I'm going in, Dad, are you coming?"

"Sure." I got up from the towel and followed her into the warm water.

We bobbed in the water, floating a little, swimming a little.

"It's almost like a warm bath," Kasie said. The sun shimmered off her wet, golden hair.

"I know, it feels good on my old bones," I said.

She swam up to me and stopped. "What's going on here, Dad? Why did the police come for you? Are you in some kind of trouble?"

"No, I'm not in any trouble," I said. "A man died last night. He was last seen at the bar. So they just wanted to ask me a few questions."

I looked around. The woman on the towel was sitting up now. I noticed she wore a big beach hat and had sunglasses on. She was watching us.

"Who were those men that came to the house? Do they have anything to do with the man who died?" Kasie asked.

"I don't know who they were."

She wasn't getting the answers she wanted. The truth was, I didn't have any for her.

"But you were concerned about it, I could tell." she said.

I nodded.

"Why?"

"I don't know," I said.

"Does it have to do with that man you are helping? The Big Tree?"

"I'm not sure," I said.

"What did they say he did? You never told me any of that."

I ducked under the water and then resurfaced.

"Last year a woman was found dead in the shallow water at the bottom of a cliff on the northern end of the island. They thought at first she fell, that it was an accident, but now they think it might not have been."

"At that place you were telling me about. The one you were gonna show me?"

"Yeah," I mumbled.

"They think the Big Tree did it?"

I shrugged. "Maybe," I said. "I don't really know."

She was quiet for a moment. She was thinking about what I said as she floated on her back in the water. She stood up in the water and eyed me.

"I don't understand. What can you do? Shouldn't the police or detectives handle that?"

"Yeah, they should," I said.

"Then why you? What can you do?"

I had no solid answer for that question, but that didn't help my daughter any. She wanted something from me to justify all this worry. Before I could mutter something, anything that might appease Kasie, I noticed that the woman on the towel had come to the edge of the water near us.

"Hello," she called and waved from the shore.

Both of us turned to her. She was wearing a navy-blue one-piece suit with a plunging neckline. The suit was held on by a thin string that went over her shoulders and tied around the back of her neck. Her skin was light brown, and her shoulder length hair was blowing in the breeze under a floppy hat that she had to keep a hand on to keep it on her head. My eyes were far from perfect, but they were good enough to see, even from over twenty feet away, the sensual curve of her hips that led to long, toned legs, the neckline that plunged almost to the woman's navel, and what was more than evident on either side of that neckline. I was conscious of my daughter there, seeing me quite obviously checking the woman out.

"Who's that?" Kasie asked.

"I have no idea," I said.

"Hi," she said again. She moved a little closer to us, her feet now in the shallow water. It was obvious she didn't want to get wet, so both of us started out of the water to see what she wanted.

"I'm sorry if I've disturbed you," she said with a smile. She looked at Kasie. "Hi there, do you remember me?"

Kasie looked at me and then back at the woman.

"From the airport in Barbados," the woman said. "We were on the same flight to St. Pierre. We were in the terminal together. We chatted."

"Oh! I'm sorry, I remember now. You're from Boston?"

"That's right," she said. "And this must be the father you came to spend your spring break with." She turned to me and smiled.

It took some willpower, but I kept my eyes up, doing my absolute best not to gawk at those legs or that plunging neckline. While keeping my eyes on her face, I noticed a splattering of dark freckles over her high cheekbones. I had seen freckles like those before and tried to remember where.

Trying to assume some sort of cool, I extended my hand to her. "Len Buonfiglio," I said.

She nodded as if she knew and took my hand. "Marcia Gould," she replied.

My mouth opened, but I caught myself before saying anything. I nodded. Now I knew where I had seen those freckles before. The woman was Deanna Gould's mother. The same woman who caught my eye as she came off the same plane with Kasie and who was escorted from the airport by McWilliams and Baines.

"Pleasure to meet you, Mrs. Gould," I said trying not to show the surprise on my face.

"Oh, please call me Marcia," she said. "Your daughter is lovely."

I grinned at Kasie. "Thanks for reminding me," I said.

"And you make St. Pierre your home, Mr. Buonfiglio?" she said. She was tall but I was taller, and she looked up into my eyes as she spoke.

"Yes," I said. "And call me Len. Or, if you want, like most do here on St. Pierre, you can call me Mr. Len, but really, I would rather you didn't do that."

She smiled playfully, and again I was reminded of her daughter. "How about Lennie? Would that work?"

I looked as Kasie rolled her eyes at me and then shook her head. "I don't think so," Kasie interjected.

Marcia Gould laughed, displaying flawless white teeth that had previously been hidden behind full red lips. "Len it is, then. Are you enjoying your time with your father, Kasie?"

"So far, yeah," Kasie said. "The beaches here are amazing."

"I agree," Marcia said. "I've been to some beautiful beaches in Southeast Asia and the Pacific, but this one is as good as any of them."

"Are you staying at the Bougainvillea?" I asked.

"Yes, I am. It's been wonderful, considering," she said.

I looked at her and then remembered why she was here. There was an awkward moment between the three of us. And then, as if on cue, Kasie said, "Dad, I'm going to lie in the sun."

"Okay, I'll be right there," I said and then turned my attention back to Marcia Gould. "I recognized your name. My condolences."

She nodded. "Thank you, Len. I'm hoping I can get closure on all of this as soon as possible."

"I understand," I said. And I could. She had waited months now. She needed answers. She needed to know what happened to her daughter. That closure meant making sure Rawle Johns was put away for her daughter's murder, that he would spend the rest of his life in the small prison in the recesses of Fort Philippe. There were many things I wanted to say and ask her about that forensics report, but I knew I couldn't. At least not now, on this beach. So I remained mute as I faced her.

She lifted her chin and smiled at me. "And I've recognized your name as well," she said.

"Me?"

"Oh yes," she said. "Your daughter gave you away during our chat in the airport."

"What do you mean gave me away?"

She looked me over. "Well, that you used to live in New York. That you have been living on the island now for several years and own a bar here."

"What else did my daughter tell you?" I asked.

"That was it, but I will confess that I did inquire about you with Clayton here at the Bougainvillea. He speaks very highly of you."

"That's nice of Clayton," I said, wondering what he told her.

"He highly recommends the Sporting Place for a casual drink and to take in the view of Garrison. I hope to see that view before I leave the island." She looked me over when she said that.

I said, "Maybe that can be arranged."

The water continued to lap at our feet as we faced each other. The hot sun was drying my chest and hair. Her eyes seemed to look me up and down, and then she grinned. The vibe coming from her was subtly sensual — the same vibe I got from those fifteen minutes with her daughter but much more powerful coming from this woman. The similarity between mother and daughter was almost eerie.

"You're a popular man here, Len, from what I hear."

"Not really," I said.

She laughed. "Oh come on, are you really modest or is that an act just to impress me?" she asked in what seemed like a whisper.

I looked her over. She was truly beautiful.

"Do I need to impress you?"

That caught her off guard. I saw her nibble her lower lip. "No," she said. "I've done my research."

I took a breath. Of course she did. My New York past was there on Google for anyone to find if they wanted. And I'm sure she did her googling. I didn't want to get into any of what she might have found. Not here.

"I should get back to my daughter," I said.

"Yes of course," she said hesitantly. "But, Len..."

I turned back to her and wondered if I gaffed by what I just said. I thought about the grieving mother. It had been almost a year, but how does a parent ever resume a normal life after the death of their child? I didn't ever want to know.

"Maybe you and Kasie can join me for dinner here at the Bougainvillea? The food is really remarkable."

"Yes, Tito is a magician," I said. "Kasie is only here a few more days, but let me check."

"Thank you," she said with a smile. "I'd love your company."

I nodded again.

I wasn't sure of Marcia Gould's motives, and for the moment at least, gazing at that freckled smile and everything else, her motives just didn't matter.

"Dad, you're not gonna go all creepy on me, are you?" Kasie said to me as I joined her in the sun on the big beach blanket.

"Creepy? What are you talking about?"

"I saw the way you looked at that woman," she said.

"That obvious, huh?" I put my sunglasses on and leaned back on my elbows.

"Um...yeah," Kasie said.

"Guilty," I said as I threw up my hands. I didn't know what else to say to her. She caught me. "Was it really creepy?"

"Borderline," she said. "But if it makes you feel any better, she had that same look."

"I don't know, Kasie, she didn't look creepy to me at all," I said.

She laughed at me. "I'm just teasing, you Dad. You're single. Go for it. She's beautiful and real classy. God that bathing suit. What that must have cost her, but from the way it looked on her, worth every penny."

I kept my mouth shut on any assessments of Marcia Gould's swimsuit. It was already bad enough I was borderline creepy. "So what did you guys talk about when you were in Barbados?"

She shrugged. "I don't really remember. She asked what I was doing traveling alone to St. Pierre. She was surprised, I guess. So I told her about you living here."

"And what about her?" I glanced over at Marcia Gould. She was packing up her belongings and folding up her beach towel.

"Just that she was from Boston and that it was her second time visiting St. Pierre."

"Anything else?"

"Nothing I can remember, Dad. Why all the questions?"

I kicked at the white sand. "Because she is the mother of that girl who died here. The one I was telling you about who had the accident and fell off the cliff."

Kasie let that sink in. "I didn't know. That's so sad."

"Yeah, it is."

"But why is she here now? Why would she come back here?"

"Apparently she had her daughter's body examined in Boston, and what they found connected her daughter's death to the man you saw being arrested. She came to see that he was arrested. She wants to find out how she really died. She doesn't think her daughter could have slipped or killed herself."

"And the Big Tree's mother wants you to help prove that he had nothing to do with the girl's death."

"Yeah."

"Can you do that, Dad?"

I laughed. "If you know, tell me," I said. "Anyway, she wants to have dinner with us one of these nights that you are here and before she goes back to Boston. You up for that?"

Kasie chuckled "No, Dad, she wants to have dinner with you. She was just being nice about inviting me. Don't let me stop you."

"I'm not going without you," I said.

"Now you're being creepy. It's fine. I don't mind one bit."

I looked over at Marcia Gould. She smiled and waved before turning to walk through the cobbled path back to the Bougainvillea. My eyes lingered a bit longer at her and then thought about those freckles...and a few other things.

13

We ate our rotis on the beach towel and then went for another swim before packing up.

"If I lived here, I'd be on that beach every day," Kasie said as we walked through the gardens of the Bougainvillea.

"I live here and don't get here as often as I should, so what's my excuse?" I said.

We got in the Jeep. "Are you ready for a shower now?" I asked her.

She stared at me curiously. "When we get home?"

"No before we get home."

"What do you mean, Dad?

I smiled. "You'll see."

I drove inland toward St. Pierre's National Park, where the island's lush rainforest was located. On the outskirts of the park is the parish of Glencoe, where Scottish settlers who came to St. Pierre in the late eighteenth-century grazed their goats and sheep. The settlers were clannish and up until the mid-twentieth century rarely intermingled with the others on the island, be they white or black. Soon after the island's independence in the early 1970s, the Scottish families began to assimilate, and clan life slowly faded into history. I made a sharp turn into what seemed like no road at all; brush was scraping against the Jeep as I inched into the forest and then parked.

"Where are we?" Kasie wondered.

"I told you we were gonna shower. Well, the shower's right over here."

We got out of the Jeep and, grabbing two towels, I led Kasie through a barely noticeable trail. There was a roaring sound in the near distance.

"Hear that?"

"Yeah, what is it?"

We walked about forty more yards, the roaring sound getting louder and louder, until the trail ended. In front of us was an open ravine, and across it water was flowing from the peaks of the rainforest, cascading powerfully down a cliff-side and into a clear green pool.

"There's our shower," I said, pointing to the waterfall.

Kasie giggled at the impressive sight. "Can we really?"

"Of course, let's go."

I took her hand and led her carefully down the slippery slope and into the cool fresh water. "Wooo hoooo," she yelled with a big smile and swam so the waterfall could literally shower over her.

"Careful, that's a really strong jet spray," I said.

"I know," she yelled over the roar of the fall. "But it feels great!"

I swam to join her and both of us let the water massage our backs.

"What do they call it?" Kasie asked.

"Inchree Falls," I said and then told her about the parish's history and how the Scots, who claimed this area, named it for a waterfall that reminded them of one back in Scotland.

"Dad, this is beautiful," she said.

I knew she meant the waterfall, but I also thought she meant being on St. Pierre with me. The whole package. At least that was my hope. I owed her that. And much much more.

We dried off and made our way back to the Jeep. I backed out of the forest road and got back onto the main road that circled the island. There was still time before it got dark to show my daughter one more thing.

"Where are we going now?" Kasie asked as she settled into her seat and put her seatbelt on.

"You'll understand once we get there."

The road as we headed north was even narrower, with a collision course of potholes that even the shocks of my Jeep struggled with. I kept my eyes on the narrow swerving road, doing my best to avoid those potholes and the threat of oncoming vehicles speeding around blind corners. We were now on the northern tip of the island. I pulled over to the side of the road.

"Now where are we?" she asked.

"Come, you'll see," I said as I got out of the Jeep. Kasie followed. I walked tentatively with her to the edge of the cliff and a knee-high chain-link fence where a bronzed memorial was embedded in a big stone near the cliff's ledge. I pointed to it.

She read the heading of the memorial and then looked at me. "Freedom Drop?"

I nodded. She read the rest of the inscription as I stared at the blue sea beyond. The afternoon sun shimmered on the surface of the choppy water below. I remembered the first time I ever came to this spot. With Big Tree. The high tenor voice coming out of that big body added to the charm of what he was reciting, the story he told all who took his tour.

"It is here where our brave ancestors came to escape their tormentors," he had said to me. "The Caribs and the Arawak peoples were the first. When the Spanish were here on this island, they captured the indigenous people and used them as slaves. But there were many who rebelled. Who ran away. They were told by their elders that if they came here and jumped off this cliff, that their souls would always be free. And that is what they did. They would rather jump into the sky and fall to the sea below than submit to the Spanish. When the Africans came, my people, the *fante* people from Ghana, they too heard the same tales. The French were here at that time when the African slaves were brought to the island. Not all, but many chose to run here, to what they called Freedom Drop, to give up their lives instead of working as slaves for the French. So this a very sacred spot. When I come here, no matter how many times, I feel a special pull. It bring shivers down my back and make me proud that my people had the courage to resist slavery, even if it mean death. I can look down over this cliff and see the rocks and water below, and I never afraid. I know that down there...that over this cliff... all the other brave ones go to escape. In death, they are men again — not slaves. They are men who are free from bondage. And sometime the bondage right here."

I remembered him pointing to his head when he said that last bit and I wondered why. For me, that pull was different. It made me think of falling — dropping — jumping from high bridges, big buildings and steep cliffs. Whenever I came here, I did my best to block those thoughts that had haunted me ever since that day in June. The day when everything changed for me. And now, here I was, years later, holding my daughter's hand tightly in mine, doing my very best to vanquish those thoughts — the bondage in my mind — to free myself of them. If it were only that easy.

"This is where she fell, isn't it?" Kasie asked after she finished reading the inscription that summed up what Big Tree had told me.

"Yeah."

"It's horrible. But those others. They were heroic. I don't blame them for taking their own lives. Still, women — babies. This is a sad place, Dad."

"Sad, but also special. This is part of St. Pierre's history. So it is sad for you and me, but the people here celebrate this spot. This was the only place where those slaves could truly find freedom," I said, recalling Big Tree's words to me. "The drop and certain death was the better alternative. The Spanish and the French would often guard this spot to prevent their property from taking their own lives. They tried to deny them even in death."

"People can be so cruel," Kasie said.

"Yeah, they can," I mumbled.

"Do you think that woman's daughter killed herself? Or that it was an accident and she slipped? Or...someone did it?"

I didn't know what to think, only that she was dead.

"You would have to be pretty reckless to slip," I said.

"You'd have to be crazy," she said. "Or unless you had a good reason to jump. Like the slaves."

Yes, I thought, you would need a very good reason.

She peered over the ledge of the cliff to look down at the steep drop and the water crashing into the rocks that jutted from the beach below. My hand still gripping hers, I pulled her back to me. My palm was sweaty. She noticed and looked up at me. And then she moved closer and hugged me tight.

We stood together there in silence for a few moments.

"Let's go home, okay, Dad?"

I nodded. "Let's go."

I drove back around the East Road alongside the cliffs that led down to the Atlantic. It was getting late and the sun was beginning to set. Kasie had her eyes closed and was sleeping. I wondered if I should have shown her Freedom Drop. It was normally an uplifting monument to man's willingness to do anything for freedom, even if it meant sacrificing himself. But now that monument was scarred. A girl died there who wasn't fleeing slavery. She was killed there. Or maybe she wasn't. But she didn't die for her freedom, in her mind or otherwise. I knew it affected Kasie. I could read it on her face. She was discovering things about me she never knew. She was learning who I was. I wasn't sure that was a good thing. I wasn't sure she was happy with what she was discovering. I just wanted to get close to her. To make up for my not being there. To be her father again.

I turned west and approached my home. As I got closer, I noticed something by the side of the house. Something different. I looked closer as I edged toward it, slowing the Jeep down. I looked at the tamarind tree on the west lawn. The tamarind is a fruit that grows in a long brown hard shell. The fruit inside the shell is a sticky, fibrous seed. The seeds are mashed and used in drinks, sweets and sauces. I don't do the mashing or know how to make it into drinks, but others do and I gladly share my bounty with anyone who wants it. As a result, I'm often given tamarind jelly, tamarind ice cream, tamarind candy, pepper sauce with tamarind and tamarind syrup as gifts from those who use my homegrown tamarind. The fruit is always abundant, and the long shells hang down from the big tree. But there was something else hanging from the tree there that was not tamarind. Something also brown, but much bigger than the tamarind fruit. Something that made the hairs on the back of my neck rise.

The light was fading and day was turning into night; I was hoping that the impending darkness had made me see something that really wasn't there, that it was just a dark shadow. I knew though, deep down in my belly, that was a false hope. I now could clearly make out what I saw. My mouth suddenly got dry. I quickly turned to my daughter hoping to hell that her eyes were still closed. But they were open wide. And they were looking at the tamarind tree. They were seeing what I saw.

"Dad?" Her eyes stared incomprehensively.

"No, Kasie!" I shouted and tried to cover her eyes. "Don't..."
She pushed my hand away.

"Don't...look," I said. But it was too late.

She turned to me, her face was red. She was angry at me — as if I did this. "Dad!" she yelled. Before I could stop her, she quickly opened the door to the Jeep and ran toward the house.

"No...wait!" I ran after her. I needed to get into the house before her. I needed to make sure no one was in there. Waiting. The Spotted One and the Gray One were whining and barking as they ran by my side.

Kasie was crying and pulling at the doorknob. I had locked

the house when we left. That it was still locked made me breathe a little easier. I opened the door, and Kasie flew by me to her room, sobbing. I ran after her and checked her room as she threw herself on the bed, face down. I went into my room and peered into the closets. The house was empty.

I flopped down on my couch, staring blankly. The two dogs nuzzled my thighs from either side. I caressed their coats. I wanted to ask them what happened. I wanted to know why they didn't help their sister. They had no answer for me.

I could hear my daughter's sobs coming from her room. I felt a rage slowly building. I knew I had to suppress it. I knew I had to keep it inside. I was good at that, at keeping the most primal things inside. I could be gruff, grumpy with customers, with Tubby, and with others. But that primal stuff. The deep dark rage I could keep buried in my gut, now I wanted to let it loose. I wanted to do something. I wanted to act yet knew I couldn't. Not yet. I had to remember that I was not alone. That my daughter was with me. I could not lose control. Not now.

I went to my refrigerator, took out a cold beer and opened it. My daughter, who had made the journey to visit me for the first time in my new home, was crying in her room. My beautiful Kasie had to witness this. To see this with her father. I downed most of the beer in just a few gulps and then went outside to the back of the house. The two dogs followed my every move. I had a storage shed behind the house. I opened it and took out garden shears. And then I walked to the tamarind tree, the dogs at my side. When I got to the tree I tried not to look too closely. But then I didn't try anymore. I saw what they did to her.

And then I saw something else. Wrapped around the dog's broken neck was a string of golden blonde hair. I removed the

119

string of hair and stared at it. I knew what it was. I knew why it was put there and what it meant. My fist was now gripping the shears. I reared back and was about to stab the sharp blades into the tamarind tree when I stopped myself. I had to stop myself. I tried to focus, to just breathe like I knew how to when I used to prepare for a fight. Back when I was running the bars in Brooklyn, the long nights, the constant buzz, and the frenetic pace of the work took a toll on my body and my mind. To combat it I began training in martial arts. I studied and trained in Muay Thai and soon I was able to fight and started winning. After four years, I had earned a Super Cruiserweight title which came with a championship belt, the equivalent of a black belt in other martial arts. After that victory I gave up fighting but continued to train. The training helped balance me, and as part of it, I learned the flow state, the ability to use the power of the right side of my brain to help me focus clearly. I did this through daily meditation, and it calmed me, centered me and helped in my training. After everything fell apart in New York, I abandoned training altogether. It was only recently, here on St. Pierre, when I needed to put my skills into use in self-defense that I realized I had to at least keep my body in shape, which, as I got older, was no easy thing. So when we had the time, Tubby and I would work out together. Tubby was anxious to learn what I knew, but I wasn't a patient teacher. Still, we went at it whenever we could, and even though I was training again, I wasn't meditating; I hadn't had to call up that calm in many years. I needed to summon those skills now. I had to.

After a few slow breaths with my eyes closed, I loosened the grip I had on the shears and then did the only thing I could do at that moment. I cut her down.

14

I put the string of hair in my pocket and carried the dead dog in my arms to the far end of my property where I had a star apple tree. I could hear my daughter's sobs in the otherwise quiet night. The Brown One and her brothers often slept under the shade of that tree in the midday sun to escape the heat. It was as good a spot as any to bury her. I dug a small hole, placed her there and covered her up with dirt while her brothers looked on. I patted down the dirt mound. I would make a marker to indicate the grave, but that could wait.

I washed my hands using the outside hose and then pulled my phone out. I knew my voice was trembling when I talked to Tubby. I told him what happened. There was a cool anger in my tone. It made Tubby hesitate before responding to what I told him. He could sense my rage. This was a side of me he hadn't seen before.

"Go easy right now, Mr. Len," Tubby said. "Stay cool. I know you can do that. Best to sleep on this. I know what you want to do, but you know that not the way things get done right. I find those men. I find where they staying and then we figure what to do."

I just held the phone to my ear.

"Okay?" he asked.

"Yeah, okay," I finally mumbled.

"Now you go take care of your girl. That what matter most," he said.

He was right. That was what mattered most.

In time I did cool down, and when I no longer heard the sobbing from the guest room, I knocked on Kasie's door. There was no answer, but I opened it anyway. She was lying on the bed, her head buried in her pillow. I had looked forward to this visit for so long. I wanted it to be perfect. I did not want this. She and her brother Luke were my family. If I lost them what did I have?

I bent over her bed and reached to stroke her hair. "I'm sorry you had to see that, honey," I said. "I'm sorry about everything. I'm gonna change your ticket and get you on an earlier plane home. I'll take care of everything."

She turned and looked at me. Her eyes were red.

"You want me to go?" she said.

I was surprised by her question. "No...I..." I had assumed she couldn't wait to get back home.

"Dad, I came here to see you," she said. "I've been looking forward to this too, you know."

I tried not to choke up hearing her say that. But then I thought about the reality of the situation. It wasn't safe for her here anymore. Circumstances had changed. I could not put my daughter in jeopardy in any way. The responsible thing to do was to get her on the first plane off the island the next morning.

And I hadn't even thought of Kathleen. What would I tell her? She'd never let Kasie or her brother come down here again if she knew what was going on. Yet I couldn't lie to her. I couldn't hide what was going on from her. I did that once already. I had to tell her the truth. I owed her at least that.

"I don't know, Kasie. Whoever did that, if it were those men you saw, they might come back. I don't know what they want, but I'm in the middle of something that's a threat to them. I just don't know. I can't take a risk with you. You are my main concern."

"What are you going to do, Dad?" Kasie asked, sitting up in bed now.

"About what?"

"Those men. The girl who died. Big Tree. All of it. I just don't understand, I mean, you always told me you owned a bar here. You never told me you did other stuff like this. Why can't these people just get the police to help them? Why do you have to get involved?"

After what she just saw, I couldn't evade her questions. How would I ever have a relationship with her if I kept holding back?

"It's hard to explain, Kasie," I said. "This is not like New York City. This is a small place. When I first got here, I felt like an outsider. That's how people looked at me. They were friendly and I had no trouble with anyone, but I wasn't one of them. I was just another foreign investor. And then I helped a man here who was hurt by someone bad. I took care of it. I did what the police couldn't do. And for that, people started to look at me differently. I became part of their community. And that made me feel good."

"What do you mean you took care of it?"

"It doesn't matter what I did. But it worked out. For everyone here on St. Pierre. It was almost as if it was an initiation. I had to prove myself to them."

I could feel her eyes on me. She wanted more; she wanted details, but they were dirty and I wasn't going to give her that. Not after what she just saw.

"After that, others started asking me for help in matters where they did not believe the police could. Or didn't want the police involved. But it's not like this stuff happens all the time. Just here and there. Most of the time it's me and Tubby working at the Sporting Place. That's all. Don't worry about me. You just came and all this happened at the same time. I didn't plan it that way."

I tried to smile reassuringly at her.

She was thinking about what I just told her. "I won't tell Mom what happened," she said. "She doesn't have to know."

"No, she does," I said. "Don't worry, I'll explain it all to your mother."

"Really, Dad, I'll be alright. I won't get in your way. I don't want to go tomorrow. Let me stay until I'm supposed to leave, okay?"

"How about we sleep on it and decide tomorrow morning. Okay?"

She nodded, but I knew she could sense where I was going. I would not put my daughter at risk. I had to get her off the island.

We talked for a long time, and then she said she was hungry, which made me feel good. I made spaghetti with a marinara sauce I prepared from canned San Marzano tomatoes, which I bought along with a block of Parmigiano-Reggiano off a boat that came to the island from St. Lucia every few weeks. Tito, of the Bougainvillea, tipped me off about it. The boat supplied yachts, restaurants and exclusive marinas around the Grenadines with gourmet and imported foods you could never get in the local markets here: authentic olive oil, French and Italian wines, truffles, salted anchovies, Mediterranean tuna, aged balsamic vinegar, imported cheeses and even hand-rolled fresh pasta.

I had the phone number of the captain of the boat. I would call to find out when he was coming to the island and order whatever I needed, which usually wasn't much. The boat never came ashore; Tito and I would take a dinghy out to meet it. I wasn't sure if the enterprise was legal. Maybe the boat stayed offshore to avoid customs, taxes and other duty charges for the supplier. I had no doubt the business was known, but as was usually the case, it wasn't worth the time or effort for the St. Pierre government to put a stop to it.

Kasie ate ravenously. We both did. But in the middle of the meal she started to cry again. "I'm sorry, Dad. This is ridiculous. I have to stop crying."

I shook my head. "No, honey, never be afraid to cry," said the man who rarely shed a tear.

She wiped at her eyes and started to eat again until she put her fork down. "I'm going to bed," she said.

She got up from her chair. I got up with her and walked her to her bedroom. I apologized again for what she had to go through. She didn't say anything. She didn't have to.

I knew I told Kasie that I would sleep on my decision, but there was nothing to sleep on. If I was going to change her flight, I needed to do it as soon as possible. She had a ticket back in three days. Could I hold off that long? I knew I couldn't wait. I couldn't drag my daughter along with me while trying to figure this out. I also couldn't leave her here alone while I did what I had to do.

I turned on my laptop and before I even began to check on potential flights back to New York, I realized the flight from St. Pierre to Barbados did not run Thursdays, and tomorrow was Thursday. I checked to see if I could get her on a flight to another island like St. Lucia or Aruba, but it was spring break and most flights from the larger islands were booked. There was a late flight from Trinidad, but she would have to take the ferry to St. Vincent and then another prop plane to Port of Spain and most likely wait in the airport for hours before the flight to JFK. That was asking a lot of a teenager who was not experienced in travel. She would be with me at least one more day. I couldn't leave my daughter here alone and I did not want her tagging along. I knew what I had to do. I knew who I had to call.

15

I'd known Betta Baptiste since I came to St. Pierre. I knew her when she had a small shared room on Front Street and entertained male visitors to the island. I just happened to be one of those visitors back when I first visited St. Pierre, before I decided to make it my home. But I was not like her other visitors. I didn't come for what the others came for. Betta was a temptation, there was no doubt about that; it was just that at the time, after leaving New York, that part of me was an empty hole. So instead, I would take her out for a steak dinner at the restaurant at the Lime Tree Hotel, the only restaurant on the island that served steak. And we would talk. Or I would talk and she would listen, her dark eyes always probing mine. When I brought her back to her room, she would invite me in. She would ask me to stay with her. But I never did. Our quiet talks had revived the feelings of intimacy that had been dormant now for too long, and I very much wanted to accept her offers. But I just couldn't. Not this way.

Soon after those weekly dinners, Betta met another man, an Italian named Maurizio, who became more to her than someone she entertained. He said he would take care of her, and he did. Until he didn't. Leaving her with child and returning to the safe security of his family in Italy. Being a thoughtful man, however, he sent her checks on a regular basis. Those checks sustained her, so she never had to go back to the small room on Front Street. And they helped feed and clothe her son, their son, Paolo.

During and after Betta's relationship with Maurizio, she and I danced around each other. We were friends. We were more than friends. But we were not lovers. Betta was much younger than I, and though that never seemed to matter to her, it did to me. Most of all, though, was that I knew her heart and everything else remained with the man who left her. The man who gave her a child who inherited his blue eyes. I could give her many things, but I could not give her a child with blue eyes.

Though she never asked for my help after Maurizio left, she knew I was always there if she needed me. And in so doing, Tubby and I worked to complete the house he left unfinished in the foothills of Mt. Hadali. It was a small but modern house with a pretty backyard, where there was both a mango and a breadfruit tree for shade.

There was one time Betta did ask for my help. It was when she needed me to punish a man who had hurt a girl she worked with. I found out later that the same man hurt Betta in the same way years before. I was not the punishing kind; there are others who can fill that role. And in this case it wasn't me who extracted retribution for the wrong that was done. But I was involved. And for this man and for what he did, it was a pleasure.

After our history, I liked to think Betta would protect my

own daughter as she would her young son. That she would do me this favor even if I hadn't done those things for her. That her feelings for me alone would be reason enough. It was a silly thought on my part, but one I could never shake when it came to Betta.

She answered the phone as I knew she would. Before I could tell her what I was calling her for, she said: "I would like to meet your daughter."

I hadn't talked to her since Kasie had arrived. I don't think I even mentioned that she would be visiting me. It had been awhile since we saw each other. But she knew, as it seemed so many did, that my daughter was here with me.

I explained the situation to her. She listened without interruption. Betta was a woman who used words sparingly. It was part of her allure. She had an almost mystical magnetism to her. Her deep black eyes could toy with your soul. Her gentle voice could soothe even the most agitated of men. She didn't ask questions, and after I finished telling her how I needed her to take care of Kasie, to make sure she was safe, she said without hesitation, in that voice that never failed to stir me, "Please bring her over, Leonard."

Not Len. Not Mr. Len. For Betta it was Leonard. From anyone else I might have objected. Coming from Betta's lips, it just sounded right and I never corrected her on it.

"You're in luck," I said to Kasie the next morning. I had let her sleep as long as I could, but I needed her up now. Tubby was waiting for me to pick him up. She sat up in bed. "I couldn't get a flight out for you today."

"Oh, good! So I can stay with you?"

"Not exactly," I said. "I have to go somewhere with Tubby and I don't want you here alone. Not after what happened yesterday. I'm gonna drop you off with a friend of mine. She'll take care of you until I can finish up with what I have to do."

"She?"

"Yeah, Kasie. A friend, that's all."

She looked at me doubtfully. "Okay, Dad."

"No, no, she's not like that. Just a friend. Really. But someone I can trust."

Maybe I protested too much. Either way, Kasie wasn't buying it.

"Uh-huh, but you'll pick me up later?"

"Sure," I said. "You should maybe bring a change of clothes just in case I can't get over there till later."

"What are you planning to do?"

"Nothing to worry about, Kasie, Tubby and I have this under control."

Yeah, we had it under control. Whatever it was.

As soon as I pulled the Jeep up in front of her house, Betta emerged from the front door, as if she had been waiting at the window for our arrival. Tall and slender, she wore a short, light-yellow dress with spaghetti straps that highlighted her toned shoulders. Her skin was charcoal black and so smooth it often appeared as if it was glowing. When I first met her she wore her hair short and when working put on a wig with long flowing soft dark hair. She had long since abandoned the wig and in the last few years or so had let her hair grow long enough to braid into plaits she decorated with glossed shells that cascaded back from her forehead and down to the middle of her back. When we got out of the Jeep I saw her studying Kasie with a smile that revealed the gap between her two front teeth. Some might have considered that gap a slight blemish, but in my opinion it just added to her allure.

Kasie caught me looking at Betta. I couldn't hide what I was feeling, what I always felt. Betta was closer to my daughter's age than to mine. Had I crossed the line to full-fledged creepy? I tried to control my eyes. I tried to put on a different face, but I just could not. Not with Betta.

We walked the stone pathway to the front door, and before we got to Betta, three-year-old Paolo ran out and wrapped a small arm around his mother's thigh and stared not at me but at Kasie, with perhaps the same look I had for his mother. He had a mop of dark curly hair, and his skin was the color of cinnamon that only accentuated the bright blue of the eyes he had inherited from his father.

"This is my daughter. Kasie," I said to Betta. "Kasie, meet Betta."

The two smiled at each other and then Betta opened her arms and they hugged as if they were old friends. I wasn't sure how this would go. My daughter was no dummy. I knew she sensed that there was some history between us. I didn't know how she would react. I breathed a sigh of relief.

"She is beautiful," Betta whispered to me. I could see Kasie blush. "And it looks like Paolo thinks so too."

"He's so cute," Kasie said, as Paolo ran back into the house.

"He shy," Betta said with a proud smile.

I could see Paolo peeking through the screen door at us. Kasie bent to him. "Hi, Paolo," she said. "Can I come in?"

With his eyes on her, Paolo slowly opened the door for Kasie.

She laughed and turned to me. "I'll see ya, Dad," she said and then went in after Paolo.

"Thanks for doing this, Betta," I said.

"She is always welcome here, Leonard. You don't even have to ask. You should know that."

I did know that, but I always had to ask.

She put a hand on my forearm. The same forearm I broke — or should I say was broken by a very hard beer bottle wielded by the illegitimate son of the island vagrant who was murdered by both the young man and his biological mother. But that was another story and history now. The point being that it was Betta who took care of me for the few days after the incident. Her touch there made me think of what she did for me. And what she was doing for me now. I tried not to think of anything else beyond that. But it was hard.

"Please be careful, Leonard," she said, keeping her long slender fingers there. Her dark eyes searching mine. I hadn't told her any of what had happened. I didn't mention the dog. The two men. The death of Craig Frost. The death of Deanna Gould. The case against Big Tree. She got nothing from me, yet she knew that there was trouble, of that I was sure.

"Yeah, Betta, I plan on it. I just feel really bad that I have to do this while Kasie is here. It was not what I had planned."

"It will be okay. We will have fun."

16

Tubby and I stood on the side of West Road overlooking a black-sand beach and the village of Laborie. I had a pair of binoculars fixed on a sailing yacht anchored off the tiny fishing hamlet. From where we stood, I estimated the yacht to be about 150 feet. There were other boats anchored as well, but they looked nothing like that impressive vessel. For generations families had lived around this beach and took their boats out early, late or whenever the fishermen felt was the right time to catch their bounty. Just off the beach from where they lived, nets could be tossed in the water and dragged by groups of men. The result was usually a cluttered net of flapping Jacks that, when dusted lightly with flour, pan-fried and served with a squeeze of lime juice, was one of St. Pierre's great treats. Just around the bend from Laborie was Coral Beach, where my daughter and I had spent the afternoon snorkeling just two days earlier. It seemed like a century ago.

I held the binoculars closer to my eyes, squinted into it and tried to focus in on the name of the boat, but I just couldn't read it.

I passed the binoculars to Tubby.

"You are sure this is where they are staying? That they came from that boat?" I asked.

He took the binoculars from his eyes. "Absolutely. I know Linden bring them supplies on his dinghy. He see them there when he unload ice and whiskey for them."

"Anyone else with them?"

"He say they have a girl too," Tubby said.

I nodded. The girl in the bar with the tattoo on one of those dark-brown thighs and the gold hair — the one I saw in the Suzuki with Craig Frost just before he died.

I stared at the boat without the use of the binoculars. It looked just as large and luxurious without the magnification.

"Linden recognize the girl?"

"She no one from this place," Tubby said. He put the binoculars down. "What are we going to do?"

"We?" I turned to him. "This has nothing to do with you."

He looked back at the boat.

"I see there are two of them and one of you. Not to mention the girl. That one too many. These men are not from around here. They tough guys. Gangsters. Maybe Jamaican. Maybe African. Maybe from somewhere I don't know. I know you have skills, Mr. Len. But you need more than just your skills for these two."

"I don't even know what I'm going to do, Tubby."

I started back to the Jeep. Tubby followed and got in the passenger side. I drove down West Road heading to the bar.

"I need to know when they leave the boat," I said as I drove. "I have to have a chat with them."

Tubby turned to me. "A chat? Is that what you plan, Mr. Len?

Just a chat?"

"Uh-huh," I mumbled.

"Where does that leave me?" Tubby asked.

"It leaves you safely at home with your family or tending bar at the acclaimed Sporting Place, St. Pierre's liveliest and only sports bar."

Tubby hissed. "You know I be right by your side with those two. This not just one skinny drug dealer from Guyana. Or a lady preacher. These men are not nice at all and you know it. They in a different league altogether."

He didn't have to remind me. Still they came to my house. This was my problem, not his. "You have someone in Laborie who can let you know when they get off the boat?"

"It already done, Mr. Len," Tubby said. "I tell my friend Rondo to keep an eye on that boat. He know what to do."

"Who's Rondo?"

"He live in Laborie and fish there with his father. I know him since we boys and play cricket together. He a mighty fine batsman."

Tubby and most of St. Pierre called cricket their national pastime. When he had free time, he would umpire local youth games and, as I heard many times from him but was never verified by anyone else, as a boy he was considered one of the island's top bowlers, the cricket equivalent of a baseball pitcher. Since living on St. Pierre, I've tried to assimilate in many ways, but I've never garnered any enthusiasm for the game. There was baseball...and then there was cricket. You had to make a choice, and for me it was easy.

"Alright, but I don't want this Rondo to become involved. Just have him tell us when they come ashore."

"Don't you worry about Rondo. He a little man, but he fierce," Tubby said.

I looked at him. "Little?"

"That what I say, Mr. Len. But fierce. But I already tell him all this. See I'm a step ahead of you. I know what's what. But what happen when they on island? How you find them? And when you do then what? You have a plan?"

I pulled into the empty parking lot of the Sporting Place. I turned the Jeep off. "Do I look like I have a plan, Tubby?" I got out of the Jeep and Tubby followed me into the bar.

"No, you got no plan. I know this. It's always good to have a plan, Mr. Len. And it's good to have a backup plan too."

"Well, Tubby, you know what they said about best laid plans of mice and men."

"What they say?"

I shrugged. "I have no idea," I said.

He hissed again at me for making light of what he thought could be a dangerous situation, and he was probably right.

◆

The bar was empty with the exception of Mike, who was asleep on a chair, his legs spread out on another chair. He shuffled awake as soon as we entered. I took the string of hair out of my pocket and put it on the bar. Both Mike and Tubby looked at it. "They take that from some doll," Tubby said.

"Yeah, I know, it's not about what this is," I said, waving the string in front of them. "It's the message they sent with it."

Tubby took the string from me and gripped it. "Nothing ever happen to that girl on this island as long as I'm breathing. Understand that, Mr. Len." He looked straight at me. Tubby wasn't just talking the talk. I knew him well enough to know that he would always walk the walk too. I was lucky to have him as friend.

I nodded that I understood and checked my phone. There was no word from Kasie or Betta. I knew I would hear from my daughter if she was bored or needed me. No message was a good thing. I needed to use this time away from her to get things done. To do some research on that website Frost and Gould worked for. I also had to go see Big Tree and talk to him. That's how all this started. A simple pelau given to me as a token of good will from his mother. If only everything else was as simple.

"De fan break, Mr. Len," Mike said after rubbing at his face to wipe the sleep away.

"What fan?"

We had two large ceiling fans in the bar and windows that opened out to let in the breeze that, on aptly named Windy Hill road, seemed never to cease. As a result, we didn't need air conditioning. Mike pointed to the fan toward the back of the bar over the tables. I went to the wall switch and flipped it on. The fan did not move.

"He tell you the fan not work, Mr. Len. You think Mike make that up?" Tubby interjected.

"No, Tubby, but a man needs to see for himself," I said. "Can you call your friend who installed them for us?" I asked.

"Miles Carruth?"

"Yeah, him," I said dubiously. It was just another name lost in the empty canyon between my ears.

"He the one who put them fans in for us," Tubby said. "Now I think he retire and move to Florida to live with his daughter and his grandchildren there. One of his sons still here, I know, and do that kind of work. I check it out for us."

I glanced at the time on my phone. It was getting near lunch. I wanted to get down to Fort Philippe and the police station before things went quiet for two hours when most businesses on the island shut down during the heat of midday. I first had to stop at Mrs. John's house and pick up those papers I hoped she had signed. I was anxious to talk to Big Tree. I wanted to hear it from his lips that he was innocent, that he had nothing to do with the death of Deanna Gould. I also hoped he might shed some light on what she was doing on the island that got her killed.

I left Tubby and Mike in the bar and got back into my Jeep. I drove down to Mrs. John's house and parked by the curb. She answered the door before I had a chance to knock.

"Are you going to see Rawle now?" Mrs. Johns asked me before I even entered.

"I am," I said. "Have you signed those papers?"

She opened the door wider and I went in from the bright sun into the shaded living room. I followed her to the kitchen table where I saw the papers. She handed them to me.

"Have you been down to see Rawle?" I asked.

"Yes, but I don't like to see my son like that. I want him to come home. He look so sad. De man do nothing to nobody and he in shackles. Why the Lord unfair to my son? He suffer so when his wife sick and then pass. He a good boy always. I pray all day. I go to church and pray and pray, and my son still in that place where he should not be."

I listened to her. She took her glasses off and wiped at her eyes.

"What has his lawyer said?" I asked.

She shook her head and sucked through her teeth. "That man say nothing. I do not know what he do. He tell me wait. He tell

Rawle he will get him out. But my son still there."

"Okay, Mrs. Johns. I'm gonna go down there now. I'll come back later today and let you know what I've found out after I talk to him."

"Thank you, sir," she said. "When you come I have a stew chicken for you and your daughter. I hope you like stew chicken. I add dumplings instead of pumpkin. You like dumplings?"

"I do, Mrs. Johns, but you don't have to do that," I protested weakly. If her pelau was any indication, she was a magician in the kitchen. I wanted that stew, but I didn't want to appear overly greedy or gluttonous even though I was most definitely a little of both.

"I make sure not to put pepper in. Some people not from here don't like too much pepper."

"Don't worry about the pepper or anything."

"I have it ready for when you come."

I realized this was all she could offer me for my services. It would be rude of me to refuse the food. I would protest no more and just accept her offering.

I smiled. "I look forward to it, Mrs. Johns," I said and then hustled out of there.

17

I showed Emmalin Sealy the papers signed by Mrs. Johns as I entered the police station. She flipped through them to confirm that everything was in order.

"Okay?"

"Yes, it's all complete," she said. "But the magistrate has not stamped it. Remember I told you it had to be approved and stamped by a magistrate. And you need an appointment. You cannot just walk in any time." Emmalin pushed her gray-rimmed glasses up her nose.

"An appointment? Is Johns a busy man these days?"

"There is a protocol for this type of thing. His counsel must be present. And we have to arrange for someone to bring him to the visitation room. You cannot just show up."

I looked at the time on my phone. It was 11:35. "Can I make an appointment for noon today?"

She stared at me. "Mr. Buonfiglio, that is less than a half hour."

"Yeah?"

"Are you trying to be funny with me?"

"Do I look like I'm being funny, Ms. Sealy?" I said with all seriousness.

She sighed and picked up the phone. I could hear her whispering in her soft Caribbean lilt to someone. I assumed it was McWilliams. She nodded at me and I took the papers and dashed back out of the station.

The island government offices and courthouse were a five-minute drive from the police station. I zoomed up a steep hill and squeezed the Jeep into a spot. I hurried in and was directed to a side administrative office. There was a young woman at the reception desk. She stared at me. I was sweating from rushing in the heat. I blurted out what I needed — that I had to have the visitation papers signed immediately. She smiled sweetly. I expected an excuse why that could not happen. St. Pierre was notorious for its governmental bureaucracy and endless red tape, but there were ways around it. I just didn't know those ways. So I was poised and ready to unleash a heavy dose of Bronx on the poor young woman and anyone else that might come to her rescue. It wasn't going to be pretty.

But St. Pierre is also an island full of surprises, and the woman, despite seeing that my fuse had been lit, took the papers from me and with that sweet smile still intact, said: "We can do that."

I was left standing, feeling foolish, not that I cared so long as I had those papers stamped.

A few moments later she returned. "Everything is in order," she said as she handed me the papers. I glanced at the stamp and then thanked her, trying not to show my embarrassment.

I got back to the police station just before noon and shoved the papers at Emmalin Sealy. "Done," I said.

She flipped through them and picked up the phone again.

Just as I sat down on the wooden bench opposite Emmalin's desk, a man rushed in wearing a brown jacket, pale yellow dress shirt and navy blue slacks. He carried a tattered leather satchel under his arms. His too-thin tie flapped around his neck.

"Mr. Buonfiglio," he panted, clearly out of breath. He was slight with close cropped hair that was sprinkled with gray. He stuck his hand out while gripping the satchel under his armpit. "Maurice Dennard. I am representing Rawle Johns."

I got up and shook his hand.

"Thanks for coming," I said. "I didn't know you had to be present for me to talk to Mr. Johns."

"Yes, yes, it all has to be official here on St. Pierre, sir," he said. He leaned over Emmalin Sealy's desk. "Can we go back and see Mr. Johns now?"

"Someone will be out to escort you to the visitor's room," she said to us.

The lawyer sat on the bench. There were streams of perspiration running down the sides of his head.

A guard in a gray uniform came from the rear of the building and headed our way. He nodded at us. "Follow me, sirs," he said and then turned to head back from where he came.

The guard led us to a room with a big stainless-steel table and a few metal folding chairs. He gestured to the chairs. "I will go get the prisoner," he said. I didn't like the sound of that. It was still hard for me to conceive of Big Tree as a prisoner.

I folded my long frame into one of the small folding chairs. I could only wonder how Big Tree could fit on one of those tiny chairs.

"How does it look for him?" I asked the lawyer, who was

opening his satchel.

"I think it looks good, sir. They are holding him because of a DNA match. That is all. They find his DNA on the girl that does not mean he kill her. I hope to have the man home with his family within days."

"Yeah, but McWilliams told me his DNA was all over her body That's not good, is it?"

"No, but that still is not enough to conclude that he kill the girl."

"What about rape? Were they able to find evidence of any kind of sexual assault?"

"Not that I know of," The lawyer said and then added: "Mr. Buonfiglio, that poor girl fell over two hundred feet from that cliff. How could they determine anything from the shape the body was in after a fall like that?"

I shrugged. "They can do a lot with forensics these days…at least that's what I've read."

"They tell me that it is inconclusive. All they have is the DNA match. I'm hoping to have a long chat with the director of public prosecutions, Mr. Braithwaite, and see if we can clear all this up shortly."

"So he hasn't been charged?"

The lawyer, whose name I, of course, had already forgotten after our quick introduction, shook his head. "Not officially."

"Then why is he here? That doesn't seem right to keep a man behind bars who hasn't been charged with anything."

"I think they do it for the woman. The mother."

Marcia Gould, I thought. She didn't seem the vindictive type. She didn't seem malicious. But then again, if it were my daughter, I know I'd stop at nothing to get to the truth. Thinking about that sent a chill up my spine.

"How does she have that much sway here? Or is it common here to hold people who are just suspects and not charged with a crime?"

"I'm afraid it might be a little of both, Mr. Buonfiglio. I know this may not seem proper to you, but that is how we do it on our little island."

The door opened, and the guard who escorted us to the room now guided Rawle Johns inside. He was wearing a blue jump suit that barely contained his massive frame. Both his hands and legs were shackled with cuffs. He shuffled to the table. I looked at his face. This was not the Rawle Johns I was familiar with. Gone was the almost always cheerful expression. His eyes were set back now and distant. There were furrows on his brow and his mouth was turned down. He wouldn't meet my eyes as if he were ashamed to look at me.

"Cuffs? Really?" I glowered at the guard.

Rawle Johns' lawyer put his hand on my forearm in a calming gesture. The guard ignored me and pulled the chair out for Big Tree to sit. He lowered himself into the seat. I could hear the cheap folding chair creak under his weight.

"Mr. Len, I'm sure you did not expect to see me here like this," Rawle said in that melodically high voice. "And thank you for coming, Mr. Dennard."

Dennard. I swore to myself I wouldn't forget the lawyer's name again.

"No, I sure didn't, Rawle," I said once the guard had exited the room.

"My Ma sent you. I told her not to bother you with this business. I tell her this is not your worry. That you run the place up on Windy Hill Road. That have nothing to do with this trouble. But she think you can help me. She get it in her head that you will know how to get me out of this place. I do not know where she get these ideas. I appreciate that you are patient with her, Mr. Len."

"She keeps cooking for me," I said with a smile. "A pelau and a spice cake. Now she wants to make a stew chicken."

"With dumplings?" he asked.

I nodded.

"My Ma make a tasty dumpling," Rawle said. "But I tell her not to put the pig tail in the pelau. She stubborn and do it anyway. For the flavor, she say."

"I don't mind pig tail," I said. "Your Ma's a real good cook, Rawle."

"How you think I get like this, Mr. Len? I become Big Tree with her help, that's for sure."

"Yeah, but if I keep eating her food, I'm not sure it's Big Tree I'll become. More like Fat Len."

He laughed. "I know that won't be a problem for you, Mr. Len."

The frivolity suddenly stopped and there were a few moments of awkward silence. Dennard was tapping his fingers on the steel table.

"I would like to help, Rawle. But I need you to tell me everything you can about why they put you here. It has to be the truth."

"I tell you the truth, sir." He said in an almost muffled voice.

"Okay. Now tell me everything about those two days you were with her and the other writers. Based on your experience shuttling travel writers around, was she like what you were used to?"

He thought for a moment. "Mr. Len, that girl was different. She was not like the other writers."

In my brief conversation with her I sensed she was different too, but I wanted to hear it from his lips. "How so?" I asked him.

He shifted in his seat and it creaked some more. His face contorted a bit as if in deep thought. And then he looked at me. "I take them all on the island tour," he said. "I take you on that tour once, didn't I, Mr. Len?"

"I still remember it fondly, Rawle," I said.

"And on that tour you know I always stop at the Freedom Drop. I like to tell the people about our history. How some resist slavery and oppression even if it mean they give up their life. They make the ultimate sacrifice for freedom. That make me proud to be a Petey."

A Petey, I knew, was a term sometimes used to refer to a person from St. Pierre. Even though I'd been living on the island for several years, I hadn't yet considered myself a Petey. I was still a New Yorker, for better or worse.

"So you stopped there like you always do to show them Freedom Drop?" I asked.

He looked down and lay his hands flat on the table. They were enormous hands.

"We walk up to the little chain barrier, and after I point out the stone with the engraving, the others start taking pictures. But that girl did not take a picture. I stand back so they have room and she move back with me. While they all were looking out at the steep drop, that girl used both of her hands and grabbed my hand. I was surprised and tried to pull my hand away, but she wouldn't let me. Her hand was warm. I never forget. Almost hot. I think maybe okay, she frightened of the drop. Maybe she afraid of heights. Maybe she do not like being so close to the ledge. I tried again to pull my hand away, but she would not let me. I was getting nervous. Why was she doing this? What if the others saw? I worried about my job. I looked at her, and she was smiling at me. Why she smile like that? What she want from me? Why was..."

He stopped in mid-sentence as if he was about to say something he thought better of. Dennard and I gave him a moment to finish what he was saying.

"What, Rawle?" I asked.

He looked away for a moment and shook his head.

"What? What happened next?"

"As soon as the others turn back after taking their pictures, she release my hand and go back to the van to sit next to me up front before anyone else can take that seat."

I didn't know what to make of what he told me. I remembered my encounter with Deanna Gould. She made me uneasy as well, in a seductive way. Was it just her personality, or were there other motives?

"Did he tell you any of this?" I asked Dennard.

The lawyer nodded.

"And McWilliams."

"Yes, sir," Dennard said

Though the room was cool, at least to me, Big Tree was sweating through the prison garb he had on. "What happened after that?" I asked.

"After that we drive around the island and then to your place so they see the view of the harbor."

"Right, but did she say anything to you in the van?"

"She ask me some questions. She want to know if I like my

job. What I think about St. Pierre. If I happy here or would like to see changes. When I first work for the tourist board, they say don't have an opinion. Just be a good ambassador for the island. I do that always. I love St. Pierre so that's easy. But the girl want to know what I think about things."

"What things"

"Like if I want more business. If the island should add bigger hotels and expand the airport. Maybe build better roads with traffic lights. If I heard that St. Pierre might get a new very big hotel."

I thought for a moment. She had asked me similar questions in our fifteen-minute encounter. She was obviously digging for something.

"Do you know why she asked that?"

"No, but the way she ask. The way she look at me. I don't know, Mr. Len. It was just different."

He had the same impression I did of her when she pulled me aside to grill me that day.

"What did you say to all those questions?"

"I tell her I love my island just as it is. I don't need more business. I tell her we do not have room for more hotels or tourists. We are a small island."

"So it was just you two talking?"

"In the van, yes. The others were chatting amongst themselves in the back rows."

"Did she ask anything else?"

He nodded again. "She ask me if I married."

I looked at him. I could tell this was hard for him.

"I tell her that I lost my wife and that I have a boy. That we both live with my Ma."

"That's it?"

He nodded. "She was quiet after that and then we pull up to your place so they can see the view of the harbor."

I knew what happened at my place. I remember Rawle sitting alone at the bar drinking a lime squash while the others had beer or rum punch out on the back deck. I remember how the girl moved away from the group to pull me aside; to talk to me in that intense way she had.

"And after that?"

"I take them back to the Lime House. I go home and see my boy and Ma and have some supper, and then I go back to take them to dinner at the Bougainvillea."

"Anything I should know about what happened that night when you drove them? Did she sit up front with you again?"

He nodded and looked down.

"And?"

"She ask if I was joining them for dinner. I tell her no, I had my dinner."

"Anything else?"

He hesitated.

"What, Rawle?"

"I sit in the van while they dine and listen to music. I fall asleep a bit until I hear someone open the passenger door and it she."

"You mean she left the dinner to come out to the van to see you?"

"Yes, she say she want to see how I doing all alone out here. She say she tell the others she going to the ladies' room. I tell her I'm fine and that she not need to come out to check on me. I'm used to it. This my job."

"What were you thinking, Rawle," I asked. I knew what I would be thinking.

He shook his head. "I did not understand her," he said. "Why was she doing this? No writer I drive around before do anything like this. It make me uncomfortable."

"Uncomfortable, how?" I pressed.

He looked at me like I was dense. "Mr. Len, when a woman take your hand like she did mine when we at Freedom Drop, when she come and sit up front next to you and ask you all those questions, when she pretty like she was and look at me like she did? I was nervous. What I was thinking was not good. It worry me. And now here I am."

Here he was. But he hadn't finished telling me what happened.

I got up from the chair and walked around the room to stretch my legs. Big Tree's eyes followed my movements. I put my hands on the back of my folding chair and bent down to stretch my lower back.

"Mr. Len, are you okay?"

I laughed. "Yeah, but I'm not one to sit for too long without having to stretch out my back."

"You should talk to my Ma about that. With the driving I do, my back get stiff. Ma make a paste of some spices and such, cinnamon, turmeric and cayenne that she heat and put on my back. It work like magic. Calm the nerves there. I tell her to give you some."

I smiled not so much that there was a remedy for whatever ailed you here on St. Pierre, but that this man who was in serious trouble could so easily segue from retelling his experience with Deanna Gould to talking about herbal remedies. I eased myself back into that harsh metal folding chair.

"Anything happen in the van when she came to see you during that dinner?"

"Nothing. She was just there for a few minutes and then she went back to the dinner."

"And after that?"

"They come out and I drive them back to the Lime House."

"What did you do that next day? Did you see her? Did you have to drive them anyplace?"

"Yes I saw her. I drive them that day. I remember I take them to Coconut Palm and then the Caribbean Manor House."

Besides the Bougainvillea and the Lime House, the Coconut Palm and Caribbean Manor were the most exclusive small hotels on the island. When travel writers visited, they were always shown those properties. "Let me ask you, Rawle, did Ms. Gould seem interested in her work?"

"What do you mean, Mr. Len?"

"I don't know, compared to the other writers. Did you think she was interested in reporting on the hotels for the publication she was representing?"

"I don't understand. She went with them to look at the hotels and take the tour of the property. Other than that, I do not know."

I nodded. I knew I was fishing with those questions, but I had to try. I wanted to see if he knew she was not truly a travel writer.

"Where did you take them after they saw the properties?"

"They have lunch and then go on a snorkeling trip to Silver Beach."

Silver Beach was a strip of white sand about a quarter mile off the southwest coast of the island. From a distance, the strip looked like a silver jewel against the blue of the ocean.

Completely flat with just a couple of palm trees, it reminded you of those old images of deserted islands where you might end up after being shipwrecked. The beach had often been used in movies, ads, modeling shoots and other photo opportunities because of its unique look. The snorkeling was good but nothing like what you would see in and around the reef off Coral Beach, where Kasie and I had gone earlier in the week.

"You didn't go with them on the trip, did you?"

"No, I drop them off and then go back and pick up Ezran from school," he said "I take him home and even have time for a little nap before I have to go retrieve them after they snorkel."

"And then?"

"I drop them back at the Lime House for the night. I know they have the cocktail party at the hotel and the dance show, but they don't need me to drive them anywhere. I know I drive them to the airport the next morning because that was on my schedule."

"So, when you dropped them off at the hotel, was that the last time you saw Ms. Gould?"

He put his head down and shook his head.

"What happened that night, Rawle?" I asked.

He picked his head up again. "She call me later that night. I do not know how she get my mobile number, but she did. I was surprised. I was nervous."

"What did she want?"

"To see me," he said. "She say she enjoy our chats and would like to talk some more with me and can I pick her up at the hotel. I tell her I'm at home with my son and Ma who are asleep. She say she really want to see me. Can I please come pick her up."

"How did she sound on the phone? Had she been drinking?"

"I could not tell. The truth, she sound like she did always. No different. She have that teasing voice."

"What did you do?"

He looked at me. "It shames me, Mr. Len, to tell you this," he said. "But that girl excite me. The way she talk to me. The way she took my hand in hers. The way she look at me. I cannot deny that. Mr. Len, I lose my wife four years ago. It been very difficult. I miss her very much. I try hard, I do, but the girl put thoughts in my head. I wasn't sure what she really wanted from me, but I hoped it was what I wanted."

"I see." I was not there to judge what he did. I just wanted to know the facts of what happened so I could somehow help him.

"I try once more to tell her it best I not come there, but she not stop. 'Please, please,' she say. She wants to see 'Big Tree.'"

"She said that?"

"Yes," Rawle said with a nod.

I noticed Dennard shake his head in disgust. I looked back at Rawle.

"I could not resist, Mr. Len. I knew what would happen. I knew I would suffer from my choice. But I was weak. The Lord test me and I fail that test." He rubbed his palms over his face. "I always fail He."

Dennard patted the big man's back.

I waited a moment for him to compose himself. "You met her where?"

"I pick her up at the hotel and she get in the van with me. She give me that teasing look of her and then she kiss me on my cheek and say let's drive somewhere. I ask where she want to go. Somewhere quiet, she say. The whole island quiet, I tell her. She say she want to go back to where the slaves leap to freedom.

Freedom Drop. She say her mother's ancestors were slaves and yes, that where she want to go. To see it again. I try again to tell her the drive a long one and at night even longer. She hug my arm and tell me to just drive. I do what she ask, and while I drive she talk."

"What did she say?"

"She say how much she like St. Pierre. She say so many places ruined by mankind. That it would be very bad if that happened to St. Pierre too."

"What did she mean, Rawle?"

"I don't know. It's just what she say to me while I drive. It what I remember."

"What else?"

"When I get to Freedom Drop and park the van, she stopped talking. And then I remember she look around out the window in the dark and she look at her phone a few times. I see her reading something from it. She seem distracted now, and I was confused. I did not know what she wanted. I ask her if she want to get out of the van. She stop looking at her phone and say no she does not. So we sit there in the van. I say nothing. Finally I say maybe we should go back to the hotel. She laugh and say why would I want to do that? I look at her when she say that. At her pretty smile, and her legs in that short dress. I know I stare at her. And she knows I staring and she keep smiling like she does not mind that."

Rawle leaned back a bit in the tight chair. His eyes looked upward.

"Tell me what happened, Rawle," I said, pushing it now.

"My Ma does not know any of what I tell you, Mr. Len."

"She doesn't have to know," I said. "But I do."

"Yes, sir," he muttered. "I know you do."

He sighed and rubbed his face again.

"Tell me, Rawle."

He nodded and took a breath. "I just sit there and then she move up from her seat and, with that smile still there on her face, climb around to sit on my lap on the driver's seat with her back to the steering wheel.

I looked closely at him as he talked. "She really did that?"

He hesitated a moment. "Yes, sir," he mumbled with his head down, avoiding my eyes.

"What did she do next?"

He exhaled loudly. "She put her legs around my hips. She say, 'Hold me, Big Tree.' I try to stop myself. I remember I grip my hands tight to my sides. And then she start moving on my lap."

As he said that, I noticed that he closed his eyes for a moment. When he opened them he continued.

"When I smell her perfume, when I feel her warm body on me, Mr. Len, I could no longer resist. I held her like she ask and then she kiss me."

"She kissed you?"

He hesitated. "Yes, Mr. Len, and I had not been kissed like that since before my wife get sick. She then take my hands and put them on... her..." His head slumped down. "She take my hands to places she want to be touched. Places I should not have touched. I tried to pull my hands away, but she grabbed them and put them back there. I see her close her eyes while she press my hands to her. While I touched her. And then I hear a buzz. She hear it too and she open her eyes."

"What kind of buzz?"

"Like the kind a mobile phone make when it vibrate," he said.

"Did she have her phone with her?"

"Yes, I tell you that already. She check her phone before. She have a phone and a small purse."

"What happened next?"

"She look at her phone and read a message she get. And then like she no longer care what we doing, she quickly get off my lap. She open the door and look back at me and say for me not to go anywhere. That she be right back. Then she take that purse and go out the door."

"What did you do then?"

"I was vexed. What did she want from me? Why a woman do what she do and then just get up and leave like that? Why she tease me like that? I ask where she go. I say it too dark out there, to wait for me. I call for her, but she do not answer. So I get out of the van. I hear the waves below but nothing else. There was no moon that night, I remember. The lights from the van the only light anywhere."

"You didn't hear anyone else? You didn't see anyone?"

Rawle looked at me. He was about to say something and then stopped himself.

"What, Rawle?"

He shook his head. "No, Mr. Len, no one I could see or hear." His eyes were looking past me now.

"What did you do next?" I asked.

He took a breath through his nose. "I was frightened. What if the girl lost? I did not know what to do. I call for her again, but nothing. No sound. I look in the brush and walk around the cliff. I think maybe she fall and I panicked. I think of my son. I think of my Ma and I think of my wife in heaven. What was I doing there? I let Satan come to me. I let he infect me."

I waited a moment for him to compose himself.

"And then?"

He wiped at his eyes now. "I waited and waited. I walk around in the dark. But there was nothing. It was like she just poof away. I did not know what to do. She was gone. I couldn't sit out there in the van all night. Finally, I go home, but I could not sleep. I pray all night that she be there with the others when I pick them up to take them to the airport. I pray that I just dreamed what happen. When the sun come up and Ezran leave for school, I go back to the hotel. I park the van in the lot waiting. The manager, Mr. Wright, come out to tell me there is a problem. He tell me one of the group is missing. When he tell me that, I want to be sick. I want to run away and hide."

"You said nothing?" I asked.

Johns put his head down at that and shook it. "Nothing, Mr. Len. I was too scared."

The big man was sweating profusely now. He was also sobbing quietly. Dennard put a hand on Big Tree's back and patted him there gently.

"Has he told all this to McWilliams?" I asked Dennard.

"All of it, Mr. Buonfiglio. His official statement is exactly what he just told you. His only crime is that he did not report what happened to the authorities. The girl instigate Mr. Johns' advances. He touch her with her consent."

Big Tree lifted up his head. He looked at his lawyer and then at me. He could read the expression on my face. "I tell my Ma not to waste your time, Mr. Len. You cannot do anything for me. I appreciate that you come here to hear my story."

"You haven't left anything out? You didn't see her at the cliff? You didn't see anyone else? You've told me everything."

He wiped at his eyes with a tissue and then he nodded. "Yes, Mr. Len, everything. I see no one," he said, but when he said it, his eyes were not on mine. They were down at the table staring at his enormous hands.

"Do you know if they found the girl's purse and the phone?" I asked Dennard.

"They find the purse in the water, but there was no phone," the lawyer said. "They search the area and even bring in the scuba police to search the waters. They find nothing else."

The phone would have a record of who had texted Gould right before she ran off. She was there to meet someone, that much seemed obvious. And whoever it was she was to meet would know how she died. Or was the murderer.

We sat there not talking for what seemed like a long time. I remembered what Frost said to me, that he had no doubt Big Tree did not kill his girlfriend. He had some sort of conspiracy in mind. He was hinting at bigger forces being involved. I believed him that Deanna Gould was not a travel writer based on my brief encounter with her, and what Rawle had just told me confirmed it. With all that was going on, I hadn't had time to check out ThirdRail, the website they both supposedly worked for. All I knew for certain was that Deanna Gould was dead. I knew that her friend, Craig Frost, was dead. I also knew that one of my dogs was dead. There were some bad people after me, but I had no idea why. And now I knew Rawle Johns' story of what happened that night. But his story wasn't clearing anything up. I was nowhere on this.

"You know I do not do anything like this? I not hurt anyone," Rawle said to me, his eyes pleading now.

I could not conceive of Big Tree hurting anyone, but there

was something about his story that was unsettling. Something, I felt, was off about it. I just didn't know what.

"As long as what you say is the truth, Rawle," I said.

He looked at me and was about to say something more, but the guard who had been standing outside the room came in. "Time now is up," he said. He went to Big Tree and put his hands on him to ease him up from the small rickety metal chair. Rawle stood and forced a smile in my direction.

"Thank you for coming to see me, Mr. Len. Thank you for doing this for my Ma. But please, Mr. Len, I do not want my Ma or my son to know any of this. I do not want them to know what a weak man I am."

He used his forearm to wipe the remaining tears from his eyes as the guard took him away.

I did want to help Big Tree. I wanted to get him home to his mother and his son. But I didn't know how.

18

I had turned my phone off during the session with Big Tree. When I got back outside of the police station, I turned it back on and it buzzed with numerous texts and voice messages. I got into the shade in my Jeep and checked out my phone. There were multiple *Call me* texts from Tubby. I punched in his number.

"They left the boat," he said as soon he picked up my call.

"When?"

"'Bout a half-hour ago. They go into the harbor and into the Green building on Front Street."

The Green building, I knew, meant the tall (for St. Pierre) modern green-glass structure built close to the string of refurbished nineteenth century stone buildings housing many of the island's government offices. I knew that its presence caused serious controversy amongst St. Pierre's conservationists, the island's historical society and others. To many it was a blight on an otherwise historic landmarked stretch. How the building was approved I had no idea, but it got done and now it sat there, a modern anomaly on the island.

"How do you know this?" I asked Tubby as I sat in the Jeep.

"I have my friend, Rondo, follow them."

"Rondo who is little and fierce?"

"Yes he is," Tubby acknowledged.

"He might be fierce, Tubby, but the fewer involved in this, the better," I said. "Did you tell your friend why he was following them?"

"Of course I not tell him that, but he do ask me why."

"Yeah, Tubby, who wouldn't? According to your friend, are they still there?"

"They still there," Tubby said. "Rondo tell me if they leave, Mr. Len."

"Why would your friend do this for you?"

There was a silence on the line for a moment. "Because I ask him to. Why else?"

I should have known. "Okay, but tell him to be careful. They can't know they are being followed."

"I know all that. No one know they followed, that for sure."

I hung up and drove over to Front Street. I slowed as I passed the Green building. I glanced around to see if I could locate this Rondo, but I had never met Tubby's friend and I didn't see anyone watching the building. I had never been inside. I knew there were some businesses that had offices there, including the island's local tourism agency, which was a private firm hired by the official St. Pierre Tourism Authority to do most of the international outreach. Other than that, I didn't know who rented space there.

I drove away and headed toward Betta's house. I wanted to

check on Kasie to make sure everything was okay there. I knew I had to get back to the house and see about flights. I still had that string of blonde hair in my pocket. Thinking about it made it seem like it was burning into my thigh. She needed to get off the island. Though she had a return ticket in three days, I wanted to see if I could get her home tomorrow. Having her leave this long-planned vacation earlier than scheduled would not make her happy. I would just have to do my best to make it right with her in time.

The front door of Betta's house was wide open when I drove up. I immediately felt my gut tense at seeing it. I hopped out of the Jeep and moved quickly inside.

This guy Rondo was supposed to have his eyes on those two men. They hadn't left the Green building. That's what Tubby had said. I called for Betta. And then I called for Kasie. There was no answer. The front room was empty. I looked around, calling for them again, peering into the two bedrooms. I thought I heard a voice from outside. I moved through the house and pushed open the back door. My heart steadied when I saw the three of them, Kasie, Betta and Paolo, deep in the backyard of the house around the plastic inflatable swimming pool I had bought for Paolo when he turned one.

Paolo was splashing in the pool. Kasie was smiling and splashing back at him, wearing her Manhasset Track team T-shirt over her swimsuit. Betta was leaning back on the bench of the wooden picnic table near the outdoor pizza oven Maurizio had built to bake his bread and pizza before he split. She had on a bikini top and very short denim shorts that were almost identical to the ones Kasie had worn earlier in the week. I quickly and awkwardly looked away from her and focused on my daughter as I headed toward them.

"Leonard," Betta said standing up from where she was sitting.

"Your front door was wide open," I said.

"It was?"

"Yeah."

Betta was looking at me. She could see my concern. "It's okay, Leonard. Paolo must have forgotten to shut it when he and your daughter were playing in the front."

My hands were shaking. Betta saw it. I closed them into a fist to steady them. I didn't want my daughter to see what Betta saw.

"Oh, hi, Dad," Kasie said to me from the pool. While she was turned to me, Paolo began splashing her again. "That's no fair, you." She began to splash him and lift him up and out of the pool. He was wearing a white swimsuit patterned with blue sea turtles.

I felt myself start to calm down. I moved closer to the pool, but not close enough to get splashed. "You having fun?" I asked Kasie.

"Yeah, I am," she said.

I noticed that there were plastic sea turtles in the pool whose fins moved back and forth in the water. "Someone likes turtles," I said to Paolo.

"This kid is something," Kasie said as she dunked him into the water.

"Again," he pleaded with a giggle.

"Oh yeah? You want it again?"

"Yesss," he laughed.

I smiled watching my daughter play with the boy. I had made the right call bringing her here.

"Thanks, again, Betta," I said to her.

"Your daughter is very nice. You should be proud."

"I am proud," I said. "Do you mind if she stays the night. I'm hoping to get her on a plane tomorrow."

"She can stay as long as she wants and as long as you need her to. You should know that, Leonard."

"Yeah," I said.

"Is everything all right? Did it go well today?"

"I don't know, Betta. I just want my daughter safe."

"She will be. She can help me make pizza tonight."

I smiled. I knew Betta learned how to make Italian bread and authentic pizza from Paolo's father. They had started a business together on the island. That had been Maurizio's plan. And it was a good business. I was a frequent customer. The bread Maurizio made was just about as good as what I could get at Addeo on Arthur Avenue or Parisi's on Elizabeth Street. The pizza wasn't bad either. Better than anything else you could get on the island. Kasie was in for a treat.

"She's a lucky girl," I said.

She looked at me. "She is to have a father like you."

When Betta said things like that to me it was like the muscles remaining in my aging body just turned to Jell-O. I was totally powerless. I could only deflect.

"Yeah, right," I cracked. "A father who gets caught up in some bad business when he should be spending time with his daughter? I'm not much to brag about."

"Silly man," Betta said with a smile. "Can you stay with us for dinner?"

"No, I have to get back home. I need to see about getting Kasie's flight changed and I have to work out a few things."

"Be careful, please, Leonard," Betta whispered. I knew those dark eyes were on me, but I kept mine averted from hers as best I could. I wanted nothing more than to unabashedly stare at Betta, to take in her beauty. But I couldn't. I had to always look away. So all I could do was nod.

There was still no change in the movements of those two men, according to Tubby and their tail, Rondo, when I arrived back at my house. They had not left the Green building. What was their business in there? Who were they meeting with? They were working for someone on the island. There was a reason they came to my house, and I know it wasn't just to kill my dog.

The first thing I did after putting together a sandwich was to turn on my laptop. I checked the airlines and was able to secure a seat for Kasie for the next day's flight back to JFK out of Barbados. The airline made me pay in a big way for the change, but it was worth it. I was already relieved that she would be out of here and safe soon enough.

Once that was taken care of, I tried to find all the news I could on Deanna Gould's death. I was hoping there would be more information from the press in the States than what was revealed here on St. Pierre. The *Boston Globe* had a small piece a few days after it happened. I scanned it carefully and learned that Gould was twenty-five at the time of her death and a graduate of Northeastern in Boston. The paper said that she was a freelance writer specializing in travel and entertainment. It did not mention any affiliation with any particular website or publication. Her father, Max Gould, was the CEO of Pilgrim Savings out of Boston. He died from a heart condition eight years earlier. Her mother, Marcia Gould, was a former professional tennis player and now served as a board member of Pilgrim Savings and was known for her philanthropic causes both in Boston and internationally.

The article listed Deanna Gould's death as a suicide but noted that the case had not been closed and that further tests had been conducted to determine the exact cause of death. Marcia Gould, according to the story, had said that she expected a more thorough investigation and was enlisting the help of forensic experts in Boston.

I wondered if there was a follow-up article by the *Globe*, since those tests apparently did reveal the possibility of foul play. I couldn't find one. I went back to the original story and wrote down the name of the writer, Laura Song. I found the main phone line for the *Globe* and called it. When an operator picked up, I asked for Song. I was put through and got her voice mail. I left a message with my name and number and that I was calling from St. Pierre regarding the article she wrote about Deanna Gould's death. I asked her to call me back.

Next, I went to Google and typed in ThirdRail to see what that got me. The website came up and I clicked on it. When it opened, there was a headline that screamed of a Republican congressman from Ohio who allegedly ran a real-estate scam under a shadow company that funneled kickback money from government-assisted housing projects into his coffers. Scrolling down the site, there were other, similar stories about the wrongdoings of politicians on both sides of the aisle, celebrities, media moguls and millionaires ranging from political corruption and sexual misconduct to drug use and violent acts. The so-called news ThirdRail presented was conspiracy-tabloid stuff. It was flashy, gotcha millennial journalism that I knew had become popular on the internet in the States and all over the world lately. Since living on St. Pierre, I tried to block out all that garbage as best I could. In fact, I tried to screen myself from all political and sensational news. It wasn't hard living on St. Pierre. Only when one of the televisions happened to be tuned to CNN or BBC at the bar was I exposed to the world's goings-on. And even then I rarely paid attention. Why ruin a beautiful day in paradise?

The home page boasted that ThirdRail had over six million followers. I didn't know if six million was a good number of followers or not, I only knew I was not one of them. I searched the site carefully, first going back to the previous day to see if there was any mention of the death of Craig Frost, supposedly one of the writers for the site. There was nothing. Going back further, I looked for something on Deanna Gould's death. Again, there was nothing. I found that odd, but that was just par for the course for this puzzling situation I had managed to become entwined in.

My phone buzzed. I looked at the incoming number, which had a 617 area code. I picked it up. "Mr. Buonfiglio? This is Laura Song returning your call," the female voice said.

"Hi, Ms. Song," I said, surprised she would call back so soon. "Thanks for getting back to me. I'm in St. Pierre..."

"I know where you are. I know who you are," she said.

I let that sink in for a moment. Maybe contacting a reporter was not a good idea.

"Alright," I finally muttered. "I was just checking if you knew anything else about a story you wrote late last year about the death of Deanna Gould — if you've heard anything regarding how she died."

"I do, yes, but I'm not going public with any of it until

everything is confirmed."

"No?"

"I can't, Mr. Buonfiglio," she said brusquely. "There are a few loose ends that need to be checked first."

"Listen, Ms. Song. I know about Rawle Johns and his arrest here. I've heard his statement to the police. I know Marcia Gould had a forensic report done on her daughter's body to help determine Johns' involvement in her death. Am I missing something else?"

There was a moment of silence on the phone.

"Ms. Song?"

"I'm here, and I'm just wondering why you are interested, Mr. Buonfiglio. You know your call had me puzzling about why such a celebrated man leaves his hometown to live on a small island. And even more baffling is why this man is calling me about the death of a young woman. What could his role possibly be in all this? What is he up to on that island? It might make a compelling story."

I had heard enough. It was a mistake to call this reporter. It was always a mistake to talk to the press. "Thank you for calling me back, Ms. Song." Before she could say another word, my finger was on the red "end call" button on the screen of my phone.

The sun was setting. I got up from the kitchen table and moved away from my laptop to walk outside to the other side of the road. I wanted to hear the ocean and get a glimpse of the Atlantic before it all went dark. I took my phone with me. Carrying my phone at all times was becoming a bad habit. I knew people these days could not part with their digital devices.

I didn't want to become one of those people, but I justified it in my mind because I had to make sure I didn't miss a message from Tubby. There was always an excuse. So instead of gazing at the rough waters out there, a dramatic view that often calmed me, I glanced too often at my phone. There had been nothing from Tubby. What were those men doing there all day? I stared blankly at the small device in my hand. I had muted the phone after Laura Song tried to call me back. She left voice mails, but I deleted them without even listening to them. I was about to delete what I thought was another voice mail from her when I noticed that the 617 number was different than the number for Laura Song. I clicked on that voice mail and held the phone to my ear.

"Hi, Len," the female voice said. "This is Marcia Gould. We met the other day at Heaven's Beach. I hope I'm not being too forward, but I was wondering if you and your daughter would like to join me for dinner at the Bougainvillea tomorrow night. If not tomorrow, we can try the next night. I'm here on the island until Monday of next week."

I heard her laugh nervously before continuing: "I don't usually invite almost strangers to dinner, but you two seemed perfectly delightful and I haven't had much company while I've been here. Anyway, I'm going on and on. If you are booked and have other plans, I understand. Please return my call at this number."

I was surprised by the call. And I had to admit it wasn't a bad surprise. The image of Marcia Gould on the beach immediately came to mind. Maybe I could use that dinner to find out a little more about her daughter and what she suspected about her death. I wondered how she got my phone number. I know

I never gave it to her. I tried to remember if either Clayton Teel or his partner, Tito, of the Bougainvillea had my number. Either way, did it matter?

I redialed the number, and after several rings she picked up. "Len, hello," she said, sounding as if she had to run to the phone. Call me old school, but it still was surprising to me that even complete strangers knew it was me calling just by programming my name into their phones.

"Did I call at a bad time?" I asked.

"Not at all. I just got out of the shower and now I'm getting myself made up for dinner," she said, as if I needed that bit of information. "I've been invited to dine at the prime minister's home. Woo-hoo," she added playfully.

"Fancy stuff," I said. "You must be quite the honored guest."

"I know, right? I have no idea why, but who am I to refuse an invitation like that? I hear the house is something special."

"Yeah, I've been there a couple of times, but never for a private dinner. It's an old plantation home. Very eighteenth century."

"Too bad I didn't bring anything eighteenth century to wear," she quipped. "Oh well, they'll have to accept me in my modern-day glory."

I thought for a moment about her modern-day glory. Was she purposely teasing me or was it just her way?

"I take it you got my message," she said.

"I did," I said. "Sadly, Kasie is leaving tomorrow."

There was a hesitation on her end. "Oh, that is too bad," she finally said.

"But I thank you for inviting us," I said.

There was another hesitation.

"Len, just because your daughter will not be here to

chaperone us, you won't have dinner with me alone? Is that what you are saying?"

That was what I was saying, but it was definitely not what I was wanting. I tried to think of how to answer that.

"No," was my brilliant response.

"No you won't have dinner with me without your daughter or no you were not saying that without your daughter you won't have dinner with me alone?"

"Now I'm confused," I said. "Let's start this over."

"Okay," she said in what sounded now like a throaty whisper. I swallowed.

"What time should I be there?" I asked.

I could hear her laugh softly. "You're cute," she said. "Seven-thirty for a cocktail at the bar first?"

There was a beeping on my phone meaning I was getting another call. I could see it was from Tubby, but I had no idea how to put someone on hold while taking the other call, so I ignored it. I would call him back after I got off the line.

"That sounds like a plan," I said. "I might even get there at seven twenty. I like to be early for cocktails."

"And I like the way you think," she said. "Now I must continue my pre-dinner ritual and plaster on my game face."

"Enjoy it," I said.

"Oh, and give my regards to Kasie. Wish her a safe trip home."

"I'll do that," I said as I hung up.

"Where you now?" Tubby asked as soon as I called him back.

"I'm at home."

"They on their way there," he said.

I looked around the empty house. "Are you sure?"

"I'm sure, Mr. Len. A car pull up to the Green building. A

woman get out and the two men get in and drive away."

"Where are you?" I asked Tubby.

"Driving over to you," he said.

"Don't do that. Don't come here, Tubby," I said. "Go over to Betta's. I want to make sure they don't take a detour."

"They don't take no detour," he said. "They coming to you."

"How do you know? Is your buddy Rondo following them?"

"He is," he muttered.

"Tell him to stop. Tell him thanks but we don't need him anymore. And you just get on over to Betta's. I need to know my daughter will be safe."

I'm not sure if he was listening or not.

"You hear me, Tubby?"

"What you gonna do, Mr. Len? Those men are bad men. Get out of there. There two of them against one. And who know if they have firearms or not. All you got is your hands and legs. That don't work against a gun. Please."

"Just go check on my daughter," I grunted and hung up on him.

He was right. My hands and legs would be no match for guns. So I had to get to them before they could use their guns — if they had them. Maybe they just wanted to talk to me. Or maybe they wouldn't use their guns. A man could dream, couldn't he?

I went around to the back of the house and opened up my storage bin where I kept shovels, rakes, and garden tools, as well as the most useful tool of all, a machete, known on St. Pierre as a cutlass. Every household on the island was equipped with at least one cutlass. Among their many uses were to clear brush, to swipe at sugar cane and to split open coconuts. Each morning, all across the island, men, workers and farmers headed to their small plots, cutlasses dangling from their waistbands as if holstered. We kept a couple of cutlasses in the bar to slice open fruit to add to drinks. Guns were rare on St. Pierre, and as a result so was gun violence. To obtain a permit for a gun required a substantial tax, an extended and rigorous background check and even a public hearing as to why you were applying for the permit. There was no substantial game to hunt. There were rodents that were caught, usually by hand, and sometimes served in stews, but nothing else that would warrant the use of a hunting rifle. Guns were often smuggled in illegally but if discovered by the authorities, dealt with severely. The zero-tolerance penalty for possession of an illegal firearm was a thirty-day jail sentence for a first offense, and that was just for possession of one gun. It got harsher from there. As an alternative to guns, the cutlass was often used in crimes of passion. And the results were usually not very pretty.

I grabbed the cutlass and gripped the handle. My palm was sweaty. I wiped it on my pants and squeezed it tight again. The cutlass wouldn't stop a bullet, but it was the best I could do.

The two dogs had been following me all evening, from my walk to stare at the sea and on to the storage bin in the back. It was as if they sensed what was coming. When I got back into the house, I flicked off the lights. I had a small high-voltage LED flashlight in my pocket. I thought about sitting in the living room in my chair facing the window, but that would leave my back to the front door. I chose to lean against the kitchen counter facing the door, where I could see if headlights were coming up the hill.

I knew, as Tubby said, these were bad men. And despite my sweaty palms, I really wasn't afraid of what might be coming.

The dogs took a breather and plopped down around my feet. I smiled as I saw them there. When they first gravitated to me and my home here, I was wary. Dogs, much less three of them, were not in my plans even though they were low maintenance. They took themselves out, so they didn't need walking. I felt responsible for them and made sure they had food and water in their bowls every day and even had them examined by the local vet. In return, I guess they became my St. Pierre family. But my family was now one less. I thought about that as I waited.

While I sat there in the dark, I called Kasie. I had to tell her that she was leaving the next morning. And I wanted to hear her voice. "It's just one more day, Dad," she pleaded. "What's one more day?"

"Honey, it's important. You saw what those men did. I can't risk your safety even for one more day. I will call your mother to explain it all to her."

"You will?"

I knew that wasn't going to be an easy phone call. I just hoped that after I confessed everything and maybe with Kasie's help after the fact, my ex-wife would give me another chance with my children. I wanted to see my son. I wanted to have him come down here when he was older and could travel on his own like Kasie did.

"I will," I confirmed.

"Mom's not gonna be happy to hear it," Kasie said.

"Don't I know it. I'm sorry, Kasie, really."

"I know, Dad. I've had fun anyway. Betta's real nice and you were right about the pizza. It was good. I just wish I could stay longer."

"Yeah, me too." I was choking up.

"You okay?"

"I'm good," I said.

"Um...okay. Love you, Dad."

"I love you too. I'll make sure I pack up all your stuff here and pick you up tomorrow morning."

She hung up just as I noticed headlights coming up the hill. They were here.

19

The dogs got up and moved around me anxiously. They could hear the motor of the car approaching. I hadn't thought of what I would do with them. They would bark. They could get hurt. I should have put them in my bedroom and closed them in there. I just didn't think of it and now it was too late.

I heard chatter from outside. It wasn't English. It wasn't Spanish or French either. It sounded like what I heard on some of the other French islands — Creole, but this Creole I was not familiar with. I peeked through the window enough to see the two men, one dark-skinned with braids, the other taller, with short hair and lighter skin. They were on my front lawn. The Spotted One growled. The Gray one was whining and pacing in circles near the front door.

I watched in the dark as the taller one went to the Suzuki that was parked alongside my Jeep on the curb in front of the house. He came back from the vehicle with something in his hand. The one with the braids kept his eye on my front door. He held out his hand and the other placed what he had retrieved from the Suzuki into it. I could see clearly enough that the man with the braids now had a gun.

"Buonfiglio," the man with braids bellowed in his sketchy English. I moved out and away from the window and kept quiet. The Spotted One started to bark.

"Buonfiglio," the same voice repeated. "*Louvri Moute*."

And then there was a banging on my door. "*Ouvri pot la*!"

The Gray One was scratching at the door and whining louder.

I kept away from the door. I wanted to get the dogs and drag them back into my bedroom out of the way, but I couldn't now. I gripped the cutlass tight.

I could hear them but didn't understand what they were saying. It was as if they were arguing, not sure what to do. I peeked again at the window. I saw the taller one shake his head at his partner and head back to the Suzuki. He got in, started the car and drove down the hill. The other man remained on my front lawn holding the gun. He started toward my front door. I stepped back out of the way again. The dogs were barking wildly now.

I could see the doorknob move as the man tested it to see if it might be open, though of course if it was locked. I moved to the other side of the door, pressing my body flat against the wall. And then there was an explosion. The wood around the doorknob shattered. There was another explosion. There was now a hole where the doorknob was. The dogs continued to bark, the shots flying above them. They scampered around the room. I saw a large dark hand reaching in to open the door. I held the cutlass at the ready. The door was swinging open. And then I heard the horn from my Jeep begin to honk. My front door remained partially open. The Jeep horn kept honking. Someone was in there. Tubby. I cursed to myself. I told him not to come and now he was trying to divert the man from the house.

I went to the open door. The man with the braids was turned away from me and heading toward the Jeep and Tubby. He was moving faster now, with his gun out. I ran out of the house toward him, looking for Tubby but not seeing him anywhere. The dogs sprinted past me. I could hear their fevered breathing as they ran.

"Tubby!" I yelled, the man right in front of me. He wheeled around to face me and raised the gun. I kept running at him. I needed Tubby to get the hell out of there. I was sure the man was about the pull the trigger and I didn't care. He seemed startled that I would keep coming at him. And then I heard growling and a tearing sound and knew the dogs were at him. They were ripping at his ankles. He yelled in pain as they sunk their teeth into his flesh. He aimed the gun away from me and toward the dogs. He was going to shoot my dogs. In one quick motion, I swiped the cutlass down and onto the hand holding the gun. He screamed and the gun — and a good portion of his upper hand — flopped to the ground.

He tried to hold his shattered hand with his other hand as the dogs continued to rip at his ankles. He fell back onto the ground. The dogs were about to go to his face, but I grabbed them both and pulled them away. They fought to get out of my grasp, but I held them tight by the scruff of their necks.

"Okay, it's okay," I whispered to them to calm them, and soon their tongues lapped at my face as I stroked their coats.

The man was crying in pain, writhing on my lawn, holding

the bleeding stump. I saw the gun a few feet from where he lay. I quickly picked it up and then tossed it toward the back of my house. And then I remembered Tubby. I turned toward my Jeep.

There was a man standing a few feet from me who was most definitely not Tubby. He was small, and from where I stood, he looked like a child. I moved closer to him. "Who are you?" I asked.

"I am Rondo," he said, a slight smile on his face.

"Rondo?"

He just nodded.

So this was Tubby's friend. The mighty fine batsman. I looked him over. Though he was small, he wasn't what you would consider a midget or a dwarf. He just didn't grow tall as most of us had. He was stocky and bald, with coal-black skin and an intricately braided beard. Despite wearing a tank top and shorts, there was sweat beading over his compact muscles.

I looked around. There were no cars parked nearby. "How did you get here?"

"I bike here," he said, pointing a few yards down the hill where a bike was flat on the ground.

"You were able to follow them on your bike? Up this hill?" I couldn't conceive that he could follow them on a bike.

"I a bike champion in my youth," he said proudly.

My mouth was open. The man saved me. He saved my dogs. Tubby was right. He was little but he was most definitely fierce.

"Where's Tubby?"

"He go see on your daughter," Rondo said.

I thought for a moment: Tubby actually did what I asked. And then I remembered the other man; the taller one with the light skin. Why would he leave? "Shit," I muttered.

I ran to the back of the house and looked around the lawn in the dark. I found the gun and brought it back to Rondo. "Shoot him if he tries to get away." The man, still cradling what was left of his hand, was moaning softly. The blood kept coming from his ankles where the dogs broke his flesh there, but mostly from his hand. I could see he was going into shock.

"This man go nowhere," Rondo said. "He die soon though if he not see a doctor to fix he."

I went back into the house, grabbed a few dish towels, my keys and my phone and hustled back out.

Rondo nodded and took the towels. He started to wrap the man's hand tightly.

"I'll be back as soon as I can, Rondo. You okay to stay?"

"Where I go?" he asked with a shrug.

"Thanks." I bounded into my Jeep and headed down the hill, one hand on my steering wheel, the other calling Tubby. There was no answer. Next I tried Kasie. Again there was no answer. Finally, I called Betta, but she too did not answer.

I sped down toward Betta's house, taking those sharp turns recklessly and not caring, just hoping I wouldn't run into an oncoming vehicle at this late hour. I saw the Suzuki parked about 100 yards from Betta's house. I slowed and then pulled past it. All the lights were on and the door was wide open. I ran out of the Jeep and into the house.

My eyes scanned the front living room as soon as I entered.

"Dad!" Kasie ran to hug me.

Betta had Paolo in her arms where he was half asleep.

Tubby was sitting in the living-room chair holding a bottle of beer. There was a towel around one of his feet. Lying on the couch next to the chair was the taller of the men, the one who, in the light of the room, looked Asian. His eyes were closed but he was breathing.

"You should have seen Tubby," Kasie said. "That man tried to break in. He had a gun. Tubby...well...he kicked him in the head."

Tubby grinned at me. "You know the *Te Tat* you teach me and we work on? Just one strike and the man here go down. Easy."

Tubby was referring to the Muay Thai roundhouse kick that uses the full rotation of the hips and drives the shin and/or foot into the victim. I didn't know what to say. Tubby was there for my daughter and for Betta and Paolo. He kept them safe. All I could do was stare in awe.

"You never tell me what a man's hard head can do to a foot. I have a bruise there for sure. Now I have to explain now to my wife how I get it." Tubby indicated the towel filled with ice that was on his aching shin. "You take care of things at your place, Mr. Len?"

I nodded.

"What's he mean, Dad? Did something happen at your house."

"The other man came."

Kasie hugged me tighter. "But it's okay? The dogs?"

"Yeah, they're all good. Tubby's friend Rondo helped me out."

Tubby smiled. "What I tell you about Rondo?"

"You were right, Tubby," I said and then looked down at his foot. "I know that hurts, but we need to clean up some stuff now. We need to get back to my house."

"Clean up stuff, Dad?" Kasie asked, her eyes on mine, wanting more.

"It's not as bad as it sounds, Kasie," I said. "Trust me." I wasn't about to tell her that there was a man on my front lawn minus half of one of his hands. "You ready to go, Tubby?"

He said took a long chug of the beer and got up tentatively, taking the ice off his foot. "Let's go," he said.

I looked at Betta. "I'm sorry this happened here, Betta," I said.

She looked back at me and held her son tight to her. "I need to put Paolo back to bed," she said. She wasn't happy. Why would she be? A man came into her home with a gun. And it was because of me.

I kissed Kasie and told her I would be back to pick her up in the morning. Tubby and I lifted the unconscious man and dragged him into the back of the Suzuki which then Tubby drove, following me, back to the house.

The man on my front lawn was murmuring in pain as we pulled up in front of my house. The other was still unconscious lying in the back of the Suzuki. Rondo was squatting, looking at the man on the lawn. He had a bottle of Carib in his hand.

"I very thirsty," Rondo said, smiling and holding up the bottle of beer.

"I'm glad you helped yourself, Rondo," I said and meant it. I owed both men much more than a cold bottle of beer.

Tubby limped over to see the damage done to the man with the braids. He hissed through his teeth and shook his head. "You gonna bring them inside?" he asked.

"Why would I get my house all bloodied up, Tubby?"

I could see that the towel was soaked through. The blood kept coming. He needed medical attention. I looked down into his now glassy eyes. "You killed my dog," I said to him. And then I pulled the string of hair out of my pocket. I dangled it in front of him. "You think I let this pass? You think you get away with threatening my daughter?"

I glared at him and despite the pain I knew he was enduring, there was still a glint of disdain as he looked back at me.

I turned to Tubby. "You recognize what language they speak?"

"Creole. But different from what I hear some people speak on St. Lucia and Guadeloupe. I think it might be Haitian."

"Do you understand it?"

He shrugged.

"What do you want with me? Who sent you to me?" I asked the bleeding man.

He stared blankly back at me.

"My dog." I shook my head at him. "My daughter."

The look of shock and fear disappeared. Now there was only hate in the man's eyes. "*Koulangyet Manman'w!*" he spat.

I looked up at Tubby. "What he say?" I asked.

Tubby shrugged. "You think I know what he say?"

"I know what de man say," Rondo said.

We both looked at him.

Rondo snickered. "I hear de talk like that sometime when we fish deep out near de other islands. De man say 'fuck you.' Dat what de man say."

Tubby looked at me. "He say 'fuck you' to you, Mr. Len. Now we gonna torture him to get him to talk?" he asked.

"Torture? Tubby, you've been watching too many old Chuck Norris movies."

Tubby looked at Rondo. "Who this Chuck Norris?" Rondo shrugged and shook his head.

Before I could tell them who Chuck Norris was, I heard my dogs growling at each other. I saw that they were fighting over something near the front door of my house. I got up and went over to them. The Spotted One had what was left of the man's hand in his mouth, the Gray One was trying to grab it out of his mouth to get some of it, but the Spotted One wouldn't let him. I pulled them apart and held the Spotted One. "Let go," I commanded. The dog looked at me. I tugged at his scruff. "Let go!" I said, louder now, and the dog finally dropped the mangled hand.

I took the hand and went into the house with it, making sure no blood dripped on my floor. I grabbed a plastic bag and dropped the hand inside.

"What you gonna do with that?" Tubby asked.

"I don't know. Maybe they can sew it back on him or something."

Tubby laughed. "You too nice, Mr. Len, giving de man he hand back."

"Yeah, I'm Mr. Nice Guy, Tubby."

"Yeah, now what we gonna do with them men?" Tubby asked.

What we did was tie them up with sturdy plastic bindings. Both of the men, I noticed, had identical tattoos on their necks. In the dark I could only make it out as an image of a grinning skeleton with a black top hat, the same tattoo I saw on the woman's thigh. Once we had them secured, we dragged them into the Suzuki they had been driving, the unconscious one in the back and the other in the front. I could hear the unconscious one start to mutter in his sleep. I knew he would wake soon. We had to get going.

I had Tubby put on gloves so we wouldn't leave fingerprints — as if the St. Pierre police might actually dust a crime vehicle — and then had him drive them to St. Elizabeth Hospital. I also gave Tubby a black hoodie I had but couldn't remember ever wearing on St. Pierre. I wanted his face obscured as much as possible just in case the hospital had a security camera at the entrance. I didn't want to take any chances that he could be identified.

I threw Rondo's bike into the back of my Jeep and had him sit up front with me as I followed the Suzuki. I drove past the hospital while Tubby turned into the parking lot. It was very late and there was no one around the entrance. He dragged both bodies out of the car and left them, along with the plastic bag containing the hand, at the entrance and then quickly got into the car and drove away.

I met him on Lagoon Road, where he abandoned the car and got into my Jeep.

"I bike from here," Rondo said.

"You sure, Rondo? I can take you right to your home?"

"No, this fine, Mr. Len. I bike from here, no worries."

He grabbed the bike from the back, and I looked through the rear window mirror as he pedaled toward down the quiet road.

"You know it's not over," Tubby said to me as he slid into the passenger seat.

"I know, but at least now we'll find out who's behind all this and hopefully why. They will send someone else, but I have a feeling they will try another approach."

"I hope you right, Mr. Len. I need to work more on the knee strike in case the roundhouse miss."

"We'll work on it, Tubby," I said. "And thanks for doing what you do."

"Maybe now you realize you need backup. How you think you were gonna handle them without Rondo there, or me?"

"I had a plan?"

Tubby laughed. "Your Muay Thai skills against those guns? That your plan?"

The truth was I really didn't have a plan. I was hoping my instincts would lead me in the right direction. I knew that was lame and most likely would end in disaster. My instincts were nothing to brag about lately. He was right. I was lucky Rondo came along. And maybe next time, if there was a next time, I'd have a plan.

We drove in silence for a bit. "What about the bar? Who was there tonight?"

"You gonna worry about the bar?" He shook his head in disgust. "Mike got it."

I nodded. I pulled in front of Tubby's house. We sat inside the Jeep for a moment.

"Thanks again," I said to him. "I'm taking Kasie to the airport tomorrow. We'll talk after she leaves."

Tubby stopped and looked at me for a moment. "Say goodbye to her for me," he said. "And she be back, I know that for sure."

"Yeah," I muttered. If only I was so sure.

I went into my house, and the first thing I noticed was the black polymer frame of the gun laying on my kitchen counter. I picked it up. I didn't know much about firearms, just what I was taught in the Marines, which was, where I was stationed, not very extensive. I knew enough, however, to see that it was a 9mm semi-automatic and that it would have done significant damage to either me, Rondo or Tubby. But so would have any handgun, fully, semi or zero automatic. I took that gun and the one Tubby took from the other man and put them into a shoebox.

I wrapped a few rubber bands around the box and placed it in the storage shed with my garden tools. I would decide what to do with them later.

I was tired. I wanted nothing more than to take a hot shower and then collapse on my bed. Instead, I chose to hose down my yard where the one man bled out. I didn't think there would be inspectors combing my yard and home anytime soon, but I also didn't want flies or birds hovering and pecking at dried blood making it a little more obvious what had happened here.

Finally satisfied that I had cleaned up most of the blood, I rolled up the hose and went inside to shower. I tried not to think about what just happened while I let the warm water flow over me. I did think about what I was going to tell my ex-wife about Kasie returning one day early. And that prospect wasn't much better than the thought of further encounters with men with 9mm handguns.

In a couple of years Kasie would be eighteen. An adult. She could choose to see me or not. But I didn't want to wait those two years for her to come visit her father. The same with her brother Luke. He was younger, but when he turned sixteen I wanted him to come visit. I couldn't lie to Kathleen. Or maybe I could. I'd done it before. But she eventually found out about that one. And I've been living with that lie ever since.

After the shower, I poured myself a shot of aged rum I had picked up off the boat from St. Lucia that sold all those gourmet goodies. This rum was from Martinique, what they called *rhum agricole*. Clayton Teel, who knew about stuff like that, had told me that the rums from the French islands were the best, that they were made with sugar-cane juice rather than molasses, which was how they made it on most of the former British islands. The sugar cane gave it a smoother, almost Cognac-like quality. The label on the bottle called the amber rum *vieux,* old, and in this case, old meant aged for twelve years. I knew that back in the States the same rum sold for over fifty dollars. I got it off the gourmet boat for less than half that.

I sipped the smooth rum and sat back on my couch. It had been a long night, and it was already past two in the morning. I knew I needed to get some sleep. I had to be up early to pack Kasie's stuff and get her to the airport. But I needed this time with this rum first. I needed to decompress from the day. It seemed like a very long time ago when I sat down with Big Tree to hear his story. I hadn't had a chance to really think about what he told me, to make sense of what had happened that night. It was hard to believe that the girl could just vanish the way he described it, without a trace. But it was also hard to believe that Big Tree could hurt anyone, much less a woman. I knew it wasn't easy for him to tell me what he did, to confess his moment of weakness. We all had them. I know I did. And my weakness, though admittedly significantly more than just a moment, turned my life upside down and led me to where I was today, for better or for worse. Big Tree's moment landed him behind bars. It wasn't much worse than that.

I kept thinking about what he told me about his encounter with the girl. She had a sexual pull that was undeniable. I felt it in just that brief encounter with her. It was strong, and I'm sure she was aware of that. That pull was also evident in the way Craig Frost described her. Still, I remember Big Tree's face when he admitted putting his hands on her. He said she guided his hands to those places. But then she just turned off that sexual energy after seeing that text. How could she could run off leaving Big Tree sitting there thinking who knows what?

I sipped more of the rum. Something about his story was off. I believed him, but maybe he forgot to tell me something. There was a piece missing. I was no investigator. I should have had other questions prepared for him. I should have pushed more on what he did after she ran off. But that kind of grilling wasn't in me. It wasn't me.

Craig Frost had something important to tell me. Maybe that was the missing piece, the reason all of this happened. Maybe that was the connection between Big Tree, the dead girl and the men who were after me. Those two men came to my house to shut me up, warn me or maybe even kill me over something I didn't know. Someone sent them to me for a reason. There was a name missing. Like I told Tubby, now they would send someone else. Or maybe the big name Frost was hinting at would show up without any outside help. Either way, I was sure it would be soon and I needed to be ready. Tubby was right, I needed a plan.

I downed the remainder of the rum. I slowly pulled myself up out of my chair and went to my bedroom. I had to try to catch a few hours sleep, but my mind was a mess from the uncertainty of all that was going on. So much for decompressing.

20

As I wheeled Kasie's roll-on bag to my Jeep in the light of day, I saw that the front lawn was still damp from where I hosed it, but I didn't see any brown or red stains in the dirt or grass, or evidence of blood anywhere else.

Kasie was up and dressed when I got to Betta's house, black leggings and another one of her long track-team T-shirts. "Can't we do one more day, Dad?" she pleaded as she saw me.

I shook my head adamantly. "No can do."

Betta and Paolo emerged from the back bedroom. Paolo carried a book to Kasie.

Kasie chuckled. "You want me to read you this again?"

Paolo nodded. I could see photos of sea turtles on the cover.

"But I have to go now, kiddo," she said.

His eyes went wide and he started to cry.

"Awwww don't cry. See, Dad?" She glared at me.

"What?"

"You made Paolo cry."

"I did?"

"Yes, by making me go home a day early."

Betta took the boy in her arms. "She will visit again, Paolo," she whispered to him, smoothing down his thick curly hair. "We've enjoyed having you, Kasie."

"Teach Betta how to Skype, Dad so I can talk with them from New York," she commanded.

"Can you do that for us, Leonard?" Betta gave me one of those looks that made it pretty much impossible for me to refuse.

"Yeah, sure," I mumbled. "We should get going."

I watched as my daughter hugged Betta. It made me smile to see how well they got along. Betta glanced at me after the hug.

"I'm sorry again for what went on here last night," I said to her.

She just nodded. She wasn't judging, but I couldn't tell what she felt about it all.

"There is leftover pizza if you are hungry later," she said, keeping her eyes on mine.

The way she was looking at me...I wanted to say yes. Instead I just responded as evasively as always. "Maybe, Betta," I said. "I'll call you."

Paolo cried again, and while Betta consoled him, I escorted my daughter out of the house and into my Jeep.

The silence in the Jeep as I drove was stifling. Though she didn't show it in front of Betta, I could tell now that Kasie was upset. She was nibbling her thumbnail.

"I didn't mean for all this to be going on this week, honey," I said, hoping to sound apologetic. "It just happened."

"It's not your fault, Dad," she said.

Whose fault was it then, I wondered, but said nothing.

I parked the Jeep and rolled her bag while she carried her backpack.

"Let me," she insisted and grabbed the bag from me.

I walked with her to the entrance and started inside with her. The security checkpoint was just ahead. Garnett Edwards was in his security uniform at the walk-through metal detector. Kasie was ready with her passport and ticket. I stood next to her as she piled her bag and backpack onto the rolling security screener.

"Only ticket holders from here, Mr. Len," Edwards said to me.

I looked at him and noticed that the flight to Barbados was delayed a half-hour. That meant she had over an hour to wait in what was a pretty desolate waiting area.

"She's a minor, Garnett," I said. "And she has some time, I see, before her plane departs."

He looked around as if to see if any of his superiors were watching us. There was no one I could see. Garnett was a regular at the Sporting Place who would drop in for a few beers and sit at the bar most every night after his shift. We had several long conversations on slow afternoons. He was separated from his wife, who had taken their two children and was now living in Miami with her sister's family. She had caught him more than a few times cavorting with other women and finally, after he admitted to fathering a child with one of them, had enough. "Why a woman not understand a man just a man?" Garnett would say after a few beers. "He not meant for one woman, but that not mean he can't love one woman and the children she have with he. That not mean he can't take care of all...if he a man. Is that reason to leave? I do not think so. No, the woman just do not understand."

The funny thing about Garnett was that once his wife left

him, I never saw him chatting up the women who would come to the bar to chat up some of the men. Now that he didn't have to worry about being caught by his wife, he gave up his old habits. But that didn't mean he couldn't continue to complain that she was in the wrong to leave him over what he felt was a minor offense.

Kasie was looking up at me. We had to say goodbye here.

And then Garnett pushed the plastic box to me. "Your phone, keys, anything else from your pockets," he said in an official tone.

I smiled, making a mental note that Garnett's next couple of rounds at the Sporting Place would be on me. I emptied my pockets into the box and then, after Kasie was screened, walked through the metal detector.

Kasie grabbed her bags and we wandered to a row of plastic benches. I sat down and thought that it seemed so long ago when Tubby and I were here waiting for my daughter to arrive, yet less than a week had passed.

I reached for my phone and noticed I had a voice mail from my ex. "Looks like your mother called," I said

"Yeah, I know. I talked to her, Dad," Kasie said. "She knows I'm coming home today."

"Did you tell her why?"

"No, I told her you would. She was asking a lot of questions. She wanted to know if we were getting along."

"Yeah?"

"Don't worry, I told her we were. That it had nothing to do with that."

"I'll call her later."

"You know she's gonna be pissed," Kasie said. "Maybe we can make something up."

"No, I'll tell her what's going on." I put my arm around her and hugged her close to me.

We sat there together, staring out at the landing strip. There were a few dark clouds to the northeast. There was rain coming, but not enough to delay her flight. She would just have to get through the clouds.

Kasie turned her head to me. "Why don't you like to talk about what happened that day, Dad?" she asked, catching me unawares.

There was much I hadn't told my daughter about my life, but the biggest blank of all was that first day of June when she was just a little girl. She knew bits and pieces, but she didn't know the whole truth. Only my wife did — and that was a contributing factor to why she was no longer my wife.

"You used to smile a lot. I remember when you took Luke and me biking at Pelham Bay Park. Remember that?"

I did remember. Luke was still using training wheels. We had to go slow so he could keep up with us. We biked all afternoon, and then the four of us went to City Island for lobster. It was a happy day. We had fun as a family, but I should have known that it would not last. I already put the wheels in motion for that.

I nodded.

"Then that day happened and I remember everyone saying how much of a hero you were for what you did," Kasie went on. "My friends at school looked at me differently. They thought I had the best, bravest father. I was proud that you were my Dad, but you were always sad...and quiet after that day. In school we studied about the Vietnam War and how some of the soldiers came back wrecked mentally. They had PTSD. Same with some of the survivors and first responders of the 9/11 thing. When the towers fell. Is that what happened, Dad? You have PTSD from that day the bomb went off in the subway station? Going in to help all those people even though you could have been killed? What did it do to you? Is that why you're now all alone here on this island and without your family? Without us? Is that why you're not happy anymore? That you're not with Mom?"

"No. That's not why," I said, but I wasn't sure if I was right. If that day had never happened. If I wasn't where I was and did what I did, maybe I would still be with my family. I just didn't know and never would.

"Then why?"

She stared into my eyes. She was growing up. She would find out sooner or later. If not from me, from her mother. I didn't want that. It had to come from me.

We were alone on the plastic seats. A few other passengers were waiting for the same Liat ATR-42 turbo prop to Barbados, but they were not sitting near us. No one would hear, and even if they did, what did it matter? What would it mean to them? I had no more excuses. It was time my daughter knew the truth. I owed her that.

By the time the call was made to board the plane, she knew everything. I didn't know what to expect. I didn't know how she would react. She didn't say anything one way or the other. She didn't say I was a bad husband or a bad father for doing what I did. She said nothing about betrayal. I wasn't sure how she felt about what I just confessed. I knew I was risking losing her, but that might have happened if she found out on her own. It might have happened after what went on here. After what she witnessed.

We got up from our seats. Her eyes were red. Trying to be the tough man I really wasn't, I kept my eyes dry. "Give your brother a hug and kiss for me," I said, the first words between us after telling her my story. "I'll be up to see you guys and Uncle Pat in August," I said.

She nodded and then she hugged me tight. "It's okay, Daddy," she said and then turned and went with the others without looking back.

I watched as she boarded the plane. I could hear the buzz of my phone in my pocket. I had no interest in pulling it out to check who was texting me. I kept my eyes on the plane. I tried to look through the plane's windows to see if I could catch a glimpse of her blonde hair in one of the windows. I couldn't. The phone kept buzzing. I kept ignoring it. The plane was closed up and began to taxi down the landing strip. It gained speed and ascended into the air, the landing wheels closing up into the plane. I watched as it climbed higher and swerved northwest slightly before turning back east. I could hear my own breathing as the plane began to disappear from my sight, but before it did, I noticed that the pilot made sure to direct it away from those dark, ominous clouds that were headed this way.

PART TWO

21

McWilliams was waiting outside the terminal as I exited. He was leaning against his police car and had his hat off. I could see that his head was glistening with sweat and he was wearing sunglasses. He took them off and wiped his face with a handkerchief.

He was there to see me, of that I had no doubt.

"It's sad to say goodbye to loved ones who live so far away," McWilliams said as I approached him. "I understand that. I still get tears when I remember seeing my own daughter and her husband leave this island to live in London. I know it will be too long before I see her again. And now she has children. One grandson I've never even seen."

I didn't think he was trying to get under my skin, but he was doing a good job of it. I didn't need to hear this.

"Can we chat, Mr. Buonfiglio," he said, no more pretense of

informality or small talk.

I stopped and turned to him.

"What about?" I asked.

"The two men who visited St. Elizabeth's emergency room last night."

"What two men?"

He smiled and looked down. "One was missing part of his hand. The other had a severe concussion, from what I'm told."

"That sounds rough. I hope they will recover." I said.

"They will. In fact, they are already out of the hospital." He waited to gauge my reaction. Again, I was sure my lack of a poker face betrayed me. But I kept my mouth shut. I wanted to ask him where they went but knew that would be admitting my part in all of it.

"That's good news for them, I guess," I said as calmly as I could.

"When a man lose part of his hand from what look like the blow from a cutlass, that not a good thing. That mean it get in criminal territory. That mean this an area the police should investigate."

I stared blankly.

"Tell me what you know about them," McWilliams said.

"What could I possibly know about them?" I asked. "I'm a bar owner. I don't get involved in disputes that might result in bodily harm. Why would I do something like that and risk the good thing I've got going here?"

"But you were not at your bar last night," he said.

"I've been taking time off to spend with my daughter," I said.

McWilliams shook his head. "Why she leave early? Did your daughter not like our lovely island?"

I wondered what else McWilliams knew. He obviously had a

full account of my itinerary. He wasn't the one to snoop, yet he knew things as if he were actually doing some investigating. I'm sure he had information I could use, but then he would need to know what I was up to, which, in reality, at the moment wasn't much. It was best, for now at least, for both of us to conduct our own separate investigations.

"I think she had a good time," I said. "A school commitment came up and she had to get back earlier than she thought."

McWilliams smiled at my lie. "I see."

"Is our chat over?" I asked. "The sun is hot and I think I'm beginning to sweat."

"Yes, Mr. Buonfiglio, it's over for now. This criminal territory you entering. It best you let the authorities handle it. I'm your friend. Not your foe. I'm here to help. Remember what I tell you."

"I appreciate your friendship, McWilliams. Any criminal activity I come across, I promise to defer to you for your expert handling."

I liked McWilliams. I really did. But I needed to take care of this without his help. I had to do things my way. I always did.

There was a voice mail from Tubby on my phone. I didn't bother to listen and instead texted him and told him I would meet him at the bar. He quickly texted back that he was already there.

I got into my Jeep. I could still smell the scent of the soap Kasie used in her morning shower coming from the passenger seat. I missed her already and now couldn't wait to see her and her brother in August. I wanted them closer to me. I wanted more of them in my life. The few days with Kasie, despite being tumultuous, revived fatherly instincts that had been dormant for too long while living alone here. It was complicated, but it was there, a part of me I could not deny or shut out.

I pulled into the bar's three-car parking lot next to Tubby's old Honda. There was one more call I had to make. I got out of the Jeep and walked up the hill and under the shade of a fifteen-foot clove tree. There were buds flowering and the fragrance was intense. I picked off a bud and held it while with my other hand skimmed my phone. I took a breath and then dialed my ex-wife.

"I'm worried about you, Len," Kathleen said after we said hello. "Kasie said you were involved in some business there. What business? She was a little too vague and wouldn't tell me much. But for her to come home early like this. Did something happen between the two of you?"

"No, no. Nothing like that," I said. "We were having a blast. She's really growing up, Kathleen. You've done a good job with her."

"Yeah, yeah, spare me that, Len. What's happening down there? You know you can't bullshit me. I know you too well for that."

I thought about how I deceived her long enough. How did I do that? How was I able to hide it so easily? And then I realized it really wasn't very hard at all. My wife trusted me. She knew that there were plenty of women who came to the bars and who we hired to work there. They were actresses, dancers, models. There were countless opportunities if I wanted to cheat, but I never did. My partners did—she knew that, but me—never. I thought I was happy with my life. With my family. But then someone came into the bar who was different. Not an actress, dancer or a model. But someone else. Someone I came to need. And to love. Until I lost her. And then I lost everything.

"I've been involved in some stuff," I blurted out. There would be no more lies. "I can't really tell you how or why because I don't even know myself, but I've been doing, I guess what you would call investigative work on the side. And what I'm handling now was getting a little dangerous. I didn't want to risk Kasie's safety in any way."

There was a pause in our conversation

"Kathleen?"

"Are you losing your mind? What do you know about any of that? And I thought it was paradise down there. No crime. No traffic. Nothing like what we have up here. I thought that was one of the reasons you deserted us for that place. You tell me this and now I'm really worried."

"It's not like that, Kathleen. It's not like I'm playing cops and robbers down here. I'm helping some people out, that's all. What I'm working on now got a little rough, and I didn't want Kasie near any of it. You can understand that."

"Damn right I can. And you did the right thing, but Len, this is crazy. I think you should think about coming back here. Maybe you've been alone there too long. Maybe all that sun is affecting your brain."

"Kathleen, come on. I'm okay. You don't have to worry, really."

Again there was a long pause.

"I know we have separate lives now," she said, her voice softer now. The anger that was obvious before had faded. "You are the father to my children. I still have feelings for you, I hope you know that. I always will. And Richard knows I do and he understands. You and I have a bond that goes way back. You think I can just forget that? I miss you and think about you all the time. Your children miss you. So don't tell me not to worry. Please."

I didn't expect the change in tone. I expected to be reamed out by her for exposing Kasie to danger. For being the selfish prick that I was. I expected a tirade, instead I got a plea. I think the tirade would have been easier to take.

"Really, Kathleen, it's all right. Don't worry about me. I'm good here. Really I am. I appreciate all you said too...and I feel the same. Is Luke around?"

"He's about to leave for lacrosse practice," she said.

"Lacrosse? Can I talk to him?"

There was a pause as phones were exchanged. "Hi, Dad," Luke said, his voice suddenly deeper than I remembered.

"Hey, buddy. Everything good with you?"

"Yeah, but I've got to go to practice," he said.

"Lacrosse?"

"Yeah."

"No baseball, Luke?" I asked.

"They are both spring sports, Dad," he said. "I can't play both."

"Yeah, so why lacrosse? Last time we threw the ball, your arm was impressive."

I could hear my son sigh on the other end. "It's more fun," he said. "More action than baseball. And I might have a better chance getting into an Ivy."

Fun? Action? My son was eliminating baseball for those reasons? What was I missing? And then the last excuse. "An Ivy, Luke?"

"Yeah, you know. Yale. Princeton. Cornell."

I knew what an Ivy was but didn't know what to say about it. "I'm late, Dad. I got to go now." He was rushing off the line.

"Alright. I'm gonna call you later," I said.

"Sure, Dad," he said.

I felt my stomach flutter. That didn't go so well.

"Len?" Kathleen was back on the line. "You're gonna give him a hard time for playing lacrosse over baseball? He's a smart kid. Let him find his way."

"Yeah, I know...but...?"

"Len, let him be."

She was right. What the hell was I doing? "Give him a hug for me, please."

There was another awkward silence on the line.

"I will," Kathleen said. Her voice was cracking. "Please take care of yourself."

"Yeah, okay," I muttered. "Tell Kasie again I'm sorry and will make it up to her next time."

I waited for a response. A goodbye. Something. But all I heard was dead air.

22

I sat under the clove tree a little longer, trying to compose myself after that conversation. The hurt I caused, before and now. My wife did nothing to deserve it. And there was no way I could ever make it up to her.

I walked back to the Sporting Place. Tubby was adding bottles of Carib, Ram Stout and Heineken to the refrigerator behind the bar. I could see that he was limping slightly from the bruise on his shin. He stood up and turned around to face me. He could see my expression. He nodded. "She be back again, Mr. Len. You do the right thing by sending her home."

"I know that, Tubby," I said.

It wasn't even noon, but it was early enough for me to grab a beer. I opened a bottle of Carib and took a long sip.

"They gone, you know," Tubby said.

I looked at him.

"Someone come to the hospital with papers to get them out. The two walk out of the hospital, best they can walk, and go back to the boat."

"Who?"

"Some men. No one from here that my friend, Tyus' wife, Cleefa, who work the shift, recognize. White men."

"So now they're on the boat?"

"Yeah, and now the boat gone too," he said.

I thought about that. McWilliams said nothing about it but I was sure he knew. Whoever got those papers to get them out of the hospital without questioning by McWilliams had some pull. And then got them out of St. Pierre's waters before they could be investigated further.

"Did you ever get the name of the boat?"

Tubby wandered to the end of the bar where we had a phone, pens and paper. He picked up a stray piece and brought it closer to his eyes. "Rondo get it for me."

I took the paper from him and read: *ED's Folly.*

"Thanks, Tubby. Maybe we can do a search or something to find out who owns it."

"And then what, Mr. Len? What you do when you find out?"

I really didn't know. He was right. I could look for who owned that boat. And when I found out, what would I do? Go chasing after it? Report it to the authorities? Follow up on whoever was the owner? I drank more of the beer. The men were gone. We got no information from them. McWilliams gave me nothing. But there was still Big Tree's predicament. His mother had entrusted me to help get him out. He remained in custody, and I wasn't any closer to helping him than when I started all this.

"You under control here, Tubby?" I asked.

"Always am, Mr. Len," he said. "You go home and relax. Not much you can do about anything now."

I started for the door and was about to exit when a man, formally dressed in a dark suit with a white shirt and a tie with mini flags of St. Pierre embroidered in it, entered. He held the door open for me. There was a shiny silver Mercedes Roadster convertible parked just on the bank leading into my parking lot.

"Buonfiglio?"

I stopped at the door. "The one and only," I said.

He smiled and closed the door before I could leave.

"So this is the famous Sporting Place," the man said. He held out his hand to me. "Edward Denton."

I took his hand. He had a surprisingly strong grip. I had heard the name before and tried to recall where. I turned to Tubby. He glanced back at me and then looked down.

"How is it that after all these years with the tourism authority we've never been formally introduced and I've never been to your establishment?" Denton asked.

I remembered now. Edward Denton was the minister of tourism for St. Pierre.

"I don't know, Mr. Denton, but I guess better late than never," I said.

"Absolutely, Mr. Buonfiglio." His eyes were scanning the empty bar. He looked up at our ceiling fans. Tubby still hadn't gotten the one not working repaired. The other one was on high and the bar was cooled by it. "You are fortunate to get the combination of the sea and mountain breezes."

"Would you like a drink, Mr. Denton?" I asked. "Tubby makes a memorable rum punch."

He turned to look at Tubby.

"Yes, I know. I've had Mr. Levett's rum punches when he worked at the Yacht Club. They certainly miss you over there."

"That Yacht Club a good training ground for moving here, Mr. Denton," Tubby said from behind the bar.

"I'll take one as long as you join me, Mr. Buonfiglio," he said.

I wanted to go home. I didn't want to socialize. I was exhausted emotionally and physically after what we went through the night before. But it would not be good business to refuse the minister of tourism. And I knew, and so did Tubby from that look he gave me, that his coming here was no coincidence. We expected a visit from someone. The timing made sense. Could he be the one?

"My pleasure," I said, forcing a smile.

"Wonderful," Denton said.

He was around my age, I guessed. His skin was dark next to his white dress shirt. He had short hair and sideburns that joined a well-groomed salt-and-pepper beard. With his suit jacket unbuttoned, I noticed that he was lean, his torso muscular under that shirt. I wondered what he did to keep in such good shape.

Tubby made up the drinks and brought them to us.

"Would you like to have our drink here or out on the patio?" I asked.

"Let's go outside," he said, the smile still on his face. "I hear the view from your deck is one of a kind."

We took the drinks outside to one of the three round tables I had on the deck. Each table was equipped with umbrellas for shade. Before sitting, Denton walked to the end of the deck to stare out at Garrison Harbor and the Caribbean.

"Stunning," he said. "Good job, Buonfiglio. This is a very welcome addition to our island."

"Thanks," I said with a shrug, but though the deck was

relatively new, the Sporting Place had been around for almost five years. I didn't consider the bar an "addition" anymore.

Denton took his drink and sat at one of the tables. I sat across from him, facing the bar while he could take in the view.

"And business is good?"

"I can't complain," I said. "Your people have been sending groups here for awhile now. So thanks for that."

"My people?" He looked surprised.

"From your office. The tourism authority," I said.

"Ah yes." He nodded his head as he sipped the punch and winced at the strength of it. "Levett never fails...memorable indeed."

"Tubby's a rum-punch legend," I said.

"That he is." He took another sip and then put the drink down. "We are very happy to have you as part of our business and tourism community, Mr. Buonfiglio. This place shows your forward thinking. So often we get stuck in the past here. People like the old ways and resist the future. Progress can be daunting. So it's a pleasure to meet up with someone like you."

I wasn't sure what he was getting at. I think he was complimenting me, but I had no idea why.

"It's just a sports bar, Mr. Denton. There wasn't one on the island when I arrived, but they are really nothing new."

"See, but you found a niche here that was vacant and you filled it. We need more visionaries like you."

He was laying it on a little too thick. "A visionary? I don't think so, Mr. Denton."

"Don't sell yourself short, sir. This is where I was born and have lived most of my life. I love my home. I love my island and my people, but unless we change, we will not survive. Unless we open ourselves up to progress, we will not be able to sustain ourselves. The young people will continue to leave the island and the elders will die off. What will become of St. Pierre then?"

I sipped my punch. He was trying to tell me something without really telling me. I didn't know if it was a tactic or just the way he communicated.

"I don't know, Mr. Denton. I mean, I traveled to all the islands before I settled on this one. There was something here I found appealing. Maybe it was because, as you say, the island is stuck in the past. Sometimes it's that rush to progress that can destroy what made the place special to begin with."

"We are a long way from that problem, Mr. Buonfiglio, and we are all grateful you found us so appealing," he said and then looked around at the vista behind him. "Have you considered expanding?"

"Beyond what I have here?"

"I don't mean expanding this, but maybe opening up other establishments. You have the expertise, that's for certain."

I shook my head. "No, I'm happy with just this at the moment."

He tapped his temple. "Remember, forward thinking. Don't get trapped in the status quo. If opportunities arise, you should consider them."

Again he was hinting at something. I wasn't going to push him for what he really wanted to say. I got the feeling he was just throwing an idea out there to assess my reaction.

"I wouldn't not consider an opportunity. But I can't promise anything more than that, Mr. Denton."

"As long as you keep an open mind. We all should."

"On that we definitely agree," I said.

He ran his finger over the condensation that was forming

on his glass. "I hear you had a chat with Rawle Johns," he said, switching gears and tone as well, his voice now more somber.

"His Ma asked me to," I said.

"What did his Ma think you could do for him?"

"That's a good question and one I really can't answer. I guess she thought I have some influence here to help get him out of his situation."

He nodded "Rawle's a good boy. We've used him for many tourism functions. He's always been a reliable, wonderful ambassador for St. Pierre. When I heard they suspected him of such a thing, I was shocked."

I sipped my drink and let him talk without interruption.

"A crime like that on our island is not good for business. It was bad enough if the poor girl accidently fell from the Drop. A murder is something else entirely. News like that spreads and hurts our trade."

"From what he told me and what I've heard from his attorney, the evidence isn't that convincing. I don't know how they can keep him there without really charging him."

"This is what I tell you, Mr. Buonfiglio, about being stuck in the past. St. Pierre too often relies on archaic rules of governing. In any other more progressive, democratic society, Rawle would be free unless formally charged. Here he sits until a magistrate decides to release him."

"His attorney said he was working on that. That he would request a hearing where he would make the case to have him released," I said.

Denton looked at me and smiled knowingly. "I wish him good luck with that," he said and then, raising his glass to his lips and looking at me added: "No, Mr. Buonfiglio, these magistrates make their decisions in other ways. A powerful whisper into one's ear works much better than the diligent efforts of a court-appointed attorney."

He stared at me a moment longer and then drank down the rest of the punch, the ice rattling at the bottom of the glass.

"Now I must get back to the office and try to get a little work done," he said getting up from his seat.

I got up along with him and both of us walked back into the bar

"It was a pleasure to meet you, Mr. Denton. Thank you for visiting. I hope we'll see you again here." This time I held out my hand.

"The pleasure was truly mine, Buonfiglio," he said, gripping my hand tightly. His eyes now on mine. The way he looked at me, he was telling me something without speaking. Thinking the non-verbal message had been delivered, he released my hand and turned to the bar and smiled widely. "Tubby, you never fail. You are truly the master of the St. Pierre rum punch. This man is lucky to have you as a partner."

"And he know that for sure, Mr. Denton," Tubby said with a grin from behind the bar.

Denton laughed and walked out. I looked at Tubby and then went to the door to watch Denton get into that pretty roadster. He drove off the bank and then did a U turn, his car heading down to Garrison.

"So he the one?" Tubby asked.

"Could be," I said. "But the one what?"

Tubby snorted. "I let you try to figure that out."

"Thanks for nothing," I said.

We both knew Denton hadn't come just to inspect the bar. He had a clear purpose. After the more blunt approach, sending those two men to physically silence me — about what, I had no idea — I knew they, whoever they were, would try a different tact. Maybe there was no they? Maybe it was just Denton behind all this? He came with a message for me, but that message was unclear. He was speaking in code, talking about opportunities and whispering to judges. What was he offering me? And for what in return?

The first thing I did when I got home was to open my laptop and search the internet for anything on Edward Denton. There was a link to a St. Pierre government site that had his picture and title as minister of tourism. His brief biography mentioned his education credits, including a degree in business from the London School of Economics. I scrolled to see if there were other mentions of Edward Denton. There was a complete page of listings of a boxer named Edward Denton. I clicked on one of the links. The rum punch had made me drowsy, and I clicked on a few other links about the boxer with the same name just to make sure I wasn't seeing things. The picture was decades old, but the boxer was, undoubtedly, the same Edward Denton who had just visited the Sporting Place.

So that's where the man got his firm grip and that still-sturdy frame. Most of his fights, I noticed, took place in the 1990s. He hadn't gone to flab like many former athletes; it was obvious the man was still training. I read about some of his exploits. He had numerous championship fights around the world as a super middleweight and, according to one article, briefly won an International Boxing Federation title in 1994 in Las Vegas.

There was a photo of Denton smiling after winning that title, holding his championship belt. My phone was next to me on the bed. I picked it up and texted Tubby.

How come you didn't tell me Denton was a boxer? I wrote.

A few moments later, Tubby responded.

'Cause you didn't ask, he wrote.

I shook my head and tossed the phone back onto the bed. I started to do a search for a boat named *ED's Folly*. I had no idea where to begin, so I just typed the name along with the keyword "yacht" next to it. An endless list of yacht references came up, along with separate mentions of "folly" and "ED," but none that came together to form the name of the boat.

My eyes were heavy-lidded now. I'm not usually one to take an afternoon nap; Tubby's strong rum punch along with the lack of sleep was taking its toll. I tried to resist. I had too much to do, but I just could not keep my eyes open. I was either semi-conscious or dreaming but I was somewhere else. I was back at the bar talking to a man with an odd, off-putting smile. He kept trying to get my attention, but I was distracted by something else. I kept looking at a smaller man with dreadlocks...or braids... standing behind the man who was chatting with me. He was grinning widely and held up one hand. It was a freakishly large hand, and in it he was able to grip three beer bottles. I stared closely at the hand, watching as the hand exploded and the beer bottles dropped to the floor, shattering. The man was smiling even though his hand was gone and blood was flowing up from the stump like a fountain. I started to get up from the stool. I wanted to help him—to stop the flow of blood. He began to laugh as the blood along with the beer from the broken bottles flooded the floor of my bar. I looked for rags, towels, anything to clean up the mess. To stop the blood from flowing. But there was nothing. And the man kept laughing. Laughing at me.

I opened my eyes. My bedroom was dark. The sun was setting. I must have been out for a couple of hours. I rubbed my face and then sat up straight. My heart was pounding in my chest.

Edward Denton, I thought to myself.

E...D.

How did I miss the connection?

ED's Folly.

It was his boat. It had to be. There was no "they." It was Denton who was behind all this.

I swung my feet off the bed and went into my bathroom to douse my face with cold water. I was sure I had found the who, but I still did not know the why. I had to tell Tubby. I had to tell someone. I went to my phone and was about to text him, when I saw that there was a text from Kasie. I opened it up to see a close-up of her smiling face from a selfie she took at JFK. Under the photo, she wrote: *Home*.

I looked at her smile and started to text her back when I noticed the time. I remembered I was expected at the Bougainvillea for dinner with Marcia Gould. We had agreed on 7:30. I had less than a half-hour to get ready and be there on time. I turned on the shower and quickly soaped up. I was excited now. Things were coming together.

23

Clayton Teel greeted me as I entered through the lobby of the Bougainvillea. The reception area of the inn served as a guest lounge with luxurious furniture made from local Caribbean mahogany and was cluttered with antiques and artifacts. Teel was a slight middle-aged man, a half a foot shorter than me, with a light-brown complexion and graying, close-cropped hair. He had stylish round-framed glasses and was wearing black jeans and a loose open-collared white shirt embroidered with flowers.

"I heard we were expecting you this evening, Len," Clayton said with a welcoming smile.

"I hope that didn't ruin your day," I said.

"On the contrary, you know we always enjoy having you visit. Tito is a big fan of yours," he said.

"And I'm a big fan of Tito's...especially those lambi fritters he makes."

Lambi was a shellfish, the meat from the sea conch, that was beaten and then boiled to tenderize and served in a variety of ways including in a stew or made into fritters and fried. In the Bronx, we called it scungilli. But I never had scungilli that was anything like Tito's lambi fritters.

"If your dinner companion for the evening doesn't object, I'm sure Tito will be more than happy to bring some to the table."

"Hmmmm, I don't know, Clayton, even if she does object, I hope to..." I wanted to say to persuade her to agree, but I couldn't get those words out of my mouth. Not after spotting her at the bar, in a short, clingy white dress, her long bare legs dangling down from the barstool on which she was perched. Not after her red lips stretched into a knee-weakening smile when she saw me, open-mouthed and openly ogling her. Words just would not come.

I could hear Clayton giggle behind me. "Easy now, Len. Try to show some decorum please. You know this is a classy place, don't you?" he teased as he walked behind me.

"Yeah I know, classy and here I am. How did that happen?"

"It seems you have good connections."

"I do, don't I," I said, looking at Marcia Gould like a blushing schoolboy.

"Don't you look handsome," she said to me as I approached her.

"So I've graduated from cute to handsome," I said, hoping my humor would hide my awkwardness. "Is it because I forgot to shave today?"

"I like a man with a little facial hair," she said, her light-brown eyes dancing as she looked at me. "But I emphasize the little."

"No worries about that, I tried the beard thing. It made me look older than I really am, and that's something I don't strive for."

"I bet it looked very distinguished on you."

"Distinguished? Cute and handsome I can tolerate, but distinguished — that's going way too far, Mrs. Gould," I said.

"Tsk, tsk, tsk," she said with a sultry pout. "What did I tell you on the beach the other day? You are to address me as Marcia. None of that Mrs. Gould, please."

"Yeah, but can you blame a man who comes upon a woman such as yourself, looking definitely not very eighteenth century, and I mean that in only a positive way, who has invited a common bar owner to dine with her? He feels overwhelmed. He feels flattered. But most of all, he feels very happy to be here."

"Mmmmm," she purred. "Aren't you the charmer?"

"Yeah, I hear that all the time from the dogs that live with me."

We were flirting. But in the back of all this was the dark reality of why she was here. Less than a year ago, her daughter died tragically. Was this her way of grieving? Or was this a welcome, needed relief from the constant sorrow? I knew a little bit about grieving, but then, it wasn't my daughter who died. That I could not imagine.

She gestured to the stool next to me, one of her bare thighs close enough for me to feel the heat radiating from it. "What would you like to drink?"

She had a drink in front of her already. "What are you drinking?" I asked.

"All I know is that it is something with rum in it, and it is delicious." She turned to Clayton Teel who was doing his best not to reveal that he was listening to our conversation. "What do you call this cocktail, Clayton?" she asked him.

"Corn 'n' Oil," Clayton said. "I'm sure Len has had one."

"I have, and that sounds good to me, Clayton," I said. I'd had the drink in Barbados and even made it a couple of times at the bar when requested, which was rarely. There was no corn and no oil in the drink, but the combination of dark, molasses-derived blackstrap rum along with bitters and falernum, a sweet syrup fragrant with almond, lime and ginger, over lime juice has the look of a corn-like color floating on top of oil. I think that's how the drink got its name.

"Coming right up," Clayton said as he went to work prepping the drink.

"How was your dinner at the Heritage House with the prime minister? Were the guests distinguished?" I grinned at her.

She smirked. "Oh yes, very distinguished," she said. "Beards and all."

"Okay, now I'm curious. I want names of those beards."

"As if I could remember all the names. There were people from the government. A minister of this and minister of that, male and female."

"Did there happen to be the minister of tourism in attendance?" I asked it casually, within the flow of our conversation. I didn't want her to think I was snooping while I was flirting. Not that it really mattered.

She shrugged. "I don't know. What would make me know one beard from the other? Or one minister of this or that from the other?"

"Well, this minister was well-built."

"Like you?" She was looking me over.

"If you say so," I said. "Though this minister was not as tall as me and definitely not as cute."

She laughed. "Enough already. What was this beard's name?"

"Edward Denton," I said.

"Denton?" She nodded in recognition. "He was seated next to me. Why do you ask about him?"

"I met him today for the first time," I said. "He came to the bar for a rum punch."

"Well that's a coincidence, isn't it?"

A coincidence? I wasn't so sure.

"What did you two chat about? Was he as much of a charmer as me?" I asked.

"Oh no, definitely not. I don't even remember what we talked about. He went on about the progress on the island. How tourism is on the rise, stuff like that, most of which I admit, I tuned out."

"I would too," I said.

"I do remember that he offered his sympathies to me. It was a little awkward, the way he did it. Very official."

I just nodded.

"What is your interest in Mr. Denton?" she asked.

"Like I said, I just met him earlier today. I guess I'm curious, that's all."

She was pensive for a moment. I watched as she sipped her drink, her eyes down.

"You said goodbye to your daughter?" she asked.

"This morning," I said.

"I bet that was hard for you."

I didn't know what to say to that. This was a woman who lost her daughter. My goodbye to Kasie was nothing compared to that. She sensed what was going through my mind and her expression changed.

"Oh, I didn't mean to go there. Really I didn't. I'm sorry," she said.

I forced a smile. "You have absolutely nothing to be sorry about," I said. "It was hard, but I'll see her later in the summer when I head back to New York for a week."

"Is she your only child?"

"I have a son. He's a couple of years younger. I'm hoping he can make the trip down here next year."

She smiled and stirred her drink. Clayton placed the Corn 'n' Oil in front of me. "Enjoy, Len."

"Thank you, Clayton." I turned to Marcia Gould and lifted the highball glass. "Cheers and thank you for inviting me."

She lifted hers and both of us sipped the drink, but I couldn't take my eyes off those lips. Was I embarrassing myself? Maybe, but there comes a point when a man just doesn't care.

"It's my pleasure, Len," she said. "I enjoyed talking to your daughter on the flight over, and when I saw the two of you on the beach, it made me smile and think that you must be a good father and a good guy. A man I would like to get to know better."

I took another sip. "I have my doubts about the father thing," I said. "How good a father can I really be when I see my kids so infrequently? No, I have lots of guilt about all that."

"You shouldn't. Life takes all sorts of turns. We all do our best. So enough of that. I don't want any guilt or feelings of self-doubt to ruin our time. Deal?"

"Yeah, okay, it's a deal," I said, but wasn't sure I could keep that agreement. I wanted to ask her about her daughter. I wanted to know more about what she was really doing on St. Pierre. If her mother was aware of her life and that she was working for a "gotcha" website. If she knew the details of what Big Tree told me about the night she died. For the moment, though, I would keep that deal. I would just have to find the right opportunity to ask those questions.

Clayton brought out a basket of fried cassava sticks sprinkled with a spicy salt to accompany our drinks. I ended up eating most of them, and Marcia Gould noticed. "I think you're hungry," she said.

"That obvious, huh?"

"Uh-huh." She gave me a little smile and slid off the stool. "Let's go eat."

Clayton, who had been nosily watching our interaction from behind the bar, quickly came around to escort us to our table.

"I'll meet you there, Len. I just want to freshen up in the ladies' room," Marica said.

From where I stood, she needed no freshening, but I nodded as Clayton led me to a table in the outdoor dining area that was covered by a canopy. We were seated at the edge of the restaurant where we could see the glow from the moon on the water and hear the sea as it quietly lapped against the shore.

I watched as she made her way to our table. She smiled as she sat.

"Do you still play tennis?" I asked and then realized she never told me that she played tennis.

She peered at me with a knowing grin. "Hmmm, have you done a background check on me, Len?"

"How could I not? I was curious after you were so nice to reach out to me. I just couldn't help myself."

"Well that makes two of us," she said.

So that was it. She knew about my past in New York. She knew what I did that June morning. I wondered if that was her real motive to have dinner with me. Or maybe she knew something else about me; that I was trying to help free the man she thought did something to her daughter. I tried not to think that she had other motives for this dinner — like I did. I hoped she was sincere about what she said earlier, that I looked like a good guy and a good father. Either way, here I was, and I wasn't complaining.

"As for your question about tennis, yes, I still play but not competitively. It keeps me in shape along with my other activities. I've hit with the pro at the Lime House a few times since I've been here. Do you play?"

"Me? No. Never," I blurted out.

She laughed. "Was it such an unusual question?"

"I didn't mean it that way," I said. "Growing up in the Bronx, we played baseball, basketball and some football too. Tennis wasn't part of our world. And that's not a knock. We put all the Grand Slam matches on the televisions at the bar."

"What do you do now? You...look very fit for..." She stopped herself.

"For my age?"

"No, I didn't say that. Don't put words in my mouth. And you aren't that much older than I am," she said.

I wasn't sure how old she was, but there was no doubt, even though she had a daughter older than mine, that I was her senior by more than a few years.

"Take out the 'very' and maybe you'd be a little more accurate describing my physical condition, Marcia," I said.

"I can use 'very' if I want to. And you can't make me take it away." She smiled playfully. I could see those freckles across her cheek. And that grin. I was quickly reminded of her daughter, and how she had looked at me in almost an identical way.

"Who am I to stop you? Anyway, these days I do some martial

arts. I swim and scuba dive when I can. But that's about it."

"Martial arts? Interesting." Her eyes were dancing on me now, and I could feel them in places I hadn't felt in too long. I wasn't sure if it was a good thing or bad, but the spell was immediately broken when Tito, in his chef's whites, ambled over to our table. Tall and beefy with shaggy dark hair, thick tattooed forearms, a bushy black moustache and a three-day old beard, he held a small platter of golden-brown fritters. He put the platter down and gave me a hearty hug.

"I always remember you crazy for my lambi fritters," Tito said in his heavy Spanish accent. "My compliments."

"Tito, I knew I could count on you." I turned to Marcia. "Have you had the chef's lambi fritters?"

"Maybe I have, if I knew what lambi was."

"In Key West and the Bahamas they call them conch fritters," I said.

"Then yes I have. But I don't believe I've ever had Tito's lambi fritters," she said.

"See, Len, ask and ye shall receive," Clayton said. "Now Tito has a special menu prepared for the two of you. We won't bother you further except to bring out your dinner and refill your wine glasses."

After I devoured most of the lambi fritters, Tito started us off with a marlin ceviche, followed by his version of pumpkin soup. The main course was coconut-milk-braised mahi-mahi garnished with crushed local cashews.

"I've eaten here three times and they never treated me like this, Len. A meal prepared by the chef, especially for you. Impressive. You must have some influence here."

"Hardly," I said. "I appreciate Tito's cooking, and a chef

always likes to hear that."

"So modest," she said, her eyes twinkling again.

"Well, maybe it has nothing to do with me. Maybe it's you they want to impress," I said.

"They don't have to worry about that. They already have," she said. "I love this place. I... just wish..."

Her expression darkened and she shook her head. I kept quiet for a moment. Her charms had too easily distracted me from the task at hand. I wasn't sure if that was done intentionally or, like her daughter, just came naturally.

"I'm sorry," she said.

"No need to apologize," I said. "I can't imagine it."

She nodded and wiped at her eyes. "When Dee's father died, she was barely a teenager. I tried so hard to shield her. To protect her from just about everything. She hated me for that. She didn't want protection. So she went the other way. She was a risk taker. Always. She pushed and pushed. I warned her, and that just made her seek out anything that might be dangerous. She thrived on the thrill of it."

"What do you mean dangerous?" I asked. She was opening up about her daughter without me even prompting her. This is what I came here for. I didn't want her to stop, yet I didn't want to push her away with too many questions. I had to be careful.

"It could be anything, Len. Traveling to places that weren't safe. War zones. Countries wracked by natural disasters. She used the excuse that she wanted to be a journalist. Or that she wanted to help those suffering, but it was not just about that. It was a high for her to be in the middle of the action. Close to real danger. She could never sit still. Even as a baby she was like that. And the men. God knows how many there were. She never had a real boyfriend, but the parade of lovers, most of them older than she; she knew she had a power over them. She used a lot of them to get things — trips, adventures, whatever she wanted. But I knew one day it would hurt her. You can't always play with fire and not get burned."

She covered her face with her hands. One of the waiters came and cleared our plates. The meal had been delicious, but now there was a sour taste to it all. I had many other questions, but I just couldn't ask them. It wasn't in me.

She took her hands off her face and laughed nervously. "And here I've ruined what was a lovely dinner."

"Not at all," I said. "It's been wonderful."

"Wonderful?" She looked at me. "Now that's bullshit, Len. Maybe we should just leave?"

"Yeah...sure," I muttered and then gestured to Clayton. He came over and I whispered to him that we needed to leave and that I would take care of the check later.

"No worries," he said.

"You better not have arranged to pay for this meal," Marcia said. "I invited you. This is my treat."

I held out my hands sheepishly. Clayton laughed. "I'll put it on your bill," he said to Marcia.

"Good." She rose from her seat and I followed.

We headed slowly through a narrow hallway to the lobby. A party of four, three men and a young woman, squeezed past us, I glanced at them quickly but kept my eyes focused on Marcia Gould as she walked in front of me. She stopped and turned as we got to the lobby.

I figured this was it. Dinner was done and it was time to say goodnight. I wasn't happy about that. There was much she hadn't told me. I wanted to find out more of what she knew about Rawle Johns, about what her daughter was doing here. But most of all, I didn't want to go because I truly enjoyed her company. She was fun, smart and she was beautiful. It had been a long time since I met someone with that combination.

"Thanks for inviting me, Marcia. It was as pleasant an evening as I've had in a very long time," I said.

She raised her eyebrows at me with surprise. "You're leaving me?"

Now it was my turn to be surprised. "No...well...I thought after..." I gestured with my hands, talking with them instead of my mouth, indicating that maybe after talking about her daughter back at the table that she might want to be alone. I was bad at this. It had been too long. My social skills had turned to shit. I felt like an idiot.

"You thought wrong. Your company is exactly what I need. You are a man I can talk to...to open up to. Not all men are like that, Len. And you do it in a natural way. How did that happen?" She lifted her chin up to look at me.

"When you tend bar as long as I have, that's a skill that either comes or doesn't. For me, listening came easily."

"Mmmmhmm." She kept smiling at me and I had to admit, though it was a beautiful, alluring smile, it was making me a little uneasy. "Let's take a walk on the beach," she said, but it was more like an order.

We walked outside through the lighted garden to Heaven's Beach. She stopped for a moment and took off her shoes, leaving them at the entrance to the beach. And then, with her body close to mine, we strolled across the crescent of sand.

"You must know I wasn't just teasing you earlier when I said

I checked up on you," she said.

"Yeah, I had a feeling you were."

She stopped to turn to face me. "Why did a man who did what you did, who saved so many people, who was brave in the face of danger, run away?"

"Don't believe everything you read, Marcia. I wasn't so brave."

"There's that modesty again."

She took my hand in hers. I was surprised by the gesture but didn't pull away.

"No...it's not modesty. It's the truth."

"Was it so bad, Len? Was what happened on that day so harrowing it made you leave your family and live alone here? You were a hero. All the reports said so."

She squeezed my hand now, keeping her eyes on mine. The word *hero* made me cringe. I did not want our conversation to be about me. I did not want to think about my past. As she talked, as she asked those questions, I could feel something building inside me.

"They honored you. I read all about it. You went into the smoke...you risked your life to save them."

Stop, I thought to myself. No more talk. Please.

"And the pain you must have endured, mentally," she continued. "Trauma, I know, can make you do things you never thought you would do."

No more. I couldn't listen to what she was saying. I had to stop her. The look I gave her made her mouth close for a moment. And then I did what I needed to do. What I had to do. I took her into my arms. I stopped those words with my lips on hers, devouring them, greedy for them. I held her tight, pulling her to my chest. I didn't care if she fought to get out of my grasp and ran shrieking to the hotel. I didn't care if my reputation was ruined on the island. I couldn't stop now. But she didn't pull away. She didn't shriek. She took my lips as hungrily as I did, her need equal to mine. She wrapped her arms around my neck, her fingertips digging into my back as we kissed.

My hands were moving now, pressing into her, caressing her curves until my hands drifted down to her bare thighs. I didn't care if she slapped my hand away. It was too late. Any reason or sense of decorum was gone. I was acting purely on impulse. As my hand gripped her thigh, I felt her hand cover mine. I looked into her eyes as she guided my hand up her thigh and under her dress. She took her hand off mine there and wrapped her arms around my neck again. My hand captured the swell of her bottom and squeezed.

"God, yes, Len," she cried, and then moaned into my mouth.

I pushed her back against the thick trunk of a palm tree, pinning her with the weight of my body. She was almost panting now as she fumbled furiously with my pants. I pushed down whatever it was she was wearing under her dress and she quickly lifted her leg, curling it around my hips, pulling her tighter to me. She gasped as I entered her. And then she moved her hips as I moved mine. I could feel her nails dig in even deeper, practically drawing blood through my shirt. I could see her eyes staring straight up at the dark sky and the stars above as I drove my hips into her. I held tight inside her as a low growl I couldn't control escaped my lips. She trembled, gasped loudly and held tight, her panting subsiding. And then slowly she let the leg that had been clamped around my hips back down to the sand.

I pulled away now, bringing her gently off the palm tree. She took my face in her hands and kissed me tenderly. She smiled as she straightened her dress and adjusted what had fallen to her ankles. I tugged up my pants. Locking her arm in mine we started to walk back to the hotel without a word. There wasn't anything to say at that moment. We were about to enter into the lobby when she stopped.

"Oh...Len...I forgot my shoes," she said.

"I'll get them," I volunteered, and headed back to where she had taken them off before we got onto the beach. I found them—white sandals with two-inch heels and slender little straps. I picked them up and walked back to the hotel. She was not outside where I had left her. I went into the lobby holding the shoes by their straps. A tall thin man behind the reception desk saw me holding the shoes.

"Mrs. Gould is in the Hibiscus Room, up the stairs, first door on the left," he said to me.

I looked at him warily.

"She's expecting you," he said with a smile and a nod.

"Len Buonfiglio?" I heard someone else say just as I was about to head up the steps. I turned and saw a slight man standing in the hallway, wearing beige khakis and a coral-colored polo shirt. I stopped. "We met last week," he said, smiling crookedly.

I recognized the face. I think he was someone who came into the bar but had no idea of his name. I looked at the elegant woman's shoes I was holding. He looked at them too and smiled that odd smile.

"Eric Dunn," he said.

"Yeah?" I mumbled. The name meant nothing to me. And I was distracted and anxious to get up those steps.

"I'm sorry, you're busy. Maybe I'll catch you later." He grinned as if he knew exactly where I was going and what I was about to do.

"Okay, sure," I said with a nod and then quickly turned away from him and headed up the steps.

I knocked on the door labeled "Hibiscus."

"It's open," I heard her say from inside the room.

I opened the door tentatively. Though I had been to the Bougainvillea several times, I had never been inside a guest room. The room was spacious and filled with rare antique furniture. But the only furniture I was really concerned with at that moment was the four-poster queen bed, not so much for its historic charm, but for the fact that Marcia Gould was sitting up in the bed, a white sheet barely covering her otherwise naked body.

"Thanks for getting the shoes," she said. "Now, close the door please. I think that walk on the beach was fun, but it's time we got even better acquainted, don't you?"

She would get no argument from me on that. She smiled and let the sheet fall from her body.

I closed the door and then dropped her shoes to the floor.

The getting-acquainted process was a lengthy one. There were many things to learn about each other, and we both took the time to make sure we were careful and neglected nothing. After one of those interludes, with her body draped over mine but her eyes looking away, she asked me if was true that I went to see Rawle Johns. She caressed my chest as she waited for my answer. So she did know. Still, was that really her only motivation for all this, I wondered?

"I did," I said.

She looked hard into my eyes. "Why?"

"His mother asked me to," I said.

"Why would she do that, Len?"

I took a breath. None of this was on my mind. For the few glorious hours with her in this four-poster bed I had forgotten all the bad stuff that was swirling around my life. Now it was back.

"She thinks I can help him," I finally said. "She doesn't think he did what they say he did. She doesn't want to lose him."

She kept her eyes on me and continued to caress my chest. "You mean, like I lost my daughter?" Her nails were dragging deeper.

"No, nothing like that," I muttered.

"You can't help him, you know. He killed her, Len. He is where he belongs. And I hope he stays there until he dies." She said it calmly, but with a firm finality.

I wanted to ask her how she knew that. I wanted to know what made her so sure. But she wouldn't let me. She replaced those fingers with her lips on my chest. As those lips moved downward over my ribcage and then lower, my ability to speak was stifled. She stopped her lips for only a moment to look up at me and shake her head slowly. "You can't help him," she whispered. "Don't help him."

I looked back at her and then she lowered her head once more. There were no words spoken after that.

Soon after, I could hear her soft snoring as she lay asleep against me. I knew my body was tired, but my mind was wide awake. Was this all a set-up just to dissuade me from digging further into the true cause of her daughter's death? Was she using me for information — kind of like how I was using her? My head was spinning. I really didn't know what to think.

It took awhile but I did sleep, and when I opened my eyes, I could see through the shades of her room that it was light out. Her arm was still draped across my chest. I eased out from under it and made my way to the bathroom. I washed up and wondered if I should leave or stay. I knew what I wanted to do, but I had much that I needed to get done.

I was wiping the water from my face when I heard a cry from the bedroom. I quickly opened the door. She was sitting up now. Her hands were covering her face. Her sobs were loud through the hands.

"What happened? What's wrong?" I asked her.

She just shook her head and sobbed. Her phone was on the bed next to her.

"What is it?"

She took her hands away from her face. Her eyes were red, wet with tears. But through the tears was an angry scowl. "Did you do this?"

I had no idea what she was talking about. "Do what?"

She shook her head. "They let him out," she sobbed. "They let my daughter's killer free!

And then she covered her eyes again.

I tried to comfort her. I tried to convince her that I did nothing but listen to the man. I had no power to get him out of custody. She wasn't having it. "Just leave," she said, no longer even looking at me.

24

In the Jeep, I turned my phone back on. When it booted up there were a series of pings. Most were texts from Tubby telling me what I now knew about Big Tree. There were also voice mails from local numbers I didn't recognize. I didn't bother to listen to any of them. I wanted to get home.

I thought about what happened. How Marcia Gould had accused me of freeing Big Tree. His attorney had said that they could not hold him much longer on such flimsy evidence. But I didn't have the confidence that Maurice Dennard was capable of getting him out. He didn't impress me as particularly skilled or connected enough to pull that off.

"All you need is the right person to whisper to a magistrate." That was what Edward Denton had told me just yesterday afternoon. And now Big Tree was free.

He was offering his help without saying it straight out. He realized I would figure it out. And now, I believed, he wanted something in return for his gesture.

When I pulled up to my house, I saw Ezran Johns sitting on the front step of my doorway. The two dogs were lying by his side. I noticed a Dutch pot on the ground between his legs where he sat. He stood up and picked up the Dutch pot when he saw me heading toward him.

"Ezran, no school?"

"School out, sir," he said.

The dogs got up also when they heard my voice. They wagged their tails a little and circled me. "These guys didn't bother you, did they?"

"No, sir, but last time I here there were three?"

I nodded.

He waited for an explanation.

"One ran off," I lied.

He knew I was lying and looked at me. "I think these two like me now," he finally said.

"They always liked you, Ezran. They just didn't get a chance to really know you."

His mouth fell open at that as if he never thought of such a thing.

"What's that you got."

"My Grandma tell me you forgot the browning chicken stew she make for you the other day. She say to tell you the stew gets better after a day or two in the pot."

"Yeah, I've heard that," I said.

I held the door open for him. He entered tentatively. I told him to put the pot on the kitchen counter. He did it and then headed back to the door.

"Your Pa's at home?"

He nodded.

"How is he?"

He just shrugged and said nothing.

"You tell him if he needs to talk to me or anything, to let me know, okay?"

"Yes, sir," he mumbled.

He stood there as if he wanted to tell me something else; like he really didn't want to leave. And then he pushed through the screen door and walked down the hill. I watched him. He was moving slowly. He didn't seem happy that his father had returned.

I went back into the kitchen and put the pot on the stove. I could smell the spices as soon as I opened the lid of the pot. Did this mean my work for Mrs. Johns was over? Her son was home. Not that I had anything to do with it. But maybe I did. What more was there to do?

I poured myself a cold glass of water and plopped down on the chair facing the big window overlooking the ocean. I drank down the water and then made my way to my bathroom for a long shower before heading out to the bar.

"Did you know Denton owned that boat where those men were staying?" I said to Tubby.

I was sitting at a table at the Sporting Place. Tubby was sitting across from me. It was a Friday afternoon. Both of us should have been behind the bar working. Mike was handling things there, still helping out as per our agreement. This would have been the last day with Kasie before she went back. Technically, I was still on vacation.

"What you mean, Mr. Len?" Tubby tilted his head as he looked at me.

The stools at the bar were all occupied. The end-of-the-work-week crowd was beginning to filter in. Soon both of us would have to get up and help Mike.

"*ED's Folly* was the name of the boat, right?"

"I see that, yes."

"E...D. Edward Denton," I spelled it out for him.

"Oh, so you know that for sure?"

I shrugged. "What? You don't think I'm right?"

"E-D could mean anyone, Mr. Len. Many E-D's in this world."

"Yeah, but Denton is involved in this. After that visit yesterday, he made it pretty obvious."

"He may be involved, but that not mean the boat belong to him and those men work for him. I don't know the man. He have money, yes. I know he live in a nice house over in St. Francois where the other rich people live, but I don't know about a boat."

"Can someone you know find out if he does have a boat?"

Tubby smiled and sipped from a small bottle of Ting, a Jamaican grapefruit soda popular all over the Caribbean.

"You asking me to help you?"

"I didn't think I had to ask."

"You always say you don't want my help, but now my foot hurt from helping you the other day. You want my help, you just ask. Why play games?"

"What games?" I wasn't in the mood for a busting of balls. I got up from the table and wandered behind the bar. Tubby followed. I began to open bottles of beer for the crowd that was building while Tubby and Mike worked on making batches of rum punches, squeezing limes, opening up cans of tropical fruit juice, making sure we had plenty of bitters and simple syrup.

"Just 'cause you had a long night last night, no need to be short with me," Tubby said as he worked next to me behind the bar. "And I think I should see you smiling rather than that screw up face you wearing now after what I believe take place with that woman you see."

I thought about how we left it, her practically accusing me of turning loose who she thought was her daughter's killer. No, I wasn't smiling.

"Not good, Mr. Len?"

"She thinks I got Big Tree out. She came here to put him away for murder."

Tubby nodded. "I can see how that make it not so good."

"Yeah, well there were moments..."

"Keep those moments to yourself. Mike and I don't need that information," Tubby said.

"We don't?" Mike cracked from where he was working behind the bar.

"No we do not. That Mr. Len's business," Tubby said to Mike and then turned to me. "Those men gone and they won't come back. Big Tree back home with his family. So tell me why we looking for who own this boat now?"

"Denton got Big Tree out," I said. "And I think he did it because he wants something from me. I think it was him who sent those men to my house. To hurt me. To silence me over something I didn't even know about."

Tubby stopped what he was doing to stare at me. "Mr. Len, I think you need to go home and rest. You talking strange."

"See, that's why I keep this stuff inside, Tubby. You calling me strange. Anyway, I'm out," I said.

I left Tubby and Mike to handle the bar. I got in my Jeep, but instead of driving home, I headed to the southern tip of the island and the community known as St. Francois. A collection of modern, spacious villas and homes built over a decade ago, St. Francois was a haven for foreigners, Europeans predominantly, mostly from the U.K., looking for a Caribbean hideaway or investment. The homes were occupied usually for about two weeks out of the year by the owners and rented the rest of the year. I knew that a few of the homes were owned by wealthy local residents, but until Tubby told me, I didn't know Edward Denton was one of them.

The community was on an incline overlooking the Caribbean. Some of the amenities of living in St. Francois included twenty-four hour security, tennis courts, swimming pools, a fitness club, a supermarket, a pharmacy and an Italian restaurant. The security, tennis courts, pools and fitness club were accessible only to homeowners who paid monthly dues to use the facilities.

I didn't know which house was Edward Denton's. There were a couple of names outside the homes, but I doubted I would find Denton among them. I slowly cruised the neighborhood, peering at the gated entrances, imagining that one of them was his. I knew he held a powerful position in the St Pierre government, but didn't think the income from his civil service job would be enough to own one of these multimillion-dollar homes. Not to mention that impressive yacht. Denton had to be making money from other sources to be able to live this large in St. Pierre. I wondered if how he got his money was connected to any of this. I wasn't that savvy about the world and its workings, but I knew that the best way to get the goods on a bad guy was to follow the money. Wasn't that how they got John Gotti? Or was it Al Capone? The problem was, I had no clue how to follow money, and I didn't think I would start anytime soon.

As I drove, looking at the homes from the street, I heard a beeping sound behind me. I glanced into my rear-view mirror to see what looked like a battery-operated Smart car on my tail. The car was dark blue and had flashing yellow lights on top. I was being pulled over.

A man in a security guard's uniform, dark-blue trousers and a matching short-sleeve dress shirt got out of the car and made his way to my Jeep. I waited in the car. I had put the top back on but I had my windows open. He bent down to my open window and smiled.

"Mr. Len from the place on Windy Hill, correct?"

"That's me," I said.

"I recognize the Jeep and I recognize you," he said. "You see me at your place when the Windies play against Jamaica. Devin Cooley." He offered me his right hand while he held a clipboard in his left. I shook it.

"Devin, hi," I said, even though I did not remember him and certainly not his name. I did remember the crowd we had at the Sporting Place for that cricket match about a month ago. The bar was packed and left very happy when the Windward Islands team defeated Jamaica. Though I didn't have the rooting interest everyone else did, I was happy too. We did very well that day.

"Mr. Len, I have to ask because I spot you driving through St. Francois. Do you have business here with one of the residents? Or maybe you are lost?"

I thought for a moment about what to say to him. I knew he wasn't there to fine or report me. He was trying to help.

"Actually, Devin, a little of both. I don't actually have business with one of your residents, but I was looking for the home of Mr. Edward Denton," I said.

Now it was his turn to think for a moment.

"Is Mr. Denton expecting you?"

"No...I thought I might pop in and say hello to him." I smiled knowing that would get me nowhere, but I had other motives now.

He looked at me curiously. "Mr. Len, I'm very sorry. I can't direct you to his home unless he is expecting you. Would you like me to contact him to see if he is home and tell him you would like to see him?"

I wasn't prepared in any way for a confrontation, if that's what would occur, but I was impatient. I was ready for answers.

"Sure, that would be helpful."

I watched him scroll through the notepad he held. When he found Denton's number, he dialed it into one of those talkabout cell phones that, I guessed, was connected to an intercom system for all the homes. I could hear continuous ringing coming from the phone. Finally he clicked it off.

"Mr. Denton must not be at his home," he said. "I can leave a message at his residence that you were here to see him. Would that be acceptable?"

"Perfect," I said.

"I'll do that, Mr. Len. West Indies play the Pakis in the Asia Cup next month. Your place where I be to view that match for sure."

"We'll have it on all the screens, Devin."

He went back to his Smart car and I drove out of St. Francois. It was just a matter of time now before I would hear from Denton.

25

While I waited for the chicken stew to warm on the stove, I called Marcia Gould. As I dialed her number, I remembered her rage. How she accused me of helping to free the man who she believed murdered her daughter. Maybe I was pushing things by calling her. I wanted to make it right if I could.

But the only voice I got was her recorded message saying she was not available to answer the phone. When the tone rang signaling for me to speak, I stuttered out what I had prepared to say — that I enjoyed her company, that I enjoyed the night and would like to talk with her again. And then I didn't know what else to say, so I just awkwardly ended the call.

I put the phone on the kitchen table and dished out warm rice, the browned stew chicken and a few of those dumplings Mrs. Johns promised onto a plate. I carried it to the kitchen table and was about to shovel a serious portion into my mouth when my phone rang. I looked at the number hoping it was

Marcia Gould's, but it wasn't. It was a local number. I picked up the phone and put it to my ear.

"Buonfiglio, you don't return my calls?"

I tried to recognize the voice but couldn't put a face to it. "Who's this?"

"Edward Denton," he said.

I should have known. "What calls are you talking about?"

"Don't you check your voice mails? I left two messages for you. And now I hear you were thinking of paying me an unannounced visit to my home. It seems we are both trying to get in touch but something is preventing it. I hope it's not fate."

"Fate? You don't believe in that, do you?"

He chuckled. "I actually do, but that's a discussion for another time. Can we talk man to man?"

"Aren't we doing that now?" I said, knowing what he really meant.

"You're presence is preferred, Buonfiglio. I'd like to show you some things if you can come over here now."

"Your house?"

"No, I'm still at the office. It would be better here."

"I was just sitting down to eat," I said. "Homemade chicken stew with dumplings that's really good." I don't know why I had to tell him that, but I thought I should. Maybe it was to sound cool, unhurried. I really did want to see him immediately, but I didn't want him to know that.

"I'm not a man to deprive another of his mealtime," Denton said. "You eat that chicken stew and then come over. There are things I can do until then."

"I can be there in an hour," I said. "Where is the office?"

"The Green building. On Front Street. Do you know it?"

The Green building. So those men laying low were there with him before coming to me. "Of course, everyone knows the Green building," I said.

"That they do. I'm on the top floor. Call me when you arrive and I'll buzz the door open. The building is closed otherwise."

"I'll do that," I said. "See you within the hour."

I finished the plate of the stew and picked up the phone again. I looked at the voice mail I hadn't listened to. I pressed the icon on the phone and listened.

"I just wanted to let you know that the man you have been helping is free," Denton said in the voice message. "The magistrate must have been persuaded to release him. Please call me at this number when you get this message. Edward Denton."

The second voice mail was also from Denton and in it he sounded impatient. "Denton here. Still waiting for your call. Get back to me ASAP please."

I put the phone down. He wanted to meet at the Green building. It was after hours. Was I walking right into a trap? I thought about calling Tubby, that maybe I needed some backup, and then decided against it. This was the minister of tourism I was going to see, not some hired thug. Still, I had to be careful. I needed to have some sort of idea of what I was going to say to him. I had to have a plan. But I wasn't much of a planner. Maybe I could just improvise, go with my instincts. But I wasn't very good at improvisation, either. As far as my instincts went, I figured I was batting well under .500. So where did that leave me?

I started out to the Jeep and then took a detour, walking to the back of the house. I went to my tool storage bin and opened it. There were my shovels and garden tools. My cutlass was in there too. But I was looking for something else. I reached in and picked up the box I had placed in the bin a few days ago. I could feel the heft of it. I didn't need to open the box to know the guns were still in there. I hadn't fired a gun since my time in the Marines. Though I learned how to handle a variety of firearms back then, the experience didn't make me like them. And I still didn't like them. I put the box back, closed the storage bin and walked to my Jeep.

The only lights on in the Green building were on the top floor; the rest of the structure was dark. I parked and went to the building's front entrance. I don't know why, but I pulled the door to see if it would open, even though I was sure it was locked. I dialed the number Denton had called me from earlier. It rang for what seemed like a long time. I was about to hang up when he picked up. "Buonfiglio?" His voice sounded out of breath.

"Downstairs," I said.

"Give me a moment," he said.

I had my hand on the door handle. When I heard the buzz, I entered and walked to the elevator. I pushed the button for the top floor, the sixth. When the elevator stopped and the doors opened, I looked both ways down the hall. I saw lights on to my right and headed in that direction.

The building was quite modern by St. Pierre standards. The offices were bordered by glass partitions. From what I could tell in the dim light, very few of them were occupied. Down the hall and to my left was what looked like a spacious meeting room. Instead of a conference table and chairs, the room was equipped like a gym. There were a couple of heavy bags in one corner, exercise mats on the floor, a row of shelved dumbbells with jump ropes on hooks, and a speed bag mounted from the ceiling.

"Here you are," Denton said as I stared into the make-shift gym.

I turned to see him coming down the hall toward me. He was wearing workout shorts and a tank top and had a towel draped around his neck. As he got closer I noticed that his chest, arms and neck were glistening with sweat. My first observation when we met at the bar was correct. The man was chiseled. I knew we were in the same age range, and I had been trying very hard to keep away what age was making almost impossible to keep away. I thought I was doing a good job of it, but not compared to Denton. I was almost envious. Check that, I *was* envious.

"I thought I'd get in a workout while waiting for you," he said as he approached.

"Not a bad little gym you've put together here," I said.

He shrugged. "We have the space," he said. "We still haven't occupied the building as we would have liked, so until then...why not?"

"Yeah, why not," I said. "And it looks like you have put in the time."

"Once my days of competing ended, I could have gone either way. To go to fat like so many ex-athletes, or not to go to fat. To continue with the lifestyle that got me to that elite level, or to just slow down and not push myself so hard. To take life nice and easy."

"I guess I know which path you chose," I said.

"Mr. Buonfiglio, it looks like you also take care of yourself. You are always welcome to work out here. I hear you have studied the martial arts," he said, looking me over.

"Some, yeah."

He grinned. "Whatever it takes to keep us in shape, right? We only have one body. Why abuse it?

I didn't bother to answer that. I really wasn't there to get into a discussion about our healthy lifestyles.

"So what is so urgent that you have me here in your offices after hours?" I said.

"I can ask the same thing, Mr. Buonfiglio. What makes a man go searching for me in my own neighborhood?"

"I asked first," I said.

He smiled and wiped his face with the towel. "Follow me."

I did as told and followed him down the hall to another office. This one was spacious and filled with the usual glossy office furniture. There was a big cherry-wood desk, an ergonomic desk chair and two lush visitor chairs, while in a corner there was a brown leather couch and a glass-topped coffee table. The walls were decorated with photos of Denton with his family, in formal attire and posing with dignitaries, a framed diploma from the London School of Economics and a few oldies of him in his boxing days, including the same one I saw online where he was holding the championship belt he earned for his win in Las Vegas in 1994.

He went to a small refrigerator tucked under a bookshelf and pulled out a bottle of water.

"Do you want something to drink, Buonfiglio? I have beer."

I shook my head. "I'm good."

He drank from the bottle and then put it down on the desk.

"Johns is free. That's good news, correct?"

I looked at him. "I guess it is. They really didn't have much to hold him."

"No. That is what I told the magistrate."

He stared at me after that just to make it clear that it was he who made it happen.

"And why did you tell the judge that?"

He shifted a little in that ergonomic desk chair and took another sip of his water. "Johns has always been a good man. He has been a superb employee for us. I wanted to be there for him."

"Yeah, but what if he is guilty? What if he really killed the girl?"

"Guilty?" He hesitated at that questions. "Do you think that, Mr. Buonfiglio?"

I didn't answer. "I asked you," I said.

He shook his head. "We don't know that, and most likely we never will. Only God will know the truth of what happened to that girl that night."

"Oh really?"

"I thought you would be pleased that he was free. You were helping his mother, from what I hear. You went to talk to him."

"Yes, I talked to him. He told me his story." I didn't want to tell him more than that. I didn't want him to think I wanted his help or that I owed him anything for what he did.

He knew I was holding back on him but didn't push. He got up from his desk. I watched him walk to a wooden cabinet. He took his keys out of his pocket and used one to open it. "I want to show you something very special, Mr. Buonfiglio."

"Special? This must be my lucky day," I said. I was waiting for the opportunity to confront him on those men. I wasn't in the mood for special.

"It just might be," he said. "I told you. You are a forward thinker. A visionary. We need more progressive entrepreneurs like you on St. Pierre."

"I'm no visionary. I just own a sports bar on the island."

"Don't sell yourself short, Buonfiglio. You are more than that and you know it."

He bent over and pulled out a folder from one of the drawers he just unlocked and brought it back to the desk. "What I'm going to show you is still unofficial and needs to remain just between us. Do you understand?"

I looked at him but didn't answer. He didn't seem to care that I didn't respond. He spread out a large poster board onto his desk featuring a rendering of a property. I bent over the desk for a closer look.

"What's this?"

"The future of St. Pierre," he said.

"Looks like something else to me," I said. "Is it a resort?"

"That's right, Buonfiglio. A resort like nothing we've ever had here before: two hundred and twenty state-of-the-art rooms, restaurants, bars, a casino," he said.

That was 170 more rooms than the Lime House, the largest hotel on the island. "That's a lot of rooms," I said. "Isn't that a little too big for us here?"

"We will be able to handle it," he said. "The research has been done. A project like this will bring much needed revenue to the island along with many jobs."

St. Pierre was not a wealthy island. In my experience here, though formal employment was low, people worked. There was little vagrancy or hunger or lack of basic goods, and health care was not an issue. If one did not have a job, per se, he or she worked the land of whatever their small plot was growing enough of to offset whatever else might be needed. St. Pierre was not an impoverished place, but I knew if there were higher-paying jobs with actual benefits and chances for growth, those jobs would be welcome. More and more young adults were leaving the island for better opportunities abroad. It was a constant concern among the people here, that their numbers were dwindling. Maybe his project and the increased tourism it would bring would keep some of those young people at home.

"Take a look at this, Buonfiglio," he said. He pointed to a semi-circle of what looked like a dock. "Overwater cabanas. They'll even have glass bottoms so you can see the reef below your room. These rooms will be priced at a premium. The developer envisions the resort to be a more upscale version of the Sandals brand."

"Sounds impressive, Denton. And where would this development be located?"

He folded up the poster board and placed it back in the file. "We have so much undeveloped beachfront in the north," he said. "It's time we use that land rather than let it just sit there untouched."

"The north?"

He nodded.

"Where?"

He studied me for a moment as if he was hesitant to say.

"Laborie," he finally said.

I realized immediately why he was being hesitant.

"That's a fishing village."

"Yes, but we have plenty of fishing here," he said. "And the people living there will be taken care of and relocated."

I listened to him, but I was thinking about something else. I remembered standing with Tubby overlooking Laborie and staring down at that million-dollar yacht. Right around the bend was Coral Beach where my daughter and I snorkeled. She was nipped by a damselfish. A young family offered us papaya. Turtles nested on that beach.

And then I remembered the two men who were wandering the beach carrying electronic tablets. Men in suits. Now I understood why they were there. They were surveying the beach.

"Does this project include Coral Beach?" I asked, even though I was sure of his answer.

"That would be part of the resort yes. I know the sand is black, volcanic; that won't work with the clientele we hope to attract, but we can change that. We can bring in fine white sand."

"White sand?" I looked at him. "And the reef?"

He smiled. "Never worry about the reef, Mr. Buonfiglio. A study has been done to make sure that it will be protected throughout the construction of the project and that there will be no damage whatsoever to it. I've seen the study. It is genuine. A conservation crew from the States was hired to determine the environmental impact of the project. They gave it the green light. Really, I would never approve of a project that could harm any of the natural treasures we have here on St. Pierre. If they are destroyed, we lose so much of what makes our island so special. My participation in the project is contingent on that. So no worries, Mr. Buonfiglio. No harm will be done to our precious resources."

I didn't know much about the impact on the environment that large resorts had, but I couldn't believe that a project of this magnitude wouldn't damage that reef — not to mention the fishing, the wildlife and the area's overall ecosystem. There was a strong conservation society on the island; how did this get by them? And I knew there had to be a multitude of permits and licenses to allow construction. No wonder he was keeping this under wraps.

It was my turn to study him now. To see if he was bullshitting me. If he really meant what he said.

"How come I haven't heard anything about this until now?" I asked. "A project this ambitious, not even a rumor?"

"Those who know about it are very few, Buonfiglio. We kept it that way just for the reason you mentioned, that the more who know, the better chance that false rumors circulate."

"How far along are you with it?"

"There are just a few small details that need to be worked out before we can go ahead and announce the project and break ground. This will be an economic boon for our island. It will make us the go-to destination in the region. And it's about time."

I didn't like the sound of that. I didn't want to live in a go-to destination. But that was me. Maybe this was what was needed? Maybe this was wanted by more people than I thought.

"So I get to hear about this in advance because I'm a visionary," I said.

He beamed again. "That, and I'd like to make you a proposal. The developer has also heard of your success here and wanted me to personally present his offer to you."

"Oh, now it's an offer?"

He nodded.

"Who is this developer? And how does he know about my so-called success here?"

"I'd rather not divulge that at this time," he said. "Just know that he is a high-level officer in a very successful world-renowned corporation that is behind this project. If they are making you an offer, you should seriously consider it, believe me."

"What are they offering?"

"As I said, the resort will have multiple restaurants and bars. The developer would like you to run one of those bars as an extension of your Sporting Place on Windy Hill. You can franchise the name and have complete control of how it is operated within the resort. The developer will partner with you in a very generous split of profits, while all construction and initial expenses will be covered by them. You will be creating your own brand, Mr. Buonfiglio."

I thought about what he just said to me. That was what he was intimating when he visited the bar the other day and asked if I was open to expansion. I didn't know what he meant then. I did now. But it was all bullshit and I knew it.

"That is a very generous offer," I said. "But I find it hard to believe that my modest place could attract the interest of who you claim is a major player in the hotel industry. The Sporting Place is no Margaritaville."

He laughed. "You did say that this was your lucky day, Buonfiglio. Maybe it really is. Can I tell them you are interested? Or better, can I tell them that you are sold on the idea? It would be best if we could give them a definitive answer as soon as possible. They have others in mind for the space if you deliberate too long."

I stretched out my legs a bit as I sat there. He wasn't making me an offer. He was bribing me. In reality this was an offer to shut me up. I didn't believe there was a major developer at all. This project could be nothing more than a fantasy. But then I remembered the men in suits. I remember what Craig Frost was hinting at, how it would be a shame if St. Pierre succumbed to big-time tourism. I had to find a new tact to get to him. He was dirty. He had those men come after me. After my daughter.

I couldn't let that go. It wasn't just about false rumors that the project was top secret. There was something else he was hiding.

"Did you know I had three dogs, Denton?"

He shifted a bit, his expression changing. "Dogs? No. What does this have to do with what I've just presented to you?"

"I only have two dogs now," I said. "One of my dogs was killed not too long ago. Someone wrapped a rope around the dog's neck and hung her from a tree. Why would someone do such a thing?"

He stared at me but said nothing. He tapped his fingers on the desk. "Mr. Buonfiglio..."

I didn't let him finish. "And if that wasn't bad enough, my daughter, who is sixteen and who you knew was here visiting me this week, got to witness that. Should a sixteen-year-old girl have to see a dog hanging from a tree, Denton? You need to send people to intimidate me? To fuck with me? To harass my family?"

He genuinely looked surprised and sat up straighter. "I don't know what you are saying, Buonfiglio..."

"The men who killed my dog came to see me. They wanted to hurt me. Why?"

He shook his head. "This has nothing to do with me, sir, if that is what you are implying."

"Those men were staying on your boat. They were with a woman..."

"My boat?"

"I saw that woman and those men with Craig Frost."

"What woman. Who is Craig Frost? This is rubbish."

"I thought you would be slicker than this, Denton. You can't even lie like a pro," I said. "The man who was found dead at

253

LuJean's. I know you know what I'm talking about. I know fake news when I hear it. It's got to do with this project, doesn't it?"

"You think I'm lying?" He stood up from that beautiful ergonomic desk chair so he could look down at me. "You are talking nonsense. I've heard of some of your exploits here on St. Pierre. They mean nothing to me. I'm no low-class drug dealer. I'm no pepper-sauce pervert. It's best you leave now before you really get yourself hurt."

But I wasn't ready to leave. I could tell I was getting to him. That's what I wanted. It was part of my half-cocked plan to push him hard. But now I was improvising. I had to keep going at him.

"You knew that girl too, didn't you? Deanna Gould? The one who fell from Freedom Drop. Or was she pushed? Big Tree didn't do it, did he? Someone else did."

He moved from behind the desk to where I was sitting. He glared down at me. I got up from my chair so now it was I who was looking down at him. Being taller wasn't necessarily an advantage. In fact it could be a disadvantage. I didn't care.

"You better keep your mouth shut, Buonfiglio. I had you come here to offer you something most men would beg for, and you disrespect me. You talk like a crazy man now. Crazy talk gets a man hurt."

"You put your hands on that girl, didn't you, Denton? You couldn't resist her, could you?"

"You're mad," he spat. "You don't know what you are saying."

He was probably right about that, but that wasn't going to stop me. There was a method to my madness. I was going with my gut. I was winging it. I wanted to see what my crazy talk would get me. It was all I had, but if I was right, it would get me exactly what I wanted.

"Or was it something else? She knew about this little project, didn't she?" I got into his face as I spoke. "There's something rotten about it. Frost knew, and you had those men take care of him. You thought I knew, so you had them come and muzzle me. As you can see, I don't muzzle well. And now you're offering me a piece of your project." I shook my head at him.

"You think you have the answers? You have no idea," he spat.

I had to go at him harder. I couldn't let him turn this around.

"You wanted to shut that girl up just like you want to shut me up with this offer. She was a pretty girl, wasn't she? She was hard to resist. You put your hands on her, didn't you? What else did you do, Denton?"

I glared at him. He seemed confused. He didn't know how to react. One of his eyes was twitching. The things I was saying were just coming from me as if I had no control. The words could be rubbish, as he said. But from the way he was reacting, I didn't think so. I had him now. I knew I did.

"You pushed her off the Drop, didn't you? You used Johns? You set him up. You murdered that girl..."

Before I could say another word, he let loose with a rapid right jab. I was ready for it and ducked my head back enough so that the blow just grazed my cheek. This was exactly what I wanted. This is where I hoped it would go.

I moved back away from him. I needed space. He needed closer contact. He crouched into his fighting position, fists up, torso moving. I stood on my toes, my knees bent ready to react. He came forward and landed an uppercut into my ribs that shook me but didn't put me down. I expected more, frankly, from what I saw of him, but maybe now the power was gone and only the strong shell remained.

I came around with my fist and drove it into his temple. He staggered but I was sure he had been hit much harder in his day. His day, however, was long gone. He came back with a round-house right that I blocked easily. His moves were reflective of his age, slow and ponderous. But his age was also my age. Did that make us equals in this match? I didn't think so. Now, with my eyes focused on my target and not wanting this to go on much longer, I pivoted my hips, keeping my weight on my right leg. I then lifted my left leg up and as fast as I could, swung my foot through his face at his mouth, knocking him back onto his desk. His mouth was open and bloody, and he was breathing hard. He didn't get up.

I bent over him. He put his hands up in a gesture of surrender. He didn't have to. I wasn't going to hit him again. It was really just a glancing blow, but I had hit what I had aimed for. I put my fingers into his mouth. He flinched and closed his eyes, thinking I was going to hurt him. I searched through his mouth. I knew I had kicked out at least one tooth. That was the idea. That was the plan. I couldn't find it in there and then saw it on the desk. It was coated in blood. I took the tooth and put it in my pocket. I looked at him sprawled on his desk. His chest was heaving.

"You don't know what you're doing, Buonfiglio," he panted. "You've made a big mistake."

I tried not to hear him. I didn't want to hear him. I wanted out of there now. I wasn't happy with what I'd done, but it was over. I did what I needed to do. I had to live with that, as I'd lived with so much more.

I turned and hustled out of the office without another glance at what I left behind.

26

Sleep came in fits and starts that night. I kept going over what I had done. How I had acted. I had no real plan going in to see Denton. I just had my gut. When I was there, face to face with him, there were no doubts. I was confident I was doing the right thing. I was sure I had connected the dots. Even my bold accusation that he killed Deanna Gould felt right. She had dirt on him. He did it to protect himself. He had Frost killed for the same reason, and then tried to intimidate me with those men. When that didn't work, he made that gesture to get Big Tree out. He thought I would appreciate it. And then he went further by bribing me. He figured that if I came in on his plan, I wouldn't talk. All of it was to keep me quiet about what was really going on with the "future of St. Pierre."

I kept asking myself why else would he throw that first punch if what I was telling him didn't have some connection to the truth? Why else would he react so violently to what I accused him of?

But later, in the quiet dark of the night when the mind goes to those shadowy places, I wasn't so sure. I had no hard evidence to connect him to anything. What if I provoked a physical confrontation for nothing? What if he just didn't like what I was saying and the way I was saying it? What if I was all wrong? It wouldn't be the first time.

Those were the questions that kept me up most of the night. A strong dose of coffee and the bright morning sun helped clear my head a bit. I didn't know what to expect now. The blood-stained tooth was on my kitchen counter. Using a small pair of tongs, I placed it in a plastic bag and zip-locked it closed.

I had my coffee in my big chair facing the window that overlooked the Atlantic. I watched the sun rise high in the sky and waited. After what I did to Denton, something had to happen. I would hear from him again. Or I would hear from someone. But after awhile, with only the sound of the dogs padding around me, I heard nothing. I was impatient, and I was restless. I couldn't sit around all day waiting, so I got up, showered, dressed and went to work.

"Denton have no boat," Tubby said.

It was just after lunch, and the bar was almost empty. Herman Dark and Dwight Aldridge were at a table with open beer bottles in front of them. They were staring at a golf tournament taking place in a desert somewhere on the West Coast — California or Arizona; deserts all looked the same to me.

"What do you mean he has no boat?" I was on a barstool next to Tubby. He hadn't said anything to me when I came in. He looked me over curiously, as if he didn't know me. I wasn't sure what was going on with him.

"I say he have no boat. You ask me to find out if that *ED's Folly* a boat belong to Denton. I tell you I find out and I did. He have no boat. I check with my friend in the marina near St. Francois and also ask around other marinas. No one hear of a boat called *ED's Folly*. And no one ever see Denton in a boat at all."

I felt my stomach clench. I knew he wasn't wrong. If Tubby spread the word, the word usually came back to him and you could count on it being accurate. What else was I wrong about? I wondered. I thought about that feeling I had lying in bed trying to get to sleep; that I had made a big mistake.

"You go see him, didn't you?" Tubby said to me but wouldn't look me in the eye.

I couldn't answer.

He shook his head in disgust. I didn't have to answer him. He knew that whatever I did wasn't good.

I got up from the stool and moved behind the bar. I took a Carib from the refrigerator and opened it.

"What you do to him?"

I took a long gulp from the bottle; the beer felt good going down. He knew I wouldn't tell him.

So it wasn't his boat, I rationalized to myself. Maybe it was their boat. Those thugs. Or maybe they stole it. But that was hard to believe...it was a million-dollar yacht. Men like that who did the work they did didn't own million-dollar yachts. Still, that didn't mean I was wrong about those other things. That didn't mean those men weren't working for him.

I saw Herman Dark and his friend peering through the open door to the bar. They were looking at something outside. I watched as they both straightened in their chairs when McWilliams, in his uniform, strolled through the door followed by Sergeant Rodney Burris. Both policemen removed their hats as they entered.

McWilliams and Burris walked to the bar. Tubby got up and came around to stand next to me behind the bar.

"Thirsty, McWilliams?" I asked.

"I wouldn't mind a Malta," he said, referring to the non-alcoholic bitter brew that, for its supposed powers to invigorate a man, was popular on just about every island I had been to.

"What about you, Burris?"

"Coke, please," he said.

Tubby got them their drinks and opened the bottles.

"Let's have a chat, Mr. Buonfiglio," McWilliams said, indicating for me to come out from behind the bar.

I looked at Tubby and then took my Carib and went to join the supeintendent. Burris sat on a stool with his soft drink. Could Denton have called McWilliams and made a complaint against me? I couldn't believe it.

"The deck?"

"That would be best," McWilliams said, and the two of us headed outside. I guided him to a table with one of the umbrellas to keep us out of the midday sun.

He sat. I settled into a chair opposite him.

"What are we chatting about, McWilliams?"

"You were seen leaving the Green building last night," he said. "After hours."

I took another sip of the beer.

"Am I being followed?"

He didn't answer. He kept his big bloodshot eyes on me.

"Do you know, Mr. Buonfiglio, that it is the great honor of my life to serve St. Pierre as I do?"

"I have no doubt about that, McWilliams," I said, and I wasn't kidding. But why was he telling me this?

"Good. I appreciate your concern for the people of this island. I know you are trying to help, but I need you to stop. I need you to step away."

"Stop what?"

He shook his head. "You are a smart man. You can understand what I am telling you. I know you can. I respect you, Mr. Buonfiglio. I believe I deserve the same respect. So I ask you nicely now. Let me take care of my island."

I grazed my fingernail over the paper label on my beer bottle, shredding it from the glue that held it to the bottle. I was making a mess on the table as I thought about what he was telling me. He was waiting for me to acknowledge his request.

"You take care of St. Pierre, McWilliams," I said. "I won't prevent you from doing that. But you can understand a man taking care of himself and what is his, can't you?"

I heard him suck through his teeth at what I said. He knew he didn't get what he wanted out of me, but his demeanor remained as it always was: calm, assured, deliberate. He got up from his seat and left the barely touched bottle of Malta on the table.

I followed him back into the bar. He glanced at Burris, who abruptly left his stool. Both men put their hats back on and proceeded briskly out the front door

"You in trouble?" Tubby asked once we knew McWilliams was in his car and gone.

"What makes you think that, Tubby?"

"What you do to Denton? Did he summon the police?"

"No, Tubby," I said.

"Then why McWilliams want to have a chat with you in private like that?"

"McWilliams likes to send messages without really putting anything into the message. He makes you fill in the blanks."

"What he say in the blanks?"

"To stay out of his business," I said.

"That nothing new for McWilliams. He always tell you to stay out of his business."

"Yeah, but I'm not sure what his business is. He knew I was with Denton last night. They saw me leave his office."

"They either watching you or watching Denton. That much pretty clear to me," he said.

I thought about what Tubby just said. Did he also suspect Denton of something?

"You still not tell me what you did to that man." Tubby was pushing.

"That may not have been his boat, Tubby, but the man is dirty. He's involved in something that got people killed, not to mention what they did to my dog. They were going after Kasie."

"What he involved in?"

I thought about telling Tubby about the planned resort at Laborie. I knew that he was loyal to a fault. Why then did I think I should not let him in on what Denton told me? If I asked him to keep it between us, he would. But bad things were happening to those who knew about the project. I remembered how I felt when I heard the shot at my house the other night. I thought the man was shooting at Tubby, that he was there to risk his life to save mine. He protected my daughter, my family. And he also had a family, young children. No, this was too dangerous.

He sensed my trepidation because he had gotten plenty of it

from me before.

"We partners, Mr. Len. You hurt me when you don't let me into your business," he said.

Now he was going for my guilt. The more he knew me, the more he realized my weak spots. He was trying to make me feel bad and doing a good job of it.

"It's for your own good," I said.

"That what you always say, and then it turn out to be for your own good that I'm around. Say it not so?"

That was something I could not say. So I said nothing and decided to head back home.

27

The weather had changed, and there were heavy clouds hanging over the island as I drove home. Soon it started to rain. The top of my Jeep was down but I wasn't going to pull over to put it up. I'd just get a little wet. It wouldn't be the first time.

I rushed into the house, letting the dogs, their coats matted from the rain, in with me. It was torrential now, the front coming hard from the southeast and splattering against my picture window. I felt a vibration from my phone. I had the volume off as I usually did. I looked to see that I had a voice mail. It was from Marcia.

In a cool, detached tone, she thanked me for calling her and said she was leaving the island the next morning. She mentioned that she had enjoyed meeting me and spending some time with me. She wished me luck with the bar and to give my regards to my daughter when I next chatted with her. That was it. I wanted to hear more but there was nothing.

I didn't have to check to know she would be taking the 7:30 Liat ATR-42 to Barbados. That plane, I was sure, would eventually connect her with a flight to Boston. I looked at the tooth I bagged on my kitchen counter. Denton's tooth. I knew what I had to do.

·

I spent the rest of the afternoon and evening searching on the internet, trying to find any clues about Denton and that proposed development. All I got was more information about Denton, first about his boxing career and then about his success as a businessman and his tenure as minister of tourism for St. Pierre. I searched for proposed resorts on the Caribbean. There were notices of a few with overwater cabanas and casinos that were in the planning stages on other islands, but no mention of St. Pierre.

The rain stopped, and the skies cleared enough so I could see a bright half-moon leaving a streak of light over the Atlantic. I went back to read about Denton. Now I was looking at his business history, to see if there was anything I could find in there that would tie him to a big-name real estate or resort developer. I knew that as minister of tourism, he worked closely with the lodging and cruise-boat trade.

I found myself looking back again at his boxing career. I came once more to the story of when he won, briefly, the super-middleweight title. I studied the picture that was associated with it, the one where he was holding the championship belt in Las Vegas. I hadn't bothered to look closely at the caption. I did now, and besides acknowledging Denton's victory, the caption identified the two men on either side of him. One man was his manager, Terry Richards; the other was a balding, smiling white man identified as Norman Dunn, owner of the Dunn Vegas Palace and Casino.

The accompanying story about the fight mentioned that the ten-round decision had been somewhat controversial. But I was more interested in the fact that the fight was held at the Dunn Vegas Palace and Casino. That picture of Norman Dunn, owner of the venue, smiling next to the victorious Denton rang a bell somewhere. I had heard of Dunn, knew he owned a few properties in New York and several hotels and casinos around the world. I kept looking at his picture. Was this the connection? Dunn was a big-name developer. But the picture was from decades ago. What relevance could any of it have to what was happening in St. Pierre now? I felt I was missing something. The answer was buried somewhere in the clutter of my brain. And the harder I tried to grasp it, the more it eluded me.

I went to bed, restless again. The nagging feeling of something being just at the tip of my memory kept me up for I don't know how long. I dreamed it was raining again. I heard water, or waves, splashing against my windows. And then I was out in the rain, the wind was blowing, and I was naked but I didn't care. I was on the cliffs overlooking the ocean. I knew there were mountains below, sharp peaks that were formed from the lava spewed out by volcanoes millions of years earlier. Those mountains, in the delirium of my dream, appeared like natural stakes. If one fell from the cliff's edge, he would surely be impaled. I didn't want to look down. But I did.

My head hurt when I woke, almost as if I had a hangover. I had just one beer earlier in the day, so I knew that wasn't it. Maybe it was the rain, the low pressure from the day before. I swallowed two aspirin and took a shower, hoping that would clear my head. I needed coffee, but I didn't have time. I looked at my clock. I had just a few minutes. I grabbed the zip-lock bag from the kitchen counter and hustled out into my Jeep so fast, I didn't realize until I reached for my phone that I had left it at home. I also didn't realize, until I returned home an hour later, that I had walked right past a plastic bag with a rubber band around it that was lying in front of my door.

She was in the small security airport checkpoint line when I got there. I parked and rushed out of the Jeep.

"Marcia," I called to her as I approached.

She turned to me. She smiled, a forced one to be sure, but a smile nonetheless.

"Len, you didn't need to come," she said.

"I know, but here I am." I tried to smile.

She looked me over, studying me. Now I didn't know what to say to her. I moved along with her as the line headed closer to security. I pulled the zip-lock bag out of my pocket.

"Take this," I said.

She furrowed her brow as she looked at it. "What is that?"

"Bring it to that place where they did the DNA test. It might be a lead for you."

She looked closely at the bag and grimaced. "Is that a tooth?"

"Yeah, have it checked out. There might be a match."

She held the bag by its edge. "A match?"

"Yeah, someone I think might have been involved with your daughter's death."

"You brought me a tooth?" She stared at me in disbelief.

Hearing her say that, it did sound ridiculous. And maybe it all was.

"How did you get it?"

"It doesn't matter. Just have it checked out. If there is a match, let me know."

She kept staring at me and then shook her head. "I'm done here," she said brusquely.

"Wait...will you do it?"

She stopped walking. "So you haven't heard then, have you?"

"Heard what?"

"You really don't know?"

"What?" I stared at her.

She stared back as if she didn't believe me, and then said: "He's dead."

I had no idea what she was talking about. "Who's dead?"

"The man you thought you were helping. The man who murdered my daughter. Rawle Johns."

My head was throbbing at her words. The aspirin I took earlier had no effect now. I just stared at her, not really comprehending what she was telling me.

"I don't need this," she said, handing the zip-lock bag back to me. "It's over, Len. A man with no guilt would not take his own life. An innocent man would not do that."

I listened to what she was saying without responding. I had nothing to say. I had nothing.

"I have to go now," she said. "I wish you well." And then she turned away from me.

I watched her as she disappeared through security, my fingers on the bag with Denton's tooth. I was in the tropics. The average daily temperature on St. Pierre ranged from eighty-one to eighty-nine degrees, 365 days out of the year. But I was chilled. My toes were cold and my mouth was dry. Could she be wrong about Big Tree? It had to be a mistake. At least that was what I hoped.

I rushed back to my Jeep and reflexively went for my phone, but again, when I felt nothing, remembered I had forgotten it in my haste to get to the airport. I zoomed home wanting to call Tubby and find out what really had happened. As I rushed inside, I almost stepped on the plastic bag that had been left at my doorstep. I picked the bag up. I was curious as to what it was, but I needed to get to my phone first. I looked on the kitchen counter, but it wasn't there. I dashed into my bedroom and saw that it was on my dresser. I grabbed it and turned it on. As soon as it powered up, I was bombarded by a series of pings indicating voice mails, texts and emails.

Tubby's texts were the most prominent. He also left more than a few voice mails. I knew what they were about, and instead of listening to or reading them, I just called him back.

"Why Big Tree do that to himself," Tubby said as soon as he picked up my call. "This whole thing too sad for me now. Where you been that you don't answer my calls?"

I let it sink in. It was true what Marcia Gould said. I knew it was but had held out hope.

"Mr. Len?"

"Yeah, I'm here," I mumbled. "I was at the airport. I forgot my phone and had it off all night."

"So you just find out?"

"Yeah. Tubby, tell me. What did he do?"

"What you think he do?"

I took a deep breath. "Tell me."

"He go there and do what the others do," Tubby said.

"The Drop?"

"They run from their oppressors. They run to freedom. What he running from, Mr. Len?"

I didn't know what to say to Tubby. And then I remembered what Big Tree had said to me at Freedom Drop that time long ago. That a man could escape the bondage in his mind. And I remembered him pointing to his temple. Maybe that was what he was doing. Maybe he was running away from himself. I knew a little about that. But my flight took me here — to this island. Not off a cliff.

"I don't know, Tubby," I mumbled. I felt responsible in some way for what happened. I let my feelings for the man distort what I knew in my heart. I knew it after I talked with him, but I couldn't admit that to myself. I wanted to find anything to prove that those feeling were wrong. I had to string together an impossible conspiracy. I glanced at the bag with Denton's tooth in it. What else was I wrong about?

"I don't know, Tubby," I said.

Neither of us had much more to say at that moment. I kept the phone to my ear anyway.

"You coming here?" Tubby asked.

"I'll let you know," I said.

I hung up and went to my refrigerator for a beer. The aspirin wasn't working, but maybe a beer would. I popped it open and then thought about Mrs. Johns...and her grandson Ezran. The boy first lost his mother. Now his father was gone. I took a long sip from the cold bottle.

I grabbed the package that was left at my door and took it to my chair with my beer. I squeezed it and felt something solid inside. I hesitated a moment and then pulled off the rubber band that had wrapped it tight and opened the bag. Inside was a phone with a plastic faux white-marble case around it. It looked in reasonable condition; there were no cracks or dents on the screen. I pressed the side button to turn it on. Nothing happened. I guessed the phone's battery was dead and took it to where I kept the charger for my own phone. I tried to plug it in, but the connection to the power port wasn't compatible with mine.

I held the phone in my hand. I could see the reflection of my face on the dark screen. I wasn't looking so good. There were wrinkles that I didn't think were there just a week ago. There were bags under my eyes that seemed like a new development. I had an idea whose phone I was handling, and that should have made me feel better. But I also knew who dropped that phone off in front of my house. He was here, at my house, before he went to do what he did. And I didn't hear him. I was asleep. Dreaming. While he was running. While he ran into the clouds. And that made me feel worse.

28

There's a small business I know of just off Front Street and not far from Uncle Harvey's Delightful Roti shop. The business is run by a young man named Quincy Frank. He is known around the island as the best person to go to if you have a problem with your computer or any electronic equipment. He helped me with the Wi-Fi in my house and also fixed a glitch I had on my laptop as soon as the product warranty ran out, which was usually the case.

Quincy was just opening his doors for the day when I drove up. He smiled when he saw me and held the door open for me.

"Mr. Len, that computer running poorly on you?" he said.

"Not at all, Quincy," I said. "It's perfect, thanks to you."

"What can I do for you this fine morning," he said. "I'm thankful that storm has passed through and leave us with a lovely day."

"It has, hasn't it," I said, but it wasn't feeling lovely to me. I pulled the phone out of the plastic bag. "My daughter was in town, but when she left, she took her charger and forgot her phone. The battery is dead, so I need a charger for this phone, if you have one."

I showed him the phone.

He nodded.

"Sure, Mr. Len, I have one for that." He continued to look at the phone.

"And something else, Quincy. Could you transfer the data from the phone to, you know, a flash drive or one of those external hard drives?"

He studied me for a minute through thick-lensed glasses, then looked back at the phone. "Do you have your daughter's password for this phone?"

I hadn't thought about a password. But I needed to come up with something quick. "No, I don't," I said, somewhat unconvincingly.

He looked at me again. "Can you get me it?"

This was going to look bad, but what could I do? "Hmmm, I'd have to try to get in touch with her, Quincy. She told me she was going to be at a track tournament all day," I lied. "Is there any way you can transfer the stuff without her password?"

He smiled slightly. He knew I was hiding something but didn't push it. He understood it was not good business to get into anyone else's business. "Some locked phones are almost impossible to open up, Mr. Len," he said.

"Oh yeah? You don't think you can open this one without the password?" I needed the information on that phone. It was left with me for a reason. He gave me a reassuring smile.

"Mr. Len, I once meet a man who come through St. Pierre a couple of years ago from Cuba, I'm not sure if the man Cuban or not. He spoke very good English, I recall. This man come to my shop and want to sell me a device he say was made in Cuba that can unlock any phone."

"Did it work?"

"The man connect the device to a phone I had that I just could not unlock. The device has a microchip or some sort of scanning system that can read the code that locks the phone. It took less than a minute and the phone come unlocked. He offered me a good price on it, so I think it might come in handy here. People sometimes lock their phones accidently and forget their passwords. It can be quite the bother to try to unlock them. Now I can offer that service as well."

It was now my turn to smile. "Is that legal, Quincy?"

He looked at me. "I don't advertise this service, Mr. Len. And I trust you to understand why I don't."

"I understand completely, Quincy." I didn't say that his secret was safe with me, but the way I looked at him, I didn't think I had to.

He nodded. "Then can we proceed?"

"Proceed," I said. "And whatever you need to charge me for having to use that thing, I'll cover."

"No worries, Mr. Len. When I get the phone charged and open, what I can do is transfer the data from the phone to a computer here and then from the computer, transfer to a portable hard drive."

"Perfect. That's exactly what I want. This way I can get all her stuff to her so she can put it on her new phone. I guess losing this one gave her an excuse to get a new one."

"Yes, Mr. Len," Quincy said, still giving me that smile, knowing I was completely full of shit.

"Great, Quincy," I said. "When do you think you can have all this done for me?"

"Before closing," he said. "You just stop by then and I have it done for you."

I thanked him and got back into my Jeep.

I made the southerly turn on the roundabout at Garrison Harbor and headed up toward Windy Hill. There were cars lined up on the street outside Rawle Johns' house. I parked behind one of them. As I got out of my Jeep, I saw McWilliams emerging from the house, his hat in hand.

He looked at me, his expression glum and almost accusatory, and then he looked away. I took a deep breath and made my way toward the front door.

The small living room was crowded, and the smell of warm food filled the house. Through a few bodies, I saw Mrs. Johns seated on a couch with her grandson Ezran by her side. Shirma Bates was hugging Mrs. Johns. Shirma looked at me with recognition. She had one brown eye and one light blue, her face a mix of pigmentations. She nodded at me knowingly as she held her friend.

Ezran spotted me and glanced in my direction before looking down at his shoes.

I made my way through the crowd to the couch. Mrs. Johns saw me now. Shirma Bates kept her arm around her. I bent down to her. "I'm so sorry, Mrs. Johns," I said.

She held a handkerchief in her hand and nodded. Her eyes were red, but they were not wet. I guessed she had done all her crying already.

"You get my son home to me, sir," she said. "That was all I ask from you. I never thank you for that."

He would be still alive if he were in jail, I thought.

She took my hand and squeezed it. "Why the Lord make this path for my son?" she wondered out loud, not looking at anyone in particular. "Why he? Why make a man go through so much pain by taking he wife from he? And then this? Why?"

"Rawle, one of the Lord's chosen," Shirma Bates said.

Mrs. Johns nodded in agreement. "The Lord guide him to where the brave ones go before him. The Lord take him home in His sacred place. For that I grateful."

"Oh yes," Shirma Bates cried. "He basking in the Lord's glory now. God bless he."

They both began to hum and sing softly, rocking on the couch.

Mrs. Johns stopped singing for a moment. "There a fricassee on the stove," she said to me. "My sister make it for me. Please, sir, you go take some. I thank you for what you do for my son." She squeezed my hand again and then let go of it.

I felt my face redden. She was thanking me. She was squeezing my hand and offering me food. I never told her what her son said to me. How he could not resist putting his hands on that girl. I never told her that the girl's mother referred to her son as her daughter's killer, as a murderer. And I never would.

There were things I wanted to ask her. I wanted to know more about Rawle Johns. I wanted to know why he would take his own life. What was tormenting him so? What was he hiding? But I could never ask her any of those things. Not now. Not ever.

I noticed Ezran staring at me as if he could read my thoughts. I took a breath.

"You want to help me with that fricassee?" I asked him. I could sense how uncomfortable he was sitting there while well-wishers paid their respects. I thought he might need a little escape.

He didn't answer.

"Go help the man, boy, and show him where he find the fricassee," Mrs. Johns commanded.

He got up from the couch as ordered and I followed him into the kitchen. He took me to the stove where there was a massive Dutch oven, much bigger than the ones that were brought to my house. He took off the lid.

"It here," he said.

"Thanks, Ezran," I said. "Are you gonna have some?"

He shook his head.

I wasn't hungry in the least, but I put a chicken thigh on my plate that was smothered in a brown sauce with cassava, onions and peppers.

"You know where I live now, Ezran. And the dogs know you now. No need to be afraid of them," I said. "Anytime you want to come by to see the dogs, you can. Okay?"

He looked down again.

"You don't visit them, I'll have to bring the dogs to you, and I don't think your grandmother will like that."

"She don't like dogs," he mumbled.

"Alright then," I said. "Anytime, Ezran. Got that?"

He nodded and stood with me in the small kitchen as I picked at the fricassee. After I had made enough of a dent in my plate so as not to appear as if I wasted good food, I put it down on the kitchen counter. I squeezed Ezran's shoulder once more as I headed out.

"You come from Big Tree's?" Tubby asked me as I walked

into the bar.

"Yeah, have you been there?"

"I pay my respects earlier," he said as he leaned back against the bar looking up at one of the televisions. Mike was opening bottles of beer. There was a group out on the deck.

"Cruise boat come in last night," Tubby said.

I nodded. I looked at what Tubby was looking at. There was some sort of bike race in Las Vegas. In and around the strip. It seemed strange. Bikes in Las Vegas. Not that I'd ever been to Vegas.

Vegas?

I looked back at the television as the bikes raced past casinos and hotels. And that's when it came to me — the missing piece that I just couldn't pull up from my memory.

"What you staring at?" Tubby asked me while I was trying to recall the encounter.

"Nothing."

"Why your mouth open then?"

"Do you remember that man who was here last week who chatted me up?" I asked him.

"What man?"

"It was the day we picked Kasie up from the airport. Mike said he was a big tipper. You thought he might be a celebrity."

"A celebrity? Only celebrity I meet was Johnny Depp and..."

"Yeah you told me, Tubby. No, this guy was with a group that was sitting out on the deck. He said he was sailing through the islands."

He also said he lived in Las Vegas, I remembered now. He asked if I'd ever been there. I told him no, but then I made a crack that maybe I should put it on my bucket list. He was in his thirties. He had a funny smile, like there was nothing behind it. I saw that face and smile again. At the Bougainvillea. When I was in the lobby holding Marcia Gould's shoes. It was the same man. He stopped me there to say hello. He introduced himself to me again, but I wasn't listening. I just wanted to get up those stairs to the Hibiscus Room. More of it was coming back to me now.

"One of his group came for more beer at the bar when he was chatting with me," I said to Tubby.

"The man who wear a shirt with the Rasta lion on it that look like the man he self?" Tubby said.

"A man with braids," I said.

Tubby looked at me with recognition. Both of us knew then. We remembered it at the same time. The man had multiple tattoos in and around his neck and on his arms. And he had hands that were large enough to easily capture two beer bottles in each of them. One of those same hands, I realized now, also easily gripped a 9mm pistol. But that was before that hand became nothing more than a bleeding stump.

29

While I was still at the bar, Quincy Frank texted me that the work on the phone was done. I left immediately and drove to Frank's shop; I needed to know what was on that phone.

"I get the phone unlocked easy and then back up everything onto this," Quincy said indicating the hard drive. "Now your daughter have everything she need for her new phone."

He smiled at me when he said that...a knowing smile.

He gave me the phone that was now fully charged, a charger for the phone and the external hard drive.

"Thanks, Quincy," I said, wondering if he peeked at what he was transferring from the phone to the hard drive. I had a feeling that whatever I found would soon no longer be a secret.

I paid him, but before I got back into my Jeep, I ran across the street and bought a curry goat roti from Uncle Harvey's Delightful Roti Shop. I was suddenly ravenous.

As soon as I got home, I turned on the phone. While it

booted up, I took the roti from the paper bag and devoured it, the curry sauce dripping onto the paper bag. I washed my hands and then checked on the phone, bringing it with me to the table along with my laptop and the external hard drive that held its data.

The phone was set up different than mine, and not being well versed in electronic devices, it took me a while to figure out the icons for texts, email, voice mail and other documents. I went first to the contacts folder and opened it. There were hundreds of names and numbers. I scrolled down the list quickly; after the numbers, which featured area codes from all over the country, the names were arranged in alphabetical order. I went directly to those starting with "M." There was no Marcia, but there was a contact for "Mom." I clicked on "Mom" and the phone number came up. I cross-checked the number with what I had on my phone. It was the same number Marcia Gould used to contact me. I had been pretty sure before, but now I knew for certain: I had Deanna Gould's phone.

I went back to the top of the contact list and this time scrolled slowly seeing if I might recognize any other names. I stopped when I came to a contact listed as "ED." I clicked on it, expecting to see a local St. Pierre number, to see Edward Denton's number. Instead, the number, I knew, was from the U.S.

I turned on my laptop and typed in the area code to see where its origin was. The code was from Clark County, Nevada. My heart was pumping now.

I put the phone down for a moment and pulled up the article on Edward Denton winning the super-middleweight championship in Las Vegas. I stared at that familiar photo. I focused on the man smiling next to Denton, Norman Dunn, owner of the

Dunn Palace and Casino in Las Vegas, where the fight was held.

I did a search on Dunn. His Wikipedia biography came up first. I scanned down to his personal life, past his history as a real estate mogul and hotelier, to see his family history. He was born in New York and had been married three times. He had four children, three of them daughters; two daughters were from the second marriage, while the third, I noticed, was born the same year as Kasie and was from his current, much younger wife. The only child from Dunn's first marriage was a son. His name was Eric who, according to Wikipedia, worked with his father in the hotel and casino business.

I sat up straight.

I typed in Eric Dunn's name. I went right to the images. There were many of them. And they all looked exactly like the man who introduced himself to me over a week ago at the bar. Who wanted to talk to me at the Bougainvillea. Who was at my bar with the same man who killed my dog and who came to hurt me.

I searched the internet for information on Eric Dunn. I quickly learned that most of his ventures resulted in failure. He was involved in an upscale gentleman's club, also known as a strip joint, that was shuttered due to Russian organized crime connections, a sports-betting business with tax issues that forced it to close, and a high-end East African safari business that went belly up due to bad publicity over the treatment of some of the rare, supposedly endangered animals the hunters thought they would be able to trophy kill. He was married once to a dancer who had worked at his father's casino, but the marriage was a failure as well.

I looked back at the photo of his father with Denton. And

then scanned the images of Norman Dunn. There was one old photo of him with his first three children, who were very young at the time. Eric Dunn was in a suit that he looked uncomfortable in. There was a frown on his face, while his stepsisters, both blond, were smiling happily and gripping their father's hand.

I stared at the picture of young Eric Dunn.

Eric...Dunn.

E...D.

ED's Folly.

I read more about the Dunn hotel empire. Eric was listed as an associate vice president of Dunn Properties; the two daughters, though younger than Eric, were named as full-fledged officers, both of them vice presidents. I thought on that for a moment. It couldn't have sat well with the first born to be relegated to a lower status than his younger sisters.

I returned my attention to the phone and the text contact ED. I went to see if there were texts from this ED. There were only two. One read, *I'm here.* And then a response from Deanna Gould: *On my way.*

I knew that on my phone, the newest texts I received and who they were from appeared at the top of my text list. I wanted to see what Gould's last texts were and if her phone operated in a similar way. It did and there were several, including "Mom" and someone called "Frosty." My stomach clenched when I opened the texts from Mom.

Is everything all right, Dee? was followed by *Please contact me, I'm worried.*

There were no responses from Deanna to either.

I opened the Frosty texts.

You're meeting him now? Frosty asked her.

Tonight was her response.

Good. Nail him. Frosty wrote.

Frosty. Craig Frost?

I checked the time log and saw that there were no responses from Gould until a few hours later.

I think I might be in some trouble, Frosty, she wrote. *I think I pushed too much here. I...*

What trouble? Be careful, he replied.

Shit! He's coming after me, she texted.

Dee? Frosty wrote back.

Frosty, I'm scared. He's chasing me. I...

Who? What's going on? Dee? Frosty asked numerous times, but he got no answer, and from what I could tell looking at all the texts from people that came after, the previous one was the last she wrote. Reading it sent a chill through me. I thought of how confident she had appeared to me. I remembered that teasing, playful smile. They didn't mesh with the words I just read from her texts. Someone was pursuing her.

I looked back up at the time sequence of the texts. The text from ED, *I'm here,* came right before *I think I might be in some trouble, Frosty. I think I pushed too much here. I...* Big Tree had told me she left after getting a text. It had to be the text from ED. But then what? Big Tree? Was he the one she pushed too much...or was it Dunn?

I went back to the ED contact and studied the phone number. I pressed the telephone icon and held the phone to my ear. The phone rang repeatedly until a recorded voice informed me that the person I was trying to reach was unavailable. There was the usual opportunity to leave a message, but I decided against that. I wanted to spook him a little.

I took the external hard drive that Quincy Frank had used to download from her phone and hooked it up to my laptop. I looked to see what was in it. There were numerous files, including one labeled "SP." I was about to open it up when her phone made a doorbell sound. She was getting a call. I grabbed it. ED came up on the screen. I picked it up.

"E...D" I said into the phone, drawing out the initials.

There was a pause.

"Who is this?" the man on the other line said warily.

"Who do you think it is?" I said.

Again there was a pause.

"How did you get this phone?" he asked, not answering my question.

"Does it matter? I got it. And I got you, don't I?"

"Are you fucking with me," he said. "People learn fast not to fuck with me."

"Such a tough guy with such bad language. You were so nice and polite when I met you," I said. "And who's fucking with who?"

"Who is this?"

"Ah, Dunn, I'm hurt you don't recognize my Bronx accent. I'm bad with names, but you are pitiful with voices. I guess I have to toss you a few softballs — see if you can guess. Your partner, Denton, lasted less than one round with me, and instead of a championship belt, I got a tooth. And then there were those two other acquaintances of yours who you sent to my house. One was not very *hand*-y with a gun. The other one got off easier, but let's hope he doesn't get another concussion anytime soon."

There was silence as he thought about what I just told him.

"Buonfiglio?"

"Were you expecting the ghost of Deanna Gould?

"How did you get this phone?"

"Doesn't matter. I've got it. I've got all of it." That's what I told him, but I had no idea yet what I had. I figured that was as good a time as any to hang up on him. I knew he would call back, but I wanted to see what I had. I needed to read through Deanna Gould's files.

He did call numerous times as I scanned what was in those files, but I didn't answer. I wanted him to sweat a little more. I heard another sound from Gould's phone. She was getting a text. From ED.

When can we meet? he wrote.

I wasn't about to get into a long text session. I was ready to talk to him now.

"What do you want to meet about, Dunn?" I asked as soon as he picked up.

"Well, I know my associate here on St. Pierre made a proposal to you."

"You mean Denton and the magnificent opportunity to open a bar in your big resort?"

"Well, maybe he wasn't as persuasive as I can be. Or maybe I can offer even more in the package."

"Ain't I the lucky one," I said. "But I'm sure this generosity of yours comes with some condition."

"It's not much really," he said. "Just give me the phone, and everything I've offered is yours. Or you can just tell me what you want."

"What makes you think I want anything?" I said.

I heard him laugh. It was a cackly, high-pitched laugh. I didn't like it.

"You're human, aren't you? It's in our nature to want things. Lots of things."

He was wrong about that, but I really didn't want to have a philosophical discussion at the moment. "Maybe I just want answers," I said. "Maybe I want to know why you would threaten me and others. Did you think I knew something about your project? Did you think Craig Frost told me what he knew and that's why you sent your sailing companions to my house?"

"A smart businessman takes precautions to protect his investments. I learned that growing up."

"Yeah, I'm sure your father taught you many of his real-world lessons. I'm sure he's schooled you well on the way businesses work. Must have been disappointing to him to have your sisters surpass you on the corporate ladder. What happened there, Dunn?"

There was silence again. He was digesting that, as I knew he would. I didn't think bringing his father or his sisters into the conversation would sit well with him.

"Let's meet face to face and discuss this," he said after a pause.

I glanced out the window. The sun was just about to set, but it was already dark over the eastern horizon.

"Buonfiglio?"

"I'm here," I said. "I'd like to meet, but how can I be sure you won't do me like you did the others?"

"You think I'm like that? I'm a legitimate businessman. I'm no gangster."

"No?"

"I've got an undergrad business degree from Dartmouth and an MBA from Booth at the University of Chicago. I'm Ivy League all the way."

"I guess I'm convinced then. So I have your word Captain Hook won't show up with a firearm in his one good hand?"

"You absolutely have my word on that. It would be very bad publicity if it were known that I did some damage to the June first hero," he said.

I could hear the smile in his voice. He had a file on me too.

"But maybe I should ask you the same thing, Buonfiglio. I hear you are good with your hands...and feet. You're not going to show off your skills on *me*, are you?"

"I only do that for the privileged few, Dunn," I said. "And at my age, I have to be very selective when I expend so much energy. The recovery time is a bitch. Let's meet at ten. I'll have the phone for you. Any suggestions where?"

"Okay, ten works. I'd rather it be in a private setting. I don't want anyone witnessing our transaction, if you know what I mean."

"How about we meet at Freedom Drop. I can guarantee no one will be there at that time of night," I said. Why not end it there where it all began?

"Freedom Drop? That's dramatic. It's been quite the hub of activity lately from what I hear, Buonfiglio. Are you sure?"

"Unless there's a jumper I don't know about, I'm sure."

"Just to let you know, I can't drive these roads. You know, wrong side and all. So I'll have a driver."

"Keep your driver in your car," I said. "I don't want him coming out and disturbing our conversation."

There was a pause. "Oh, he won't, you can count on that."

"Good, then I'll see you at ten."

I cut the connection. I went back to my laptop and continued to scan Gould's data, looking over her files and notes. It took

over an hour of searching until I finally found what I was looking for. But that was just the beginning. I had a couple of hours
before the meeting with Dunn. There was someone I needed to
see and talk to. There was someplace I needed to go.

I had the external hard drive in my hand as I headed for the
tool shed. Last time I had just stared at the box that held the
two guns. This time I reached down and opened it. I pulled out
one of the guns and cradled it in my hand. And then I got into
my Jeep and drove down to Garrison. To Front Street. To the
Green building.

30

When I got back to my house, I fed the dogs and made sure they had plenty of water. I turned off my lights, locked the front door and headed back to the Jeep. Tubby called just as I was about to start it up. "Everything okay with you now?" he asked.

"Yeah sure, why?"

"You know why. The way you run out earlier, something had you going. Of course you don't tell me, so I'll have to get my island sources to find out what you up to."

"There's nothing to tell, Tubby," I said. There was no chance I would risk having Tubby at this meeting. He would know all soon enough.

I could hear the familiar hiss through the phone.

"Some day, Mr. Len. Some day, you understand I'm not trying to invade your space or anything like that. Some day you know I just want to help you. Maybe after all these years you'll let me in on what goes on in that head."

"After all these years you should know that not much goes on in my head."

"See, you try to make a joke out of it. You always do. All right then. You do what you do. Don't come looking for me when you need to get out of a jam."

"If I need to get out of a jam, Tubby, I guarantee you are the first call I make."

"Uh-huh," he muttered. "I see you tomorrow?"

I thought about his question for a moment. I thought about tomorrow.

"Yeah, you'll see me then," I said. "I'll even be there to open up before lunch. Vacation is over."

"If you say so," he said.

"I do."

I hung up and started to the Jeep. I had the phone with me. For some reason I was calm. I was looking forward to confronting Dunn. I pictured his pasty face and blank smile. He was not an impressive figure, I recalled, which was why I thought nothing of him until now. He probably realized that, and it most likely bugged him. He wanted to be a big man like his father, but for whatever reason, he just couldn't measure up. So now he was cutting corners, doing what he could to get the status and respect he thought he deserved. Deanna Gould had done extensive research on him. She might have been unorthodox in her methods and had her own personal issues, but from what I could tell, she kept clear, organized notes. She would have become a very good journalist, I think.

I had read everything she compiled. I knew about his background and his life, and that helped me get an understanding of what made him tick, what his motivations were. It was messy, and for a moment I almost felt sorry for him. But then I didn't. Gould had uncovered what Dunn was trying to do on St. Pierre, and it wasn't good. To me, what he was hoping to accomplish here wasn't worth the trouble he was going through to get it done. It wasn't worth silencing those who knew the truth. But I understood now, to him, why it probably was. He had to succeed here.

I didn't mean it to be symbolic by choosing Freedom Drop as our meeting place. I wasn't planning on throwing him off the cliff, and I was confident he wouldn't do the same to me. He might have something else in mind. In fact, I was sure he had something else in mind. That was the tricky part. I had no idea what that might be, but I was willing to take the chance. I'd done it before. And I would probably do it again. Stupid. Reckless. That was who I was now.

I got there before him. I had Gould's phone and I had my phone. I sat in the Jeep and waited. I tried to pull up an internet connection on my phone but couldn't get one. I hadn't thought of that. That was too bad. There was something I wanted to check. There was something I wanted to show him. It was part of my plan. Though I couldn't get the internet, there was phone service. I made sure of that before I left my house.

All I could hear in the open air of my Jeep were the waves below as they crashed against the rocks. Hearing it at home when the surf was rough sometimes soothed me. Tonight, however, the sound was no comfort at all.

I turned toward the road leading up the swerving incline to Freedom Drop. I saw headlights in the distance. As the headlights got closer, I could hear the car's engine. That was the signal for one last text. I hit send and put the phone on the passenger seat.

The car pulled over about forty yards from where I was parked. In the dark I could not make out who was driving; I would have to take Dunn at his word that the guy would stay in the car. I watched the passenger door open and saw Dunn, dressed in beige pants and a loose short-sleeved button-down shirt, get out of the car. He walked briskly up the hill.

"Buonfiglio," he called as he got closer.

"I'm right here, Dunn," I said, getting out of the Jeep.

I walked a few steps from the Jeep to the stone plaque.

"Hey now, be careful. Don't get so close to the ledge. We can't have any more accidents."

"Accidents, Dunn? No...I'm not planning on any accidents," I said.

I could see that familiar creepy smile now. He looked around. In the distance, lights flickered from a boat on the water. But that was it. The only illumination was the headlights of my Jeep and his car forty yards away.

"This is some spot," he said. "We are definitely going to use it in the marketing of our project."

"Ya think?"

"Absolutely. Cultural tourism, Buonfiglio, that's the big thing now. Sure, folks want their sun and their sand, but give them waterfalls, hikes in rainforests, local food, music, rum and a little history too, and it's even better. We plan on incorporating Freedom Drop and all that other stuff into the promotion of E. Dunn St. Pierre Resort and Casino."

"Gambling isn't legal on St. Pierre, Dunn. And E. Dunn? That's a lousy name. Do you really need the E?"

"This is my project, Buonfiglio. Not my father's...or my..."

He stopped in mid-sentence, catching himself. "Or your sisters, Dunn?" I helped him finish what he was going to say.

He just looked at me. It was not a very friendly look.

"So this one was is all yours, huh? This is your baby." I grinned.

"Yes, Buonfiglio. My concept all the way. And as for the gambling, we're working on that," he said. "Anyway, the resort, as I know my colleague, Mr. Denton, told you, will be spectacular, and you have the opportunity to be a part of it. We will cover all your expenses for the first two years with a fifty-fifty split in profits. All we ask is that we use your brand name, and you can manage the bar any way you like, including hiring the staff."

"Who knew I had a brand?"

"But you do, Buonfiglio. I wouldn't make this offer if it didn't make sense for us. Trust me."

"Is that right? So the girl's phone has nothing to do with it?"

The smile remained fixed. "You know that the phone is part of the deal. I want it and everything that's on it."

"You gonna tell me why you want it so badly, Dunn?"

"I'm sure you know, so let's stop with the games and just hand it over so we can get on with the deal."

"I do know," I said, staring at him now.

"I figured you did, but so what? That shouldn't affect our deal. At least I hope it doesn't. This opportunity for you is bigger than any concerns you might have on what you found on her phone."

"Really? You think I need this? You think I would sell out my country for a piece of your property?"

"Your country? Give me a break, Buonfiglio. You're not from here. This is not your country. You are an interloper, a foreign investor just like I will soon be. And without us, these countries can't exist. So let's not kid each other."

"St. Pierre exists quite well without you and me," I said. "You obviously do not understand what you're doing. It will not work here. I know it won't."

"Oh, it will work. And you know why. You know that if you throw enough money at people, they'll do what's right. That's human nature."

"People live on that land, Dunn. They have for generations. They've fished there. You are going to move them to the other side of the island, where the fishing is not the same for them? Uproot them from their homes and the land they've known all their lives? You think money will make it all good?"

"I do," he said. "It always does."

I should have expected a response like that from him. Why was I bothering?

"I read that report, Dunn. I saw what would happen to the coral reef there. I read about the damage those luxurious over-water cabanas would cause. I read about the sewage. What they would do to the local marine habitat. Sea turtles nest there. You need this so badly?"

"Enough with the sea turtles, you're breaking my heart," he said. "And don't believe everything you read. That was not a reliable report. I've had others do studies that tell me there won't be any damage."

"You mean the study you sold Edward Denton on? The one commissioned by that so-called think tank in Texas on the payroll of Dunn Properties? How much did you pay them to come up with that bullshit? And if that report was true, Dunn, why did you silence Craig Frost? You thought he knew about this dirty project and you thought he told me about it, didn't you?

Is that why you sent your thugs to my house? To kill my dog and intimidate me and my daughter?"

"That was unfortunate, Buonfiglio. I didn't know they would do that."

"What did you think they were going to do?"

"That's all in the past. Let's look to the future. I'm offering you something most men would take in a heartbeat. To be associated with a Dunn property. There's no risk for you, only profit. And I can even make sure you are well compensated on top of our split. Whatever you want, just tell me. I know your children aren't living here with you, but with this offer, they will be taken care of financially. College, whatever. There will be no worries."

"My children? You're bringing them into this?"

He put his hands up in a backing-off gesture. I knew I had to try to remain calm. Even if he goaded me with references to my family, I had to shrug it off...for now.

"Tell me, Dunn, why are you so desperate for this? You don't need it. You have your father's other properties to handle. You have a good life. Why go through all this trouble?"

His vacuous smile quickly faded. The mention of his father got the reaction I expected.

"I do need this, Buonfiglio. I've wanted something like this for a long time. Now that I have the chance and that I'm close, I'm not going to let it slip away. I'm going to make this classier than any of my father's properties. This one will be unique, and it will be mine."

"I guess it's tough living under your father's name. You don't want to be just a kid who was handed everything to him by his father, who bailed you out of all your failures. Good luck with that."

I was pushing him like I did Denton. I just hoped this time what I was doing would be the right thing.

"Now you're a shrink, Buonfiglio?" He shook his head.

"And why were you passed over by your younger stepsisters? What happened there?" I wanted to goad him more. I needed to stall some. This was moving faster than I anticipated.

"Enough of this psychobabble," Dunn said calmly. He wasn't reacting as I hoped. He was much more in control; maybe he was just devoid of any emotion. "Now...the phone, please. I tried to work this out with you, but I guess you are too stubborn. Stupid, really. Either way, I'm getting the phone."

It didn't matter if he had the phone now. As he and I stood there, what was on it was becoming public knowledge. The report he was trying to squash was about to go viral. I had sent it all to that website ThirdRail before I left. What they planned to do with it I wasn't sure, but I was confident they would blast it on their site's front page. If not, I had also sent it to the *St. Pierre Press*. Everything had been backed up. He should have known that. Who was the stupid one here?

I was about to reach into my pocket, but before I could do anything, I felt something cold and very sharp against my neck.

"*Fre mwen,*" was whispered into my ear. The voice was soft, almost sensual. "*Oh fe mal fre '-'lan.*"

I turned my head just enough to see the tip of a knife and the golden brush of hair of the dark-skinned woman who was holding it in hands with very long, equally sharp-looking nails. I quickly flashed back to the legs I saw in the green Suzuki what seemed like centuries ago. And that tattoo on her thigh. The skeleton wearing the top hat. Craig Frost got into the back seat of that Suzuki with her. The next morning he was dead.

"That was her brother you hurt, Buonfiglio," Dunn said, now with a smile on his face.

As I suspected, Dunn would not let this go without some sort of retribution.

"So much for your word, Dunn. I should have known."

"What? I didn't break my word to you. I would never do that." He grinned.

"You said the driver wouldn't leave your car. You guaranteed it."

"Yes, and you said, and I remember it clearly, that you didn't want 'him' to leave the car. 'He' didn't, but *she* did."

He lacked a soul, this man. It had been sucked out of him slowly — from his unfortunate birth and through all the years of living in the dark shadow of his father.

"Yeah, okay, Dunn. Now what?"

The woman hissed into my ear and pushed the knife in just enough to break the skin. Her breath was hot and smelled of spices — cinnamon, cloves and something exotic that I couldn't identify. I could feel a slow trickle of blood down my neck.

"You don't know what I've had to do to keep her from slitting your throat. And I still don't know if I can control her. She's a wildcat, this one. I know you like wildcats, Buonfiglio. You were with one on the beach that night. Remember, I was there. I could hear her. I heard her out there with you. Like animals. The both of you."

I started to lunge and the knife pricked me again.

"You don't want to do that. You really don't. She'll happily gut you," he said, and then nodded. "Speaking of wildcats, you know her daughter was that way too. How do you think she got what she needed from me? Bitch."

I stared at him. "So you killed her?"

He looked blankly at me. "Did I say that?"

"What did you do to her?" I needed to know now.

"Um, I did nothing, Buonfiglio. The poor girl was running away from him."

"What?"

"That's right, I could hear him calling to her. She was a tease, that one, and got much more than she bargained for with the unfortunate Big Tree, I guess."

"You saw him do it?"

He gave me that creepy smile again. I didn't know what to think.

"She wanted my help," he said. "But why should I help someone who tries to hurt me? Who was trying to ruin me?"

"What did you do?"

".I offered her help, Buonfiglio, but she resisted. That was just another of her mistakes."

He kicked at the ground around him.

"What did you do, Dunn?"

"It's slippery here," he said. "They really should put better fencing or something around this site to prevent other tragedies. Don't you think, Mr...Len?" He picked his head up and grinned, displaying teeth that were so white they almost glowed in the dark. He was mocking me.

He shut up for a moment and the silence around us was conspicuous. I could hear the woman's breathing close behind me.

"Enough on what happened to the girl. None of that matters now. Give me the phone," he barked, breaking the momentary hush.

I remained still. I thought about driving my elbow up and

into the woman's solar plexus. It would have to be as quick as I'd ever practiced the move. That knife just needed a little shove and it would puncture my carotid artery. And that would be it. I'd bleed out. I breathed in slowly and focused my hearing. I told myself I could hear the low hum of a car engine. I don't know if I did or didn't, but it was all I had.

"Get the phone," he said to the woman.

The knife pressed against my neck as I felt her hand go first to my crotch and then lower. She found what she was looking for and squeezed hard. I gritted my teeth against the pain as she laughed and said something in Creole. Her body was tight against my back. I could feel the rough tips of her nipples now. I remembered the feeling — she had done this before to me — almost as if it were a warning of what was to come. She was playing with me, and it was arousing her.

The smile left Dunn's face again. He saw what she was doing. He saw how it was affecting her. "Just bring the phone now," he commanded.

She slid her hand into my pocket and took out the phone. She pushed me forward, keeping the knife steady on my neck. Together we walked up to Dunn. He had his hand out and she gave him the phone.

"*Kite m 'fe l,*" she whispered to Dunn in a voice oozing with hate.

Dunn looked at me. He looked at her. She wanted to kill me. She was pleading with him for his permission. Just as his head tilted down in an affirmative nod, the sound of a gunshot broke the silence. I was ready for it and didn't hesitate. I quickly swung my elbow hard back into her and under her ribs. I heard a whoosh and knew the force of the blow had sent her onto her back.

I turned around in the dark. She was scrambling on the ground and wheezing as she crawled on her hands. She had dropped the knife and was frantically searching for it.

"Dunn!" I heard a voice yell from beyond. He had come as he said he would. He used the gun as I told him to. To scare Dunn. To break up this party, just as we planned. Denton.

But I didn't know now where Dunn was. And now I didn't know where Denton was. I heard more gunshots. What was Denton doing? I didn't want Dunn dead. But there was nothing I could do about that now. My eyes were on the woman.

"You lied to me, Dunn," I heard Denton scream. "You had that bullshit study paid for to protect yourself and your project. You used me."

I could see the glint of the knife about five feet from where she was crawling on her hands and knees. She saw it too now, but I got there before she did. I grabbed it, and as I did she growled and jumped on my back. I felt those dagger-like nails claw deep into my upper shoulder and neck. She wrapped her legs tight around my torso, slashing me with her long nails. As I slammed the back of my head into her head, knocking her off me, I dropped the knife. She quickly righted herself and grabbed the knife, waving it at me now.

We were perilously close to the cliff's ledge. She waved and slashed the knife at me. I reared back enough so all she did was swipe at air, but she came at me again. This time I let loose with a roundhouse kick, my right foot slamming hard into her chest, knocking her back, the knife falling from her hands and over the side of the cliff. The force of my kick sent her staggering. She was off balance as she reared back. She was going over the ledge. I tried to get to her but was too late. As she was falling, she grabbed onto the fence. She was holding on to it tightly. I quickly reached for her hand. The red and blue lights were getting brighter and the police siren louder. I gripped her hand and looked into her eyes. I started to pull her up when she stiffened. She glared at me, and with the lights from the police cars illuminating her face, gave me a look of absolute hatred. Why, I wondered? I was trying to help her, to bring her to safety. I needed to save her like I did all the others. I couldn't let her die. I couldn't let any die.

But then she made a howling sound, like that of a wounded animal, and, using her other hand, began to slash at the hand that held tightly to hers. Her nails were like knives. They dug into my flesh over and over. I tried to hold on, but the blood flowing from my hand was making my grip slick. She was wriggling out of my hand. I reached over with my other hand to try to grab her, but before I could, she was free from my grasp.

Free to drop.

I remained on the ground, both arms over the ledge. I looked down into the darkness below but saw nothing but the white-caps of the rough sea below. "Fuck," I groaned, then slowly pulled myself to my knees. Blood flowed from my shoulder and my hand where she had slashed me.

Denton was panting, standing over me with the gun in his hand. "Where is he? Where's Dunn?" He asked as he stared at me as I slowly got to my feet. "What happened here? Who was that?"

McWilliams and three other officers burst out of their cars.

"Denton, drop the gun," McWilliams ordered.

I got up onto my feet and turned back to Denton. He nodded

compliantly to the police superintendent and placed the gun gently down on the ground. I looked at McWilliams. He and one of his deputies approached Denton.

"Turn around now," McWilliams said.

"What are you doing, McWilliams?" I said to him.

He ignored me and took Denton's hands and clasped them close together while his deputy brought out his cuffs. The handcuffs were secured. Denton said nothing but glared at me as if I set him up.

"Wait, Denton's not the one," I pleaded.

One of the deputies peered over the edge of the cliff. "Someone fall, sir," he said.

McWilliams looked me hard in the eye, trying his best not to notice the blood on me. "I saw nothing," he said to his deputy.

"This is bullshit," I said. "Why are you cuffing Denton? He didn't do anything. It was Dunn."

McWilliams stared blank-faced at me. I had never seen that look from him before, and I hoped I never would again. "Now, Mr. Buonfiglio, I told you already and I tell you again. It's time you step away."

"You're wasting your time with Denton. Go after Dunn. He can't have gotten far. He's the one who did all this. He's getting away. Eric Dunn."

He looked at me. Again his face was a blank slate. "Who?"

I stood there trying to comprehend his question. I was about to say something, then realized there was no need. His question and the expression on his face was all I needed to know about what was going on here.

31

As soon I got home I booted up my laptop. My mind was trying to digest what just happened at Freedom Drop. I had lots of questions, but no answers. I checked the internet. There was nothing on ThirdRail. I was surprised. In fact, the headlines were what I saw the day before. Nothing had been updated. Something was wrong. I made sure to see if the file I had sent had gone through. It did. The file I had sent to the *St. Pierre Press* also had gone through. It wasn't my internet. It was something else.

I tried calling the police to speak to McWilliams, but all I could do was leave messages. I wanted to explain to him that he had the wrong man. That Denton didn't do anything. That it was Dunn and his scheme. And I had proof. I backed up the files on Deanna Gould's phone, but I wasn't able to copy the texts. I tried but couldn't figure out how to do it and then I ran out of time. The texts. They would implicate Dunn in Gould's death. They had to. But he had the phone — wherever he was. There was nothing I could do now.

My neck and arm were still bleeding and stung. I thought of the woman who fell. The look she gave me. I didn't understand. I never would. Why couldn't I save her? Why did another have to die? And didn't McWilliams care? Or did he just pretend he didn't see it so he wouldn't have to bother?

I washed out the wounds, but they kept bleeding. The gashes were deep. I could tell I needed stitches, but for now I put bandages on them. Sleeping was rough that night. I kept thinking about what went wrong, how Dunn disappeared. How could he have gotten away? Why did they arrest Denton? It was bad enough I knocked out the man's tooth, stupidly thinking that he had been responsible for the girl's death — and for everything else that went on. He didn't like what Dunn was up to; he hadn't known about the bogus study. When I told him what would probably happen up at Freedom Drop, he wanted to help me. And he did. He saved my life. Look where that got him.

And then I thought about Big Tree. Maybe if I didn't meddle, he wouldn't have been released. Maybe he would still be alive. And maybe if I still had that phone, those texts would implicate Big Tree. I just didn't know. I thought about what Dunn told me, that he had offered to save her but she…he didn't say it, but implied it…she slipped. What was I supposed to believe? Did Big Tree do something to her to make her run from him? To make her leap or slip off that cliff? And worse, did I let my personal feelings, my fondness for the man and his family, cloud my thinking? I didn't know what to think. My mind was a mess.

I called McWilliams again the next morning, but he still would not return my calls. The *St. Pierre Press* wouldn't come out until the next day, and their website hadn't been updated yet. ThirdRail still had nothing on the story. If it weren't for my wounds, it would have been like I dreamed what went on at Freedom Drop the night before. There was no news about it at all.

I stared at my phone and then realized I had Dunn's phone number. I quickly went through the Deanna Gould file that had been transferred from her phone onto my laptop. I found the number and dialed. There was no ring, only a harsh crackling sound followed by a woman's recorded voice saying that the number I was trying to reach was no longer in service. So much for that.

I called Tubby. If anyone would know what was going on, he would. I could hear his children talking in the background, and his wife. "We talk later," he said, rushing me off the phone.

I went back to my computer. I looked again at the history of Eric Dunn, Dunn Properties...and Norman Dunn. I looked at the countless images of the father. There were many of him with politicians, prominent businessmen, world leaders and celebrities. I didn't like what I was thinking and shut off the computer.

The cuts were still oozing. I covered them up again and then went to the doctor. I needed stitches where the woman clawed me. I couldn't remember when I last had a tetanus shot, so the doctor, just to be safe, made sure I had one. "How did you get such gashes?" he asked me.

"Playing with my dogs," I lied. "I need to clip their nails."

The doctor inquired no further.

From there, I stopped at Fort Philippe and the police station. Emmalin Sealy would not let me in to see McWilliams.

"Tell him he can't avoid me forever," I said to her.

"Mr. Len, Superintendent McWilliams is a busy man. I'm

sure he is not trying to avoid you. He is dealing with urgent matters today. The poor man hasn't even had a chance to eat the cow-foot soup his wife left for him. I know it certainly cold by now."

"So that's it?"

"Yes, sir," she said, giving me a sweet smile. "You go, and I'll make sure he know you come asking for him."

I had nothing more to say. I got back in my Jeep and headed back home.

"You know Denton been arrested," Tubby said to me over the phone when I got back.

"I was there," I said.

"You were there?"

I told him what happened. All of it. He wasn't happy that I went off without him. "If I were there with you, no way Dunn get away," he said. "If I were there things turn out differently for sure."

"But you weren't, and he did," I said. There was no reason to get into that with him again.

"I could have helped," Tubby said again.

No, you couldn't have helped, I thought. I realized that Dunn was always going to get away. That there was no chance he would be implicated here on St. Pierre. Someone made sure of that. "Did you hear anything else?" I asked Tubby, referring back to Denton. "Did they tell you why he was arrested?"

"Not sure, Mr. Len. Something about corruption."

"Nothing else?"

"Not that I know of yet. Should there be?"

"What about the woman who fell?"

"I hear nothing yet. Let me see what I learn and we talk later when you come in."

When I went to the bar later, the only news was about Denton, nothing at all about Dunn. The local television had a report that evening on his arrest on corruption charges. They weren't specific about the charges, only that Denton had been under investigation.

"Owen down at the station say it have something to do with money laundering or fraud or something like that," Tubby said.

I wasn't getting the answers I needed and didn't want to wait. I knew I was being impatient. I expected results. I expected closure. I wanted to do right. I wanted to do good. And I had done neither.

The next morning, I rushed down to the harbor to pick up a copy of the *St. Pierre Press*. Denton's arrest and photograph were on the front page. The story on Denton was brief, as all stories were in that newspaper. Apparently, he was taking money from a foreign source that the paper did not name and investing it in a shell corporation that was also not named. There were other charges, including bribery and customs tax evasion on foreign products and goods that he'd been given as gifts.

Buried under an ad for spiritual guidance was a paragraph that mentioned the discovery of an unidentified female in the water below Freedom Drop. There was nothing more in the story other than that the authorities believed that the woman's death was a suicide.

I was frustrated. I took the dogs and went down to the rocky beach below my house and threw a tennis ball to see which of the two could retrieve it faster. Neither was good at it, and they soon grew more interested in sniffing around the rocks, looking for crabs they could torture.

There was no further news on Denton over the next few days. And still nothing on Dunn. How could he have disappeared like that? He had to have someone inside who helped get him off the island.

After several days, more information was revealed about the woman found in the waters below Freedom Drop. She was identified as a Haitian national. The tattoo on her leg, the story claimed, was consistent with that worn by a gang out of Port-au-Prince. Her body had been returned to Haiti for further identification. Beyond that, there was nothing.

It was late afternoon, a week after the encounter with Dunn at Freedom Drop. I was about to head out to the bar for the night. As I was getting ready to leave, I noticed one of the island's few police cruisers pull up alongside my house. Superintendent McWilliams got out of the small car and, carrying his hat in his hand, headed for my front door. I opened it before he got there.

"Mr. Len, I hope this isn't a bad time," he said, addressing me in the more familiar, informal way.

I wanted to grab him by his shirt. I wanted to get into his face. But after a week, my rage had cooled. It was as if McWilliams planned it that way. So I just grinned. "It's never a bad time when you come for a visit, McWilliams," I said.

"Oh, is that right? Well, I'm very glad to hear that." He knew I was holding back. "May I come in?"

I opened the door and he stepped into my house.

He looked around. "It's been a busy week, Mr. Len, as you can imagine. Would you happen to have some of that very smooth rum you once offered me when I came to visit another time?"

He did look tired. His eyes were even more bloodshot than usual. He had made a few visits to my home since I started to get involved in matters that also involved him. Usually we shared a beer or nothing at all. One time, though, I remember, after my arm was broken by a disturbed young man wielding a beer bottle, we shared a shot of rum.

"You mean the rum from Martinique?"

He smiled. "Yes...from Martinique. It was special."

"I do. Let me get us both a glass."

He remained standing as I went to my booze stash in the kitchen, which wasn't very impressive for a bar owner. I had one bottle of low-grade vodka, a half-liter of British gin, two bottles of red wine, a Syrah and a Malbec, a pint of the local overproof rum and another of the island's dark, supposedly aged rum, from Karime Distilleries. But I also had that liter bottle of *Rhum Agricole*, the *vieux*, from Martinique.

I poured us each a generous shot and brought it to the couch where McWilliams had already planted himself. I sat in the chair opposite.

"Thank you, sir," he said. "Cheers."

Both of us took a swallow.

McWilliams held up his glass and pondered its contents. "Why we cannot make rum this mellow here, I do not understand," he said. "People want that rough, uncivilized stuff come from Karime. When we learn to make a rum like this, I know for sure we come a long way."

"Yeah, but not if the people want rough and uncivilized, McWilliams. You can lead a horse to water but..."

He nodded knowingly before I could finish the cliché.

"I have been informed you have been asking for me, Mr. Len. Mrs. Sealy tells me you have called and visited repeatedly. I know you must want answers. I was not purposely denying your requests. There were things I could not speak of."

"Can you speak of things now, McWilliams?" I asked.

"That depends on what things you want me to speak of."

I smiled. He had a way about him that made it tough not to get too upset with him. He seemed always in control. I admired him for that. It was a trait I wish I possessed.

"I think you know what things," I said.

"St. Pierre is my home. My family has lived on this island since we were brought here from what is now Nigeria. We were *Igbo* people. At least that is what my brother has told me. He do one of those ancestry searches. He even think a distant relative on my Ma's side escape her tormentors by throwing herself off Freedom Drop. My brother cannot verify that, but our family like to believe it so. I tell you this because I want you to know that I am proud to be a Petey. I love my country, and what I do in my humble position I always hope is for the good of St. Pierre."

I liked the man but didn't want him to charm me too much with his goodwill speech. "Your patriotism is acknowledged. But was letting Eric Dunn go for the good of the country? Were you aware of what he had planned? His big luxury resort. His signature project — the one that would make a name for him. The man wanted to destroy something beautiful here. He wanted to displace families. And he would do anything to get it. Were you aware of that?"

McWilliams sighed at my little outburst and took a sip of the rum.

"I'm aware of many things, Mr. Buonfiglio," he said, now

switching to address me by my last name, making it seem what he was saying was important and official. "I was aware of what Edward Denton was up to. Your meddling did not help our investigation. I tried to warn you about that, but you are headstrong. That can be a good thing. But not always."

"Denton told me about the project, McWilliams. He also said he loved his island," I said. "I think he might also be proud to be a Petey. When I told him about the study regarding the environmental impact of Dunn's project, the one that Dunn hid from him, he was not pleased. He felt betrayed."

"Maybe so, but there was more to it than you know. Mr. Denton had been conducting other illegal operations we had been following closely. Money had been funneled to him for a long time now for projects that never were realized. That stunt in his office...with the tooth. That could have blown our investigation. Why would you do such a thing?"

I took a big gulp of the rum thinking about that. I just shook my head.

"But none of that matters. He will have his day in court. He has counsel."

"McWilliams, if Denton hadn't arrived at Freedom Drop when he did, we might not be having this conversation. He helped me that night. Does that count for anything?"

"And where did he get that gun, Mr. Buonfiglio? You know our laws about possession of firearms," he said, a slight grin on his face.

I grinned back. "I found it on my lawn," I said. "What about the woman, McWilliams? Dunn was going to let her kill me."

He stared down at the rum in his glass. "You know what they say about how fate works, Mr. Len." He was back to calling me Mr. Len.

I did know what they said about fate. I too stared at the amber rum still in my glass. Maybe fate's mysterious ways brought me to where I was at that moment. Was my fate determined that day in June? Or was it before that, when she walked into my bar? I guess that was the mystery

"People died, McWilliams," I said, without much force.

"Yes, they did," he said quietly. "But I'm afraid none of those deaths can be directly tied to Mr. Dunn."

"No?"

"There is no evidence," he said, his head lowered. He knew all about Dunn, that I was sure. But I also knew from what he wasn't saying that his hands were tied. That someone else made the call on Dunn, and he could do nothing about it.

"Where is the justice?" I wondered out loud.

McWilliams' glass was empty. He stood up from the couch. He looked for a place to put his glass. I took it from him and stood.

"What's that they say about justice? Something about a dish best served...what is it?"

"Yeah, whatever, McWilliams," I said.

He smiled at me. "We tend to be hard on ourselves, don't we? I know I can be. My wife tell me to not worry as much as I do. How can I not worry? It come with my job."

I looked at him. "My job is to serve beer and rum," I said. "Nothing very hard about that."

"No, Mr. Len," he said. "You do more than that. And please, keep doing what you do for our island. What you do is good. I believe this even though sometimes we need to have chats like this."

I wondered what, really, I was doing for our island.

He moved to the door.

I looked at him. "Tell me, McWilliams, do you know how that girl died? Do you know the truth? Dunn was involved. I know that. But so was Big Tree. What happened? Why would Big Tree do what he did?" It was the one piece that still was left out there. If he knew, I needed to know.

McWilliams had his hat in his hand and was spinning it through his fingers, thinking how much to tell me.

"I do not know for sure, Mr. Len," he finally said.

"But you do, don't you?" I said.

"About how the girl actually die? Whether she was pushed or fell or slipped running from someone? No, I do not. And we never will. I do know that the death of his wife changed Rawle," McWilliams said. "She was sick for a long time. She suffered and so did Rawle. After that Rawle was not right."

"What do you mean, not right?"

McWilliams was looking me hard in the eye now. "You think I kept him at the fort because the girl's mother find that DNA match? Do you think I would keep a man in custody for evidence as flimsy as that?"

"I...don't understand," I mumbled, trying to understand.

"There were others," McWilliams said.

"Others?"

He nodded, looking me in the eye. "Yes, Rawle did things to others...to women. After the death of his wife. A thing like that, the loss of a loved one, is a traumatic event. Trauma like that can change a person. It can alter a man's mind in some way. Not everyone experience loss the same. It effect Rawle badly. Very badly."

I thought about that. I got what he was telling me. There was no need for him to say anymore.

"Now I must go," he said. "I thank you for that splendid rum. I have to convince them at Karime to adjust their distilling process to make something this smooth. If only for my own pleasure."

I walked out with him to his cruiser, the dogs by my side. I watched him drive down the hill. Once he was gone, I got into my Jeep. The dogs looked at me. I nodded and they both jumped in with me. Tubby was going to bitch to me about bringing them to work and let them run around in the bar. I just didn't care. I wanted them with me. They were my family here, and on this day I wanted my family with me.

32

"**Y**ou see one of those blue moons tonight, Mr. Len," Tubby said while we worked behind the bar on a busy Friday afternoon. All the stools were occupied. There was a party from the medical school at St. Elizabeth's at one of the tables, the usual Friday after-work Windward Savings crowd at another, and a dozen French couples who were sailing through the Grenadines. We were almost at overflow. I was leaving soon, but Mike would be coming in to give Tubby a hand.

"You know, Tubby, my Zio Ciccio, that's Italian for Uncle Frank, my aunt's youngest son, who was about fifteen years older than me and lost three toes in Vietnam... he used to play a song called "Blue Moon" constantly," I said. "I remember when I was a kid, hearing it coming from some tape he made. He carried around a small tape recorder with an old reel-to-reel tape on it. He said he carried it with him in Vietnam. It survived, but those toes, he always joked, didn't. There was another song he played all the time: 'There's a Moon Out Tonight.' They were what were called doo-wops. You know doo-wops, Tubby? They were big where I come from and when Uncle Frank was a kid. That was a long time ago."

Tubby looked at me. "Doo-wop? Old man, you're talking gibberish now." He shook his head.

"All those times hearing that song and I never bothered to ask what a blue moon was."

"See, just ask me and then you get a quick answer. You don't need a song to tell you," Tubby said as he opened four bottles of Carib for the medical school party. "It when you get two full moons in the same month."

"So it's not blue?"

"I don't know for sure. You look up there tonight and tell me if it blue or not."

"I'll be sure to do that, Tubby."

I was making a round of rum punches for an after-work group of six from the St. Pierre Conservation Club as I chatted with Tubby. When I bent over to grab the mix of mango, guava and pineapple we used, my half-unbuttoned shirt slipped down enough to reveal two raw thin scars near where my neck met my shoulder. I had the same streak of scars on my right hand.

"When the doctor say those scars go away?" Tubby asked, noticing them as I bent.

"In time, but if they don't, no big deal." I shrugged. I wasn't so much worried about a few more scars. It had been several weeks since the night at Freedom Drop. The stitches came out a week later, but the scars, the doctor said, might last a few months.

The other wounds, the ones that didn't show, were taking much longer to heal. But they were also healing.

Once Mike arrived for the night, I took off. I stopped down the road in front of Mrs. John's house. Ezran was waiting for me when I got there. He bounded into the Jeep. I could see his grandmother on the other side of the screen door. I waved to her from inside the Jeep. I wasn't sure if she waved back or not before I drove down into Garrison, around the roundabout, where they were finally installing that traffic light. The money for the project, I heard, was a donation from an anonymous foreign investor — there were whispers that it was a big-name hotelier from the States, though that had not been confirmed and I was sure it never would be, not that it mattered. Taking the second exit on the roundabout, I proceeded up Hillside Road to Betta's house.

The moon was up as I walked from the Jeep to Betta's front door. Betta was waiting and opened the door for me. She was wearing a long sheer linen dress that flowed over her body, ending just north of her knees. Paolo was by her side. I gave her a smile and looked at Paolo.

"You ready, kid?" I said to the boy.

He nodded shyly, his blue eyes opened wide.

I looked up at Betta. "We should be back in about two hours," I said. "He'll be in good hands."

"I know that, Leonard," Betta said. "He has been waiting all day for this."

"But I make no guarantees that we will see them," I said to her.

She smiled. "It doesn't matter. It's an adventure, and my little one likes adventures."

"I just don't want him to be disappointed."

"He won't be," she said.

I glanced at her again, trying not to stare, but with Betta, that was never easy. I made myself turn away from her quickly. I knew the move was awkward, but it wasn't like I had a choice. I led Paolo to the Jeep and put him in the backseat. I adjusted the seat belt to make sure it was on securely. Ezran was in the front and turned to smile at the younger boy. Paolo smiled back. I got behind the wheel and we headed off.

I drove back down around Garrison and then continued along the coast on North Road.

"Blue moon tonight," Ezran said.

"Blue moon," Paolo repeated from the back seat.

I turned and looked at him. He had a devilish grin on his face.

"That's what I hear," I said. "Five bucks one of you tell me what makes a blue moon."

"Serious?" Ezran said as if he couldn't believe his ears.

"Yes, I'm serious. What's a blue moon?"

Ezran shook his head. "This too easy, Mr. Len," he said. "The blue moon come when there are two full moons in one month. That usually happen twice a year."

"Blue moon," Paolo said again from the back seat, and all I could think of was my Uncle Frank and his doo-wops.

"I guess I owe you five bucks," I said to Ezran. "But you have to split it with Paolo. I think he knew the answer, too."

"Okay," Ezran said with a smile.

I slowed the Jeep as I got close. The road was dark, but I knew where I was. I eased it over to the side of the road and shut the engine.

"Here we are. Now remember, try not to make too much noise. And once we get to the beach, no lights. Did you bring a phone, Ezran?"

He nodded and showed it to me.

"Turn the flash off on the camera, okay?"

"I will," he said.

I got out and helped Paolo out of his seat. I took his hand tightly. In my other hand, I held a little LED flashlight. I used it to shine our way through the path and down the slope to Coral Beach.

Once we got to the beach, the moon illuminated the sand and shimmered off the water. I turned off the flashlight. I could see the wooden markers in the sand. I led the boys closer, and then we sat not too far from the markers. I held Paolo on my lap.

"They here?" the younger boy whispered.

"Not yet," I said.

The only sound was the lapping of the water against the sand. I caught Ezran staring up at the moon, and then we heard something. A splash and then a swishing sound like something heavy was being dragged through the sand. I smiled to myself and felt my heart beat a little faster in my chest.

"Ohhhh," Paolo shrieked and pointed.

I put my finger over my mouth to quiet him. He stood up from where we were sitting. I stood with him, keeping a grip on his hand. Ezran saw it too and rose from his seat.

From where we now stood, we could clearly see the light of the moon reflecting off the two dark eyes of one big leatherback sea turtle. The sound we had heard was the turtle's back fins brushing through the sand. It moved methodically up the beach toward us. Paolo's mouth hung open as the turtle approached the nesting area. It stopped now, but its hind fins were still swishing the sand.

I took my phone out and quickly snapped pictures, not even

bothering to see if I had the right angle, focus or size. I just hoped that the moon provided enough light for me to capture what I was witnessing. I saw Ezran do the same with his phone.

We watched the turtle as she used her hind fins to dig a cavity in the sand. Once the cavity was made, she released her eggs. There were dozens. I looked at Ezran. He was staring intently, his mouth open, and I could see he was counting to himself. When, finally, it looked like all the eggs were out, the turtle, again using its rear fins, covered the cavity with sand. Once the eggs were sufficiently protected, the turtle turned its prehistoric body and began to swish through the sand and back to the water.

"Turtle," Paolo called to it and pointed. He was on the verge of tears and pulling on my hand. "Let me go."

I let go of his hand and he began to run to the turtle. I caught up with him easily and grabbed his hand again. We walked behind the turtle as it made its way into the water, slowly swimming until it dived under. I could see the bubbles and frothy surf above where it descended, but soon the water calmed. When the turtle was out of sight, Paolo began to cry.

I picked him up in my arms. "The turtles will be back," I told him. "Maybe next time we will see the baby turtles."

I wasn't sure he understood what I was saying. Tears were rolling down his cheeks and he was bawling softly now. I knew he was tired. We had been on the beach for almost two hours. It was time to go.

I carried him back up the beach where Ezran was waiting. "What did you think?"

"A hundred and ten eggs," he said. "I counted."

"That's a lot of turtles," I said.

"Yes sir," he said, "but not all survive..."

I put my finger over my mouth again to hush him. I didn't want Paolo to hear any of that. Ezran nodded that he understood. I took out my flashlight and used it to guide us back up to my Jeep.

Paolo was asleep even before I got him into his seat. When we pulled up to Betta's house, I eased the boy out gently, doing my best not to wake him. I carried him, his warm head like a heating pad against my shoulder, to the front door where Betta waited. Her living room was on behind her. Her tall, slender figure was illuminated by the back light as she stood in the doorway. Her stiff, dark braids glittered in the light. I could feel a stirring rising up in my belly as I saw her standing there. I took a breath and tried to focus on other things. I wanted those stirrings gone. They did me no good.

When I got to the front door, I handed her the boy, who curled easily into her arms. She smiled at me and whispered a thank you. She kept looking at me in a way that wasn't making it easy for me. I felt her fingertips on my forearm and then she kissed me on the cheek. I gave her a faint smile and turned back to the Jeep.

Ezran's grandmother was also waiting in the doorway when we pulled up to her house. I didn't think I needed to escort the older boy into his home, but I stayed in the Jeep watching. I could see Mrs. Johns talking to Ezran. He turned back to me and opened the door. He put his hand up for me to wait.

From my seat in the Jeep, I saw Ezran move into the house and then emerge a few moments later. He was carrying an old silver Dutch pot. He lifted the pot and offered it to me.

"Curry crab," he said. "My Grandma tell me she make it for you."

I looked past Ezran at Mrs. Johns who stood in the doorway. She waved at me. I waved a thank you and took the Dutch pot. I could smell the briny crab and the curry sauce. The pot was warm, but not too hot to handle. I realized I was hungry.

"Thank your grandma for me, Ezran. And let me know how your pictures came out."

"Yes, sir," he said, and then returned to his house.

Before driving away from the Johns house, I flicked on some music. I scanned my playlists for what I wanted and found it easily, the reggae playlist downloaded to a phone that was now many years deceased. Each time I got a new phone I would make sure to transfer that playlist to the new phone's music library. It was a special playlist made just for me by someone also very special and also deceased. I didn't have a specific reason why, but I needed to hear it now, just as I had to hear it so many other times over the years. I pressed shuffle on the playlist, and the first song that queued up was the one Tubby had told me the name of when we were driving to the airport to pick up Kasie: "Be a Man." What I really wanted to know was why the song was chosen to be included on the playlist made just for me. I never asked, and now each time I heard the song, I regretted that I hadn't. Now I could only surmise. I didn't like to surmise. I wanted to know truths. But for this one thing I never would.

Almost as soon as I got home, I dished a huge portion of the curry crab onto a plate and took it to my kitchen table. I dug out a Carib beer from my refrigerator and opened it. I started in on the spicy curry crab. There were a couple of small claws. The dogs were under my feet. I dropped a claw for each of them. I immediately heard them crunching happily, breaking through the shells, finding the sweet meat and then finishing by eating the claws completely.

My phone buzzed with a text. I looked at it. It was from Tubby. *You hear about Dunn?*

I pulled the phone closer to me and wrote back that I had not.

Check this out, he wrote and attached a link to BBC News.

I clicked on the link, and when it came up, the headline read: "Eric Dunn to Develop Resort and Casino on the Outskirts of Port au Prince."

A resort in Haiti? I went on to read the accompanying story that said that Eric Dunn, acting on behalf of his father, his sisters and the Dunn Properties Group, would oversee the planning and development of what would be the first major international resort on that "troubled" island.

"It's a major challenge, but my brother is up to it," Dunn's sister, Lisa, was quoted in the article. "We look forward to Eric bringing the Dunn brand to Haiti with a world-class resort. We believe that this project will be just the beginning of progress and opportunity in Haiti."

I wanted to smile. I should have smiled. I knew what this was. They wouldn't even let him speak for himself. He had his younger sisters do the talking. Dunn's father was a cruel bastard, that much was true. I almost felt sorry for him. And then I didn't. This was his punishment. But he deserved much worse.

I texted Tubby. *Justice?* I wrote.

Ha Ha, he texted back. *Good luck with that.*

Tubby had no trouble smiling. He had no trouble laughing. Still, I couldn't smile or laugh. It wasn't enough for me. I wanted more. I always wanted more.

I washed down the remains of Mrs. Johns' curry crab with the beer as I sat back in my chair facing the dark Atlantic. I was listening to music on the small speakers I had in my living room. Yusef Lateef was on the flute. This was from a jazz playlist that was created by Betta's husband, Maurizio. Before he deserted Betta and St. Pierre, he and I would hang out at the bar or at his unfinished home, and he would play some of his favorites — the Modern Jazz Quartet, Lee Morgan, Herbie Hancock, Ornette Coleman and Lateef, to name just some. Maurizio's enthusiasm for jazz was contagious and almost equaled his passion for making bread.

The phone, where all my music was stored, was by my side. I glanced at it. "Nubian Lady" was the name of the track I was listening to. I should have known Maurizio would put it there.

I searched for the pictures I had taken on Coral Beach. Many were blurry or too dark, but there was one that caught the head of the turtle and those ancient, reptilian eyes. I attached the photo to a text to Kasie while I continued to listen to the music.

You know what this is? I wrote to her.

Within seconds I got a ping. I looked at her response: *What!!!*

I almost smiled and then there was another ping. I looked at what she wrote: *A sea turtle???*

I slowly punched in my response: *You got it, smart girl.*

Another ping. *Dad!!*

My phone said "Kasie is typing a message." I waited for it. I didn't have to wait long.

I want to see one.

With U!

I could hear Kasie's voice in the text. I could almost feel her presence. But they say almost only counts in horseshoes and hand grenades. I didn't care. At this moment, in my empty home, I would take whatever I could get.

I kept staring at her words and knew now that I was smiling. I was sure I was.

My fingers were not working like they should at that moment but I settled them and typed back: *You will.*

Brian Silverman

Brian Silverman's writing career has spanned over 30 years. He has written about travel, food, and sports for publications including the New York Times, Saveur, Caribbean Travel and Life, Islands, the New Yorker, New York and others. From 2004 through 2013 he was the author of the annual Frommer's New York City guide book series. He co-authored, with his father, Al Silverman, the acclaimed **Twentieth Century Treasury of Sports**. His short fiction has appeared in numerous publications including Mystery Tribune, Down and Out Magazine, and Mystery Weekly. His stories have been selected to appear in The Best American Mystery Stories in 2018 and 2019, and The Best American Mystery and Suspense Stories 2021. **Freedom Drop** is his first published novel. He lives in Harlem, New York with his wife, Heather and his sons, Louis and Russell.

Acknowledgements

There are many to thank who gave their time and support in the process of completing this work. I am fortunate to have inherited genes from the creative mind of my mom, Rosa Silverman. Her artistic flair combined with what I gleaned from my writer/editor father, Al Silverman, gave me an inherent advantage most writers do not have. I'd like to thank my go to first reader, Phil Falcone. He and I killed bugs together a long time ago and even back then I recognized his BS radar along with his subtle appreciation of art, whether it be literary, cinematic, or on a canvas. John Silbersack, with his vast experience in the genre, offered much needed and helpful advice. Ethan Ellenberg stewarded the book, steering it to many people and despite their resistance, stuck with it and with me. When I met Charles Salzberg decades ago on the dusty Great Lawn as a softball rival, I had no idea that once we both retired from that game, that he would introduce me to the community of crime writers. I thank him for that and for his continued support and friendship. Reed Farrel Coleman deserves a nod for taking an early look at the book and, as is his style, pulled no punches in pointing out flaws I was blind to. Christine Pepe's savvy editing helped polish the rough edges of my earlier drafts. Finally, I thank Ehsan Ehsani, who was the first to give me a platform for my work. His faith in my writing was always there and a balm to this writer's sometimes fragile confidence.